High praise for NAOMI RAND'S

EMMA PRICE

and

STEALING FOR A LIVING

"The author combines an intelligent, well fleshed-out cast of characters with a swiftly moving plot that is studded with surprise."
St. Louis Post-Dispatch

"Rand keeps her eye on the crime and its impact on its various victims . . . we never lose sight of where Price's compassion rests—with those she loves and those whom she's pledged to serve."
Boston Globe

"Engaging and complex, Emma is a true original who deserves many future adventures."
Publishers Weekly

"An entertaining sleuthing and procedural mix."
Library Journal

"[An] exploration of evil at its most slippery and self-justifying."
Kirkus Reviews

"Emma Price felt like a friend from the first page; a brave, sassy, smart friend."
Alice Elliot Dark

Books by Naomi Rand

STEALING FOR A LIVING
THE ONE THAT GOT AWAY

STEALING FOR A LIVING

AN EMMA PRICE MYSTERY

NAOMI
RAND

AVON BOOKS
An Imprint of HarperCollinsPublishers

This is a work of fiction. Names, characters, places, and incidents are products of the author's imagination or are used fictitiously and are not to be construed as real. Any resemblance to actual events, locales, organizations, or persons, living or dead, is entirely coincidental.

AVON BOOKS
An Imprint of HarperCollins*Publishers*
10 East 53rd Street
New York, New York 10022-5299

Copyright © 2003 by Naomi Rand
ISBN: 0-06-103121-6
www.avonmystery.com

First Avon Books paperback printing: December 2004
First HarperCollins hardcover printing: June 2003

Avon Trademark Reg. U.S. Pat. Off. and in Other Countries, Marca Registrada, Hecho en U.S.A.
HarperCollins® is a registered trademark of HarperCollins Publishers Inc.

Printed in the U.S.A.

10 9 8 7 6 5 4 3 2 1

To David, Travis, and Cody

For my mother, Anna

Acknowledgments

I would like to thank those who made this book possible. First and foremost, my mother, Dr. Anna Tulman Rand. She made me believe that women were meant to juggle careers and motherhood. I would never have been able to become a writer without her encouragement, and her example. I want to thank my helpful readers, my husband, David, for going beyond the call of duty and for going without many a good night's sleep while he read this manuscript. Thanks to Nicole Bokat and Sasha Troyan, both amazing writers, who offered support and a smart read. I am grateful for the wise editorial advice of Carolyn Marino. Thanks also to those others at HarperCollins who have made the process a pleasure: Jennifer Civiletto, whose warmth and efficiency is greatly appreciated, Alison Callahan, who is a similar pleasure to work with and know, and Tim Brazier, who makes me laugh and is a consummate professional. This book would never have gotten published without my wonderful agent Flip Brophy's help. I can't ever thank her enough for being both a dear friend and the best representative of my work I could hope for. And, finally, a heartfelt thanks to Robert Jones, who had faith in me at a time when I had almost given up. I miss you.

STEALING
FOR A LIVING

'Twas the Week Before Christmas

There was a crick in Emma Price's neck. A lump in her throat. An ache in her lower back. All the classic signs of infection. If I get sick one more time this winter . . . Emma thought. That doctor over at the clinic had scoffed at her notions. No, she did not have Epstein-Barr. There was absolutely no hint of Lyme disease. Emma was not convinced. Something was lurking in her bloodstream, undiscovered, ready, willing, and able to attack at will. Her resistance to infection had fled, gone to the Himalayan highlands, moved in with the Urks or whatever tribe it was that lived to an obscene age on a diet of yogurt and goat cheese.

From Labor Day on, Emma Price had been prey to colds that turned into flu, sinus infections that managed to linger, her body apparently an all-too-safe harbor. In an attempt to do what she could for her bankrupt immune system, Emma dosed herself with vitamin C for good health; olive leaf, a gray dingy mass inside a capsule; echinacea to satisfy the cold bug; B_{12} to hold down her premenstrual jitters; glucosamine to fortify her ever-aching joints; E because it was good for the heart; and ginkgo biloba for, gosh, oh right, Emma reminded herself, that deteriorating memory. Forty-one. The prime of life. Could it get any better, she wondered?

This morning, it definitely could. Glancing at the clock, she was stunned. It was already after nine. She had said she would show up at the door of her ex-husband Will's apartment at nine-thirty sharp. That meant she was supposed to be ready, willing, and able to vault out the door . . . well . . . now.

Emma took the stairs up to her bedroom two at a time. Goal number one, ignore the mess of clothes that lay tangled on the floor of her bedroom. Goal number two, avoid looking over at the exercise bike that was gathering dust and had become a dropping-off point for those books that would never be cracked open, underneath them a pile of magazines that dated from sometime last summer, and balanced precariously on top, bills that would clearly never see the full light of day. Goal number three, vault over the mess and into the shower.

Nine-seventeen found our girl Emma discovering the last clean pair of French-cut jockey briefs left in her top drawer and tugging them onto her dripping wet body. She added jeans, with a zip and a snap, then revived a pair of socks she'd thrown on the floor at some point in, hopefully, the very recent past, adding to this motley assortment a long-sleeved shirt, plus a burly lumberjack sweater. Emma did not attempt to dry her lustrous locks thoroughly. And she certainly did not tempt fate by taking a glance at the unkempt and unreasonably aggravated woman of middle years in her full-length mirror. If she had, she knew pretty much what she'd find: a tall, reasonably thin version of her former self. Instead of waist-length dark hair, she was now a redhead with a blunt cut. Her nose, always aquiline at best, seemed more prominent than ever, and those dark circles under her eyes gave away her lack of even one good night's sleep. Emma escaped from all this, leaving her bedroom, and taking the stairs down two at a time, into the hall. She retrieved her coat, a hat, warm mittens, then opened the front door.

"God, I am so royally fucked," Emma said, because snow was piled waist high, literally barring her exit.

By nine thirty-eight, Emma was playing a new role, damsel in distress. She waved her arms wildly at an enterprising teen with a shovel who charged her a cool twenty to clear a path down her front steps. By 10:04 she was down to street level and around the corner, taking a left. There she discovered that the residents of Hoyt Street in Boerum Hill, Brooklyn, had been conspiring against her.

Ten-eleven found Emma back, with her own shovel in hand. Feeling like an itinerant miner, she dug, and dug, and dug her way down Hoyt Street to the next corner. By ten-seventeen, she had carved a path to the parking lot where her chariot waited.

Word of the day?

"Eventually."

Eventually she would get inside the barbed-wire fence, after warming the lock with a match so that the key didn't stick. Eventually she would dig a path to her car, because dig she must. She would open the door, stick her key in, and listen to the motor not turn over.

She would rev and rev and almost flood the damn thing, but eventually it would catch. Then she would try to back up and find that she had no traction. She would climb out and go to the local bodega, where they would have several cardboard boxes that she could break down and stick under her tires, providing the necessary traction to get the slipping, sliding vehicle moving forward, not sideways, and out the gate, onto Wyckoff Street.

Up to the corner of Bond. Turn and turn and turn again.

Emma finally made it onto Smith Street, the main drag. The plows had done their work and cleared a path in that infamous New York fashion. Snow had been dumped on top of the cars that had parked on either side.

There was really no need to place a call to her ex-husband. She'd be arriving any minute now to retrieve her darling nine-month-old daughter and slightly petulant twelve-year-old son. So what if she was over an hour late? She had good reason!

"Ugh," Emma said, punching in the number on the cell phone, praying internally for a miracle, for William Price III to answer the phone instead of that other creature.

"Hayes-Price residence."

It was definitely not her lucky day; these were the dulcet, insipid tones of Jolene Pruitt Hayes, her ex-husband's current flame and one of the major reasons their marriage had headed south.

"It's Emma."

Jolene knew that, of course. Caller I.D. gave no one

any privacy. You couldn't even dial the wrong number without being exposed.

"Nice to hear from you." Jolene made sure to add the long, condemnatory pause, then called out, "Will, it's for you."

As Emma waited, she felt the burn of those little stalactites of ice Jolene had shivved through the phone line. Then there was a cough, and Will said, "I thought there must be a problem."

Had he looked out the window lately? Emma knew better than to ask. Sometimes you tossed that snowball, and the next thing you knew, an avalanche was roaring down. *I never said I was perfect*, Emma thought, a trifle defensively. Indeed, if Will wanted to play the blame game, he'd have to take a number.

Last night. Just last night, Emma had joined Dawn Prescott, her boss at New York Capital Crimes, and three hundred of Dawn's closest personal friends. In the room she'd counted five judges; the former Manhattan D.A. Reggie Moses, who was raising money for a run on the governor's mansion; two city council persons; and a host of Connecticut lime-green country club members, many of them members of Dawn's immediate and extended family, every one of them blue-eyed, and Aryan-blond. Dawn's parents had rented the entire Gramercy Tavern for the night, which Emma knew had to have cost more than her entire yearly salary. The scripted invitation, done on cream stationery, had read, A CELEBRATION OF DAWN.

Dawn's fiftieth.

This birthday had been Emma's cross to bear for a long, long while. Dawn's daily nervous breakdowns had begun in the early fall. Around the time, Emma noted, when she herself had developed her own mysterious physical symptoms. An "aha" moment if there ever was one.

"Oh shit," Emma said aloud. It all made such perfect sense. Let's face it, Dawn had never been a picnic to deal with, Emma admitted. And these days, she was, well, past impossible. For "testy," read "hostile." For "difficult," "perverse." For "a little off," the zinger, "certifiable." There had been daily knock-down-drag-out fights over the lack of paper in the copier, histrionics about a misplaced message. Coupled with the rising hysteria, Dawn's ability to track down the one poor benighted coworker who had not gotten the message the rest of the staff was sending. She'd corner her victim and have at him. Eight people had quit in the last four months. The word was out, which meant forget about finding replacements, even in this, the worst job market in the last ten years.

To cope, much of the staff had resorted to vice. Round the corner, a squad of Capital Crimes employees chain-smoked. The lunchtime cocktail was also de rigueur. In the back room, the refrigerator was stocked with a rotating six pack and a bottle of Chardonnay.

Emma had been the lone holdout, refusing to chastise Dawn. Perhaps it was because she was the one who was closest in age. Or perhaps it was their friendship. Emma knew that Dawn had a well-earned reputation as a peerless litigator, but she also understood why Dawn was so invested in the job. Dawn's home life was virtually nonexistent. There was no husband, and no current significant other. Dawn had never had children. Once, her solo status had been something she gloried in, but no longer.

Emma sympathized with Dawn's growing desperation, but knew better than to step into the path of the oncoming high-speed train. Emma knew from experience with their own clients, the more desperate people got, the more dangerous they became. For the party, she had decided she needed to provide herself with an escort, someone who would offer her the best possible defense from the potential slings and arrows that Dawn might cast. This was why she'd begged Laurence Solomon to accompany her.

Emma made a hard right at Cadman Plaza. In passing, she noted the oversized evergreen, decked out in its very best holiday finery. Next to it, a towering plastic menorah, with one candle lit. The holidays were supposed to be a time of joy. However, Emma had never quite bought in to that premise. It was partly her upbringing. Her dad had been an unrepentant Commie, revering Castro instead of Stalin. His descriptive term for the season had been "Idiot's Delight." According to Sy, old jolly Claus was a "capitalist tool." His irreverence spawned by a Marxist critique mingled with an innate Jewish disdain for the gaudiness of this Christian spectacle. Her cultural Jewish dad had even gotten down on his knees to spin the dreidel with his daughters. Meanwhile, her mother, who had a tender spot for anything resembling pomp, had conspired against him in a minor key, purchasing a spindly three-foot evergreen in a pot at the local Sloan's supermarket, the tree that, like her mom, put safety first. The deep-green color of the needles was the natural by-product of a layer of fire-retardant chemicals.

It was eleven-seventeen when Emma finally arrived in front of Will's building. Too bad there was no sign of her ex, or her kids. And no place to pull over.

Emma pressed redial on the cell phone.

"Price-Hayes residence, Will Price speaking."

"I'm downstairs."

"Great. We'll be with you in five."

Too bad she couldn't exactly sit here and wait. The street had been cleared, but snow-drenched cars made it impossible for traffic to make its way around her. Emma drifted to the corner, made a right, and immediately jammed on the brakes to avoid rear-ending a taxi. She had become part of a chain of cars, some blaring horns. Immediately checking her rearview mirror, she discovered she was trapped.

So Emma stepped out. Striding along, she discovered the problem, a car, half in and half out of its igloo-like parking spot. The tires shredded snow as the driver made another attempt, and the car pitched forward, then stopped, held there in a vicious teeter-totter, before sinking back, once again disgraced.

Three men surrounded the vehicle, huffing and puffing along with it.

"Could you guys back it up and let us get by?" she asked.

"Lady," one of them said, and added nothing more, switching his attention back to the task at hand. This should not be my problem, Emma told herself. But it was. In fact, everything was.

Take last night, for example. She'd met Laurence at the door of the restaurant and they'd stepped inside together. The coatroom attendant had taken their coats—his, peerlessly virgin wool, long, elegant, and sleek; hers, bought at the end-of-season sale last year at Century 21. Then they'd been greeted by the birthday girl herself. Dawn had on an elegant ivory wool pantsuit. Her streaked blond hair had been pinned up into an exotic mess, tendrils framing her face. Emma couldn't help wincing, internally, at how gaunt Dawn looked.

"So this is who you've been hiding away," Dawn said, reaching for Laurence Solomon and gripping his hand. Luckily, Brian Pinsky interceded almost immediately, emerging from the seething mass of the unfed.

"Hey guys," he yelled, grabbing Emma by the arm and leading her and Laurence off to a clutch of fellow degenerate coemployees. Once safely away, he leaned in conspiratorially and asked, "Can you fucking believe it?"

"Believe what?"

A waiter floated by, hoisting a tray of immaculately constructed hors d'oeuvres. Emma admired the brash chimneys of meat, crushed vegetables, and melt-in-your-mouth pastry. Why decide, she thought, taking one of each. She had one in her mouth and was chewing vigorously when he said, "About Dawn's adoption."

Brian had slung his free arm around his partner, Richard.

"Excuse me?"

"I thought you knew. I mean, of anyone, you'd think Dawn would tell you first."

"Well, she didn't," Emma admitted.

"No?" He managed to raise an eyebrow, to display incredulity. "Apparently she's already done the paperwork. Dawn was stressed about what they might ask her, you know, considering she's single. She asked me if I thought the Chinese would assume she was gay, and should she make it clear that she wasn't. Such a nice way of putting it, her words were 'wouldn't it be worse if they thought she was gay, when after all, well, she really wasn't.' To which I said, no, you're just a tactless, self-involved heterosexual bitch."

"Brian," Emma cautioned, looking around to see how far away they were from the maiden of honor. She seemed safely out of earshot, but one never knew.

"Actually she was a little more circumspect than that. Let me give her full credit. She said she'd heard that the powers that be in charge of the adoption service were put off by certain 'unconventional lifestyle choices.' Darling Dawn was afraid she might say something wrong. Something to create suspicion." Brian was an authority of sorts, Emma told herself. After all, he and Rich had adopted two bouncing babies themselves, a fair-haired brother and sister from an orphanage in Vladivostok.

"And you said?"

"The god's honest truth?" The mischievous look in his eye said, "not quite yet." "I suggested bribing them. Maybe she'll get arrested. Then we can do that whole spy game thing, break her out and spirit her across the border to freedom." A dot. A dash. Then the real deal. "I told her to give a big tip to the interpreter, in advance," he confided. "You want them on your side and you know how Dawn is. I mean, my god, if they even translate close to what comes out of that mouth!"

"I can't believe she'd consider adopting," Emma said, half to herself.

"Consider. You really are out of the loop. She's booked a flight Thursday morning at six. Next stop, Beijing."

Amazed didn't cover it. Dawn had kept this a complete secret. It was unfair to feel hurt, but Emma realized she was. Dawn claimed to consider her such a close friend, why keep this private?

"Well, more power to her," Emma said, attempting to at least appear magnanimous.

"And heaven protect that little baby." Brian's gaze strayed upward.

At that precise moment, Laurence had returned. He'd gone to get them drinks and she hadn't exactly noticed his absence, but his presence was something to remark on. He looked profoundly uncomfortable and more than a little pissed off. Emma decided she shouldn't have brought him just as Laurence spun a glass of chilled white wine her way.

"Dawn's adopting a baby," Emma said.

"More power to her." Laurence didn't raise his glass, just downed the contents greedily, making a pointed surveillance of the crowd.

She caught what he was doing and did it too. Her old friend Reggie Moses, currently state attorney general and former Manhattan D.A., was talking to Judge Epstein. Reggie had his arm around his wife's back. Other than the Moseses, and Laurence? No other dark-skinned guests present or accounted for, unless, that is, you included the wait staff. One offered her a tender morsel, and she partook; shrimp wrapped in a cunning prosciutto blanket.

Well, that had been last night's bad news. Or the beginning of it, anyhow. Today, Emma had a very different problem to contend with. Another man had joined the group of three. Four strapping men seemed to be consulting the oracle in an effort to release the trapped vehicle. One gesticulated. The next shook his head. The third shoved the fender. Stepping up, she offered a fig leaf.

"I've got some cardboard in my trunk. You could try putting it under the tires."

Not even a "lady," this time. The same man who had offered that exasperated response before simply glared. His pal said, "We've got this under control."

Really?

Men with their forty-nine percent. Returning to her car, Emma decided that the resentful looks the members of this group sported were the mirror image of the one Laurence Solomon had worn throughout that miserable evening.

To stave off the discomfort she was feeling, Emma had decided to drink. After the third white wine, a warm buzz had settled in. Deciding a scouting party was essential, she'd left Laurence in Brian's dubious care and gone off to check the seating arrangements. The tables were lovely. Large enough to seat ten comfortably, they had been covered with lime-green damask linens. The centerpieces consisted of red candles with tasteful sprigs of holly and poinsettia adorning them.

Emma scanned the names until she found her place card. But Laurence's wasn't there. Not on either side. Not at that table. He was all the way on the other side of the room. Forget this, she decided, and attempted a neat sleight of hand, finding a card to make an even exchange, a man for a man as it were.

"Hey," Dawn said, grabbing her shoulder as she attempted to switch. "What gives?"

"I need to put Laurence with me," Emma said, dropping her own voice into a nearly silent register. "He doesn't really know most of these people."

"I spent hours working out the seating," Dawn said pointedly. "Can't you please just let it be?"

Was it fair to say no? More than fair, considering the circumstances. "I can't," Emma said. She would have been happy to trying to explain why a little more clearly, but Dawn's sour look made it obvious she wasn't in the mood. "It's my birthday," she said. "But of course, you have to have it your own way." Then off she stalked.

Dawn's displeasure did nothing to dissuade her. Emma had the place card in hand and was barreling back to complete her mission when she saw Laurence, standing by the table, talking with Judge Harold Levy. Levy was known as the Silver Fox because of his mane of overripe, china-white hair. He'd been a widower for a good ten years and seemed to have an endless supply of gay divorcées to squire.

"Emma Price," Harold said, graciously kissing both cheeks and giving her a final, shakedown squeeze. His hair was fully shaped and permanently massed on top of his head, a miracle of men's hair gel. Emma extricated herself, then plunked Laurence's place card down next to her own. Which was when she heard the voice of doom.

"So, how did you make out?"

Turning, Emma saw that the voice with the distinctive nasal twang belonged to a woman in her early fifties. She was wearing a dress that might have been one of Emilio Pucci's bravest designs, purple, black, and tan op art ovals clinging to all the wrong places. She was apparently speaking to Laurence. And he was staring blankly back.

"Marilyn Rothstein," Harold interjected, claiming ownership.

"I showed you and your wife the La Biancha house last week. Marilyn Rothstein from Weichert?" Her hand slid down and emerged from somewhere with a business card, which she flourished.

"I'm sorry, you've made a mistake," Laurence said, as always the master of cool.

"Don't be silly," she began, apparently used to the brush-off, and why not? She was a realtor, after all. Luckily, Harold interceded before it could get too ugly. "Marilyn, dear, this is Detective Laurence Solomon, he's with Brooklyn Homicide."

"Oh my. But I thought . . . I hope you didn't take offense. I mean, it's a natural mistake."

"Reggie Moses is over there," Laurence said, pointing across the room at his apparent double. Even the most casual survey of the two made it clear that there was no resemblance other than skin color.

Marilyn, poor benighted Marilyn, blushed so deeply it looked as if she might explode. Then she bolted.

Laurence took his seat. He unfolded his napkin and

set it on his lap, then poured the scented olive oil onto the side plate. Reaching across the table, he ripped a piece of bread from the half-cut loaf and dipped it in, raised it to his mouth, took a bite, chewed, swallowed it down, wiped his mouth free of crumbs, then announced, "Good bread. You might want to try some."

The man was wicked!

Miracle of miracles, the car in front of her moved forward. Emma pursued, doing a box step, right to Montague Street, right again and back to Will's building. He'd emerged and was shading his eyes from the ferocious light, courtesy of the almost immaculate snowfall surrounding him. He wore a dark blue ski parka.

Pulling up and waving, Emma couldn't help finding humor in the cluster of tags hanging off the zipper. Will was terrified of heights. The one time they'd tried downhill skiing, he'd had an anxiety attack on the kiddie slope. She assumed the nubile Jolene had taken his jacket for a ride or two without him. Either that, or they were provided at the store where he'd also acquired those hiking boots that looked rugged enough to climb Everest. On his head, he had plopped one of those multicolored, court jester–style Nepalese hats.

He leaned down and lifted nine-month-old Katherine Rose, already strapped into her car seat, and Emma leapt out to offer a hand. She directed a shy entreaty of a smile toward the car that was stuck behind her, making sure to avoid direct eye contact with the driver. Waiting because someone else needed you to was not something the citizenry of New York enjoyed. For a few weeks after 9/11, there had been a thaw. People were gracious to one another. Drivers didn't try to mow down pedestrians at crosswalks. Strangers greeted each other with a fond "hello." It was almost small-town friendly, wonderful, but also totally unnerving. Emma fondly remembered the surge of relief she'd felt when she drove around a corner and narrowly missed a pedestrian who graced her with the standard Brooklyn greeting, a raised middle finger.

New York was New York again.

This meant it was every New Yorker's birthright to take offense—as the driver behind her now did, sitting on her horn. Home sweet home, Emma thought contentedly.

Will had the car seat inside and was leaning in to secure the seat belt. Their elder son, twelve-year-old Liam, was at the rear of her 1989 Volvo wagon, shoving his electric guitar into the back. Emma went around behind to help him with his amp and overnight bag. Then they both got in, Liam taking the passenger seat beside her. "Wait a second," she wanted to say, "you're not old enough to sit up front." But of course he was. Emma blinked and tried to readjust. Where had that sweet little boy fled to, and when had he morphed into this lumbering, decidedly goofy wanna-be teen with the deepening voice and the fuzzy mustache.

Will was handing over the diaper bag.

"I'll see you guys Monday night," Will said, bending in and ruffling Liam's hair, the newest style a mix of red, green, and gold on top of a dark black, almost natural base. Will then dropped a benediction of a kiss on his baby daughter's forehead and shut the back door.

Emma slammed her own door shut and put the car

into drive. But then she heard the tap, tap, tapping on the driver's side glass.

Here it comes, she thought. And I'd almost made a clean getaway. "Yes?" she asked, rolling down the window.

"You've heard, right?"

"Heard what?" Emma felt her pulse ratchet up three notches. It was her automatic response whenever anyone cued up the possibility that she might be blindsided by a piece of news.

"Eleanor Hammond. She's been murdered."

The woman at the wheel of the car behind her was marshaling a beep, double beep, triple beep chorus. Will turned and yelled, "Just wait!" Then he leaned back into the car, tucked his hand around her upper arm, and said, "It's been on the radio all morning. If you need to talk, call me."

2

Detective Laurence Solomon could make out the daughter's voice through the closed double doors. "You don't have a clue! As usual."

Then the son's retort. "What usual are you referring to, Leslie?"

Certainly a valid question, considering their present situation. It was their mother, Dr. Eleanor Hammond, lying dead behind the swinging door to the kitchen.

A hissed "ssh" came from the living room. Laurence attributed it to Bob Crescent, a professorial type who had arrived with the daughter. Leslie Hammond had wanted to see for herself, and in order to gain that perspective, she'd stormed past the trio of officers assigned to keep the crime scene pure. What she found inside brought her up short. Her seventy-eight-year-old mom, doing a close reading of Friday's Metro section, with the back of her head blown off.

Laurence had grabbed her then, Bob helping him lead Ms. Hammond back to the living room and settle her onto the couch, where she broke down completely—sobbing, wailing, screaming.

"Hey." O'Malley's voice was soft. Her redheaded,

blue uniformed self came out from inside the dining room. "Any news?"

"No one's confessed quite yet."

"Hope springs eternal."

It might, but he knew what he'd been handed. The apparent execution of Dr. Hammond would require special diligence. As an abortion rights activist who had spent time arguing her case in front of a half century of politicos, Hammond had proved herself adept at stoking controversy. In death, she'd require tender, loving care. Too bad, when you considered the timing, it being a week before Christmas and all through this house . . . Laurence couldn't help cursing Saint Nick for dropping the two of them this stocking stuffer. He knew Caitlin was doing the same, thinking hard about how Christmas Day could come and go without a break, she with three kids under the age of five. A sigh came out of her mouth, then an embarrassed flush.

"Here," he said, and hooked his finger, backing them both up and closing the door to the dining room. He noted the oak table with its ring of six uncomfortable-looking high-backed chairs. The curtains were drawn tight, leaving the room in eternal semidarkness, fitting considering the task presently at hand.

Laurence paused to admire the newest member of the squad: Caitlin O'Malley, her Irish eyes shining, her hair tucked back into a perfect French braid. He'd swap her for the Miguel Ruizes of the world any day. Where Miguel had been sloppy, Caitlin was meticulous. And driven. She had something to prove to her dad and her three brothers, all career officers. There were some who muttered that having a woman watching their back meant leaving themselves open to mischief. Laurence heartily disagreed. Besides, he knew all about being singled out as different. Maybe being a black male didn't set him apart on the force, but making detective had. Next year, when he took the sergeant's exam, he'd be even more exalted. And ostracized.

Laurence had been a member of One Hundred Blacks in Law Enforcement Who Care since its founding. The organization was there to give back to the community, offer guidance, grants, intelligent options, and a place to regroup. Which was why he was the last one on earth surprised by the news that the powers that be, mostly white, all paranoid, had been tapping the organizers' phones lo these many years.

His dad had said, "The man wants it this way, or else. You got to slide down under his radar screen to get by." He'd disbelieved then, even more now, and had never adopted those tactics. Still, despite the talk about change, despite all the agitation and the lip service that got paid to everyone being equal, the department was pretty much run by home rule, and home meant white, then male. The unspoken code was, if you stayed put, the "man" felt good, even good enough to offer you a little bit of charity and a pat on the top of your nappy-haired head. If you made a move, he got nervous, started convincing himself that a revolt was brewing, and you were the kingpin thereof. All this was his long way around to admitting he had sympathy for Caitlin, who had confided in him that her most fervent desire had always been to make her father proud by moving up the ranks to the giddy heights of lieutenancy.

"A lot of partials out on the back porch," Caitlin said.

The porch was where the perp had waited for the good doctor, sliding up the back stairs to take his best shot. One was all it required. Then he or she had walked off, conveniently before the snow fell. No signs of a B and E. No signs of entry at all as far as he could tell.

"Kendrick's upstairs," she said. "Want me to go check what he's got?"

A nod and off she went. He stayed put, trying to assess what little he did know for sure. The vic's son, Joshua Hammond, had gotten off Virgin Air Flight 71, direct from Heathrow. He'd taken a cab in from the airport and arrived to find his mother in situ. By then, the snow, which had been falling since six Friday evening, had piled up to a good foot and a half, and they were getting hail, to boot, in the early morning. By the time it tapered off, squads from the local precinct had marched in, then out, then he'd come along with O'Malley and two more assisting off the homicide squad.

Not exactly an opus. Laurence was ready to echo Caitlin's sigh. What staved it off was a bestial grunt from the direction of the kitchen, then Carter, the M.E., booming out, "A one and a two and a three, hoist her up." Carter, yet another cross to bear. In his thirties, with that spry goatee, Ducane Carter liked to pretend that being the medical examiner meant overseeing an all-night party, the kind they threw when he was an undergrad at Dartmouth and the president of Psi Theta Gamma fraternity.

Laurence stepped out to catch him, and met Carter as he vaulted through the kitchen door. That boyish, freckled face, the crew cut, the little smirk of a smile.

"All yours, Solly," he said.

Laurence controlled the impulse to say "Don't call me that" and asked, "What can you tell me?"

"Not much. The blood spatters were tight, controlled. It's possible the perpetrator used a silencer. Time of death? Judging by rigor I'd make it between six and nine A.M. yesterday. That and the egg cup. She liked hers soft boiled." Carter snapped his gum. "Got to go," he added.

What's missing from this picture? That was how Laurence tried to view a crime scene once the body was carted off. On the flowered plastic tablecloth a mix of blood, dried egg, and pottery shards remained. And a singularly whole coffee cup, tipped on its side, pretty much dead center. Laurence stepped across the room to the porch door and opened it. Out here it was starkly cold, the kind of weather that makes you pull your muffler tight.

Caitlin had been thorough, dusting for prints in the most unlikely spots. And out here there were spots aplenty. Laurence felt hemmed in by the piles of newspapers and magazines, plus the carcasses of withered houseplants. A worktable was littered with broken china and stray hardware. Underneath it, three recycling bins were topped up to the brim and beyond.

Laurence opened the door out to the backyard and took the stairs down, listening to the telltale creaks as he went. The snow was almost untouched and deep enough to reach to his knees. It was a small yard, centering around an old tree that branched up and up, diligently, making for the sky and all those hosts of planets.

Laurence found it peaceful despite the current business of death that was being carried on inside the house. He noted how the access route to the back was pretty much barred, high fences skirting all sides of the yard.

The snow had long since stopped falling. The sun was too bright, reflecting off the whiter than white surface. And every so often a wind blew up, chasing the snow with it, off the tree branches, off the tops of the fence posts and into the air. Laurence opened his mouth to grab a taste and the flakes melted on his tongue, bringing him back to the virtues of remembered youth, the way it had felt to take a clean run down that slope in Morningside Park, getting a brace of snow in his mouth as the hubcap he'd been using as a flying saucer picked up speed.

Laurence shoved his hands into his warm pockets, then turned and climbed back up the steps. He took a second look around the porch and sadness gripped him. This old lady's life was laid bare and it wasn't only how she'd died, it was how she'd lived, saving, construing a reason for the bundles that rose up, not only yesterday's news, but medical journals too, white covers with insignia on them of a coiled snake and staff. The topmost was a *Journal of the American Medical Association* from back in 1991, surely worth preserving, if only for the lead article, "Gastric Disorders and Their Link to Hyperthyroidism."

Opening the door back in, he held it and took a panoramic view with his Nikon. On the monitor screen he saw the unremarkable: faded olive green kitchen cabinets, baby blue and lemon yellow wallpaper with scenes of little Dutch boys and girls playing a game of take the pail to the damn well, drop it down, jump in after. The sink was old-fashioned, two basins for the price of one. There was an aggressive drip, drip, drip from the leaking faucet.

Old people treasured their independence, and what he was seeing convinced him that Dr. Hammond was no exception to the rule. Seventy-eight and still practicing downstairs in her home office, and over at the family clinic she'd founded on Flatbush. She'd lived here all alone, no home health worker, no assistant doing her shopping or checking on her status. The way it seemed, she might have been one of the lucky few, a burden to no one from her first day, right up till her last.

Laurence tugged open one of the kitchen cupboard doors. Dust motes rolled in the breeze like a band of refugees on the road to nowhere. It made him feel sorry, and not just for Hammond; he felt bad for old people in general, stacked up in homes, shoved out of sight, or worse. There was more than a trace of personal sentiment attached, true. He'd swung past the hump of forty blissfully unaware. And then six months ago he'd lost his virginity. Sailing up for a layup over at the Y on Third, he'd missed his step and fallen, twisting up, lying there groaning. They'd had to send him over to Long Island College Hospital in an ambulance. Six weeks on crutches. And another four in a soft cast. Now he wore a brace if he played, iced himself down religiously afterward, and tried not to swear the long, holy night through.

"You're crazy," Emma would say, then leave it alone.

He knew how it was supposed to be a lesson. There were plenty more these days, often enough he'd have to get out of bed slowly, one leg tingling before it touched down, numb after. Those first forty years you spent feeling impervious; after that, your body creaked, your joints gave out, maybe they stuck plastic and pins in to hold you together like a goddamn tin man.

Enough, he told himself. No more feeling sorry for your sorry ass.

Getting back to the job at hand, he felt a surge of relief. Spotting a calendar hanging on the far side of the ancient refrigerator, he stepped up and saw it was December. The right month, but not the year; 1994. Ortho-McNeil was wishing everyone the very best this holiday season. The photograph showed a reindeer standing tall and proud on a strip of Arctic tundra. Underneath, their promo, CHOOSE ORTHO FOR EVERY WOMAN'S UNIQUE CONTRACEPTIVE NEEDS.

3

Emma Price was in the middle of feeding Katherine Rose. Let the machine pick up, she told herself. But when it did, it was Dawn. "Emma, are you there?" The frantic edge made it sound as if she'd gotten lost in the woods and was cell phoning in for rescue. Emma reached across the couch and, in doing so, jiggled Katie enough to cause a squeal, then a full-fledged, desolate shriek.

"Oh Christ," Emma said aloud into the receiver.

"So you are there." Dawn sounded a little too self-satisfied, especially considering Katherine's insistent wail. "We've got a possible client in your neck of the woods."

Her neck of the woods was a typical overstatement. Brooklyn was a very large borough; indeed, it had once been a city all its own. This was a fact that no one except Brooklynites seemed to recognize. Greenpoint was nowhere near Boerum Hill. With no traffic on the roads, a situation that occurred between three and four in the morning, Emma could have made it to the 94th Precinct in three quarters of an hour. However, this was Saturday, and not just any Saturday, the Saturday of the

week before Christmas. Dawn had apparently never
heard of gridlock alerts. Not to mention that the city
had had its first major snowfall in two years.

Still, duty was duty. Hers was to be lead investigator
for New York Capital Crimes and, in that guise, offer
up the best possible representation of a client's motivation, thereby avoiding death penalty prosecution, or at
least a rendering of a capital sentence. Which meant
that the earlier she arrived on the scene, the better.

An hour later, Emma was stuck on the Brooklyn
Queens Expressway, or as she liked to dub it, "the road
to nowhere." On the up side, she'd been able to listen to
the news reports and had discovered that their client
was Roland Everett, a disgruntled ex-employee at a
textile plant in Greenpoint. He'd shot the three Hasidic
Jewish owners at point-blank range, then taken out
scissors and cut off their payess.

Kinky . . . and sacrilegious. Emma couldn't wait to
meet him.

Switching to NPR, she found a program devoted to Dr.
Eleanor Hammond. Eleanor was giving a rousing speech
to her acolytes on the steps outside the Supreme Court. "I
wanted to be a surgeon, but I was dissuaded," Eleanor in-
toned. "Back then, women were shunted off into the
netherworld, pediatrics, or obstetrics. You don't give a
child sharp objects to play with, right?" That hoarse
laugh followed. Emma felt tenderness well up. She saw
Eleanor at the dinner table, telling some off-color joke,
then leaning back in her chair, and enjoying it too. "They
had good reason to be afraid, I suppose," Eleanor added.

Emma switched the radio off. There was a stab of
pain when she thought of Eleanor and how they'd left

things. She couldn't help but remember the last time they'd seen each other, totally by accident. Emma had been in the midst of a heated battle with two-year-old Liam, who was throwing a tantrum because she was refusing to buy him a stick of Dubble Bubble gum. She'd been leaning over his stroller, where he was, thank God, strapped down, and trying to reason with him, and someone had tapped her on the shoulder.

"Emma."

The voice had startled her. She'd known who it was, even before she'd turned and seen the damage the years had wrought. Eleanor still had that picture-perfect posture, and that bone-white hair, pulled back into a braid, but she was old, so old. She wore a long skirt and an orange short-sleeved silk blouse, the silver squash necklace overlaid at her throat.

"How are you?" Eleanor had asked warmly.

Thoroughly flustered, with a screaming child, all Emma had been able to come up with was, "Good."

"This is your son, then?"

The thought of disowning him did occur to her, but Emma relented. "Yes," she'd agreed.

"It's a difficult age, but of course, you're coping."

It had been a generous comment. One that Emma could hardly refuse.

"I guess," she had ventured, totally embarrassed. The way they'd left things, it had been years and years, an eternity. You couldn't make it up in one awkward moment. So they had stood there instead, the squalling child their centerpiece, all the things that Emma might have said flying away so completely.

"Well, don't be a stranger," Eleanor said finally,

lifting her hand in a peremptory wave that Emma realized was meant for whoever she was meeting, then starting off.

A stranger might not owe you anything, Emma thought, but the debt was huge when it came to Eleanor. Dr. Eleanor Hammond had been her mother's oldest, dearest friend. Josh had been her running buddy. That house had been like a second home for her.

I should have called out "Wait!" Emma told herself. I should have done the right thing, I should have offered something. Emma felt the tension in her body that came with her impulse to choke back tears. She shook them off, shook herself free, told herself that driving on a day like today was hard enough, trying to navigate each flooded patch of highway that emerged, without warning. The temperature had risen precipitously, wreaking havoc.

She forced herself to return to the present and discovered she was almost at the Greenpoint exit. There. Emma maneuvered her aching, moaning vehicle down the ramp, then decided to go for it, vaulting through the pool of water at the bottom. The car coughed and threatened to die, but Emma coaxed it with a "come on, do it, baby, do it." They made it across and up and through the yellow then red light that she was not about to stop for, considering.

Emma drove past empty lots and factories, then a neighborhood of apartment towers. She passed Hasidic Jews making the pilgrimage on foot, and segregated by sex, dark-coated, fur-hatted men, their sideburns curling into payess and women in groups, their heads covered with scarves, hats, or wigs. As the streets grew more residential, the inhabitants changed ethnicity; Hispanic women pushing baby strollers, then Boho-looking white twenty-somethings. Emma glanced over at her handy-dandy Brooklyn map. Meserole was three more blocks.

Three news vans huddled together for warmth at the far end of the street. Emma purposely turned the corner and found a spot. On her way back she scoped out the territory, then made an end run. By the time Judy Lomax, from Eyewitness News, had spotted her and called her name, she had made it up to the top of the station house steps. Don't look back now, she reminded herself, and didn't, as she skidded through the door, reaching for a marble column to keep herself from slamming into the desk sergeant.

They'd seen odder, apparently. He didn't even look up until she made an "ahem" noise, then took his time, scrutinizing her I.D. in full. Finally, he released her on her own recognizance back into the interior of the station house. Emma weaved around the maze of intake tables, catching snippets of conversation as she went. The whine of a kid wearing a do-rag telling the officer across the desk, "I didn't see him no way, man." In the next cubicle a voice was saying, "You're taking the Giants? Why not just take me out for lunch, that money's good as gone."

The officer at the door of interview room C let her in. Dawn sat on one side of the table, scribbling away diligently. On the other, handcuffed to his chair, was Mr. Roland Everett, a close-cropped, heavyset black male of uncertain years.

"Sorry I'm late," Emma said, sitting down next to Dawn and waiting for her presence to be acknowledged. Dawn did, finally, with a jerk of her head.

"Emma Price," she said gruffly, by way of introduction.

"Pleased to meet you." Roland Everett had a deep, deep voice and a pleasant smile.

Once seated, Emma made a lengthier physical assessment—no signs that he had suffered at the hands of the police, no flowering bruises, no split lip.

"You the one who tells whether I'm crazy?"

"Ms. Price is our investigator," Dawn said evenly.

"No head doctor? I thought you were all het up about getting me to see one." He cast his gaze on Dawn, let it stay there, level and decidedly hostile.

"That's later on." Dawn's voice was perfectly modulated, impartial, and professional. But Emma saw the lines on her face, the tension in her jaw; it told a different story, one of fatigue, and an impatience that lay just below the surface. Considering his present straits, Roland Everett was unlikely to care about pissing her off. But Emma knew better.

"What's this girl here gonna investigate anyhow?"

"I'll be contacting all of your relatives and friends," Emma said. "I'll talk with coworkers, with teachers, with members of your church, if you attend one. I'll build a profile."

"Profile me up? You're saying I'm godless. I got myself a church. I know where and how the savior's gonna land."

"Do you? That's good news," Emma offered, deciding that it couldn't hurt anyone to deflect his rage her way.

"You disbelieving me?"

"Not at all, if you can tell me the location, I'll go meet up with him. Or her."

Roland shook his head, but he was fixed on her now. "I'm not no crazy man. I told your lady friend here. I'll tell you too. Ask anyone out there. Those three had it coming."

"Why would that be?"

"Because." And a hmmph. He sat back.

"Because why?" Emma asked, and moved her leg so that when Dawn went to kick her, she found a vacant space instead.

"You ruin a man's life, there's got to be retribution."

"How did these men ruin your life?"

Emma kept her eyes pinned to Roland.

"They took away what was mine. Mr. Weinstein knows about it. You go ask him, if you're so curious."

"Mr. Weinstein?"

"He's my lawyer, which is what I told your friend over here. I don't need but one."

"Mr. Everett, I explained that to you. Stewart Weinstein has decided not to represent you. Which makes me what you've got." A significant pause, then Dawn added, "Unless of course you choose to represent yourself." It sounded to Emma as if she would like nothing better.

"You'd like it that way, wouldn't you? Well, I'm not falling. You got to have yourself a lawyer. People always suing your ass round here." His sly grin was showing he knew how things worked.

Stewart Weinstein was his counsel? Emma turned Dawn's way to make sure she'd gotten this right. Dawn ventured a terse nod, implicitly understanding her unstated question. Weinstein had a reputation for taking on very public cases, but his clients were almost always pure of heart, and left of center.

"Mr. Everett suffered a job-related injury," Dawn said, offering a shorthand version. "When it came time to collect disability, his employers refused to pay out."

"There I am, laying in my hospital bed when Marie finds out," Roland Everett muttered. "Cheap bastards went and pulled the plug on my insurance, and when I go and call them up, thinking it's some mistake, Mr. Ben Dov gets on the line and says how I'm the one got it wrong, how it was all a great big misunderstanding. He's all patient, explaining to me how there wasn't no coverage at all for what went wrong with me. No disability coming my way either so I shouldn't go expecting it. All that time, all those years, I kept on sitting tight. Marie wanted me to go out there and get something better, but I told her, baby, you got to trust them, they're good people." As Everett told the story, his demeanor underwent a subtle shift. His body began to wither, his voice took on a tremulous quality. He wants my sympathy, Emma noted.

"You were in no position to argue, I expect," she offered, thinking this might be enough.

"That's what they thought too," he pointed out. "Good people, huh? They take care of their own and no one else."

Deflecting his anti-Semitism for the moment, Emma asked, "What kind of injury had you sustained?" She was beginning to connect the dots; his eyes were striated with blood vessels, and his tongue kept lashing over his lips, indicating dry mouth—that, plus the mood swings, drugs had to be involved.

"Mr. Everett's spine was crushed. The doctors had to fuse it together. For a while it looked as if he'd be paralyzed. He's in constant pain."

"Not a day I don't suffer," he said.

Which meant opiates, Emma decided, and God knows what else. At least they had a shot at proving diminished capacity.

Dawn added a few more details to round out the picture. "They've been litigating against the Ben Dovs for six years. This last November, Mr. Everett received a judgment in his favor. It was a substantial judgment," she added. "Three million plus. The Ben Dovs filed for bankruptcy a day later."

"Wow," Emma said, and felt embarrassed by her impolitic outburst.

Everett seemed to like it, though. He smiled a winner's smile. Considering his current shackled state, it was more than a little ironic. "You know how those people are. Got themselves pillows stuffed up with money. Think a poor black fool like me can't get between them and their filthy lucre."

Now there was an interesting word choice. Emma didn't like Mr. Roland Everett, not at all. But she was still willing, ready, and able to provide an explanation for his actions. Emotional stress, plus an addiction to painkillers. His bigotry would have to be kept under wraps if at all possible. Curious, considering it, that Weinstein had taken him on. The cutting of the payess fit with the way he was spewing out invective. Emma was no psychiatrist, but she thought one explanation was a need to emasculate the Ben Dovs. Death wasn't enough to make up for what he felt he'd lost.

"My wife Marie's from the Deep South, down near Oxford, Mississippi."

"Yes?" Emma offered. Roland had changed course and she couldn't help but feel a sense of relief.

"She comes up here real young. Her mom and dad both dead, so she and that bitch sister of hers head here, stay with their cousins."

"Mr. Everett's wife left him in November," Dawn said.

"Sister of hers was the one that started it. Never could keep a man for herself so she got all up in Marie's face, saying I'm unsuitable. Thanksgiving, we have ourselves a fine dinner and then she clears off the table, says she's got something to tell me, and tells me, right in front of the girls, how she and them are going. Says she can't stand being round me no more with my negative attitude." Roland was gathering steam again, then something happened and his body sagged. Tears broke out in the corners of his eyes. "Imagine. Imagine her sayin' that."

Dawn slid something her way. Glancing down, Emma saw the wife's name, Marie Everett, an address out in Queens, and a phone number.

Dawn managed to contain herself until they got out the back door, to the alley behind the station. "Slip, sliding away," Emma hummed the song unconsciously, then realized why. She wanted to do the same to Dawn, who was having none of that, diligently keeping pace.

"How do you like our Mr. Everett?" she asked, not even attempting to mask the sarcasm.

Emma knew why. Like was hardly the word she would feel comfortable using, considering the context. "Diminished capacity," she ventured gamely.

"The drugs, you mean? Not an option."

"Why?"

"Before your tardy arrival Mr. Everett explained that he needed to maintain a clear head. No fool he, as he so eloquently explained. Therefore, he decided to forgo his pain medication, not for one day, not for two, for an entire week."

"What's he on?" Emma asked.

"You name it, he's taking it. And yes to your next question, every one of the medications is addictive."

"You believe him?"

"The toxicology will either bear him out or not. But my guess is he's not lying. He doesn't seem to see the need for it." There was something else, Emma could tell by the way Dawn's voice lowered, as if she were about to share a deep, dark secret. "There's a witness. She said he popped a handful of pills right after he finished shooting. Let me amend, right after he played Barber of Seville," Dawn added. "Apparently he got himself a drink from the watercooler and took them, one at a time."

"There's a witness!" This had not been reported on the news.

"Yes indeed. The Ben Dovs' executive secretary was in the room during the shooting. He told her to get under the table. When he was finished, he leaned over and mentioned she might want to call in the police."

"Crazy."

"And yet, entirely noncertifiable. I noticed you decided not to mention your own Semitic origins."

"Some things are better left unsaid," Emma noted. "Weinstein represented him after all."

"Yes, though God knows why. I forgot to mention

the real humdinger. One of the Ben Dovs is married to Moshe Levin's daughter."

"Moshe Levin as in developer Moshe Levin?"

"Yes."

"Shit."

"Your eloquence is, as always, astounding."

"Thanks," Emma offered wryly.

"You've got to admit, Mr. Everett has done himself proud."

Emma told herself the absence of the "our" in front of Everett's name signaled nothing. "You think Weinstein took the case because of the link with Levin?" she asked.

"Could be, Stewart loves publicity."

"I wonder why we never heard about it. Or had you?"

Dawn shook her head. "I'm guessing he discovered his client was a little unreliable, in fact, a first-class bigot. May I add, off the record, how heartily sick he makes me."

"That's not the point," Emma reminded her. Usually it was Dawn doing the reminding. And there had been plenty of opportunities. In the last few months their caseload included a mass murder at a bar, a distraught ex-boyfriend's slaughter of his girlfriend's parents and baby daughter, and a drug dealer who'd killed one of his runners in a dispute, then gunned down a twelve-year-old eyewitness.

"By the way, I'm adopting a baby," Dawn said.

There. There it was. An interesting segue.

"I heard about it from Brian."

"Did he tell you when I'm leaving?"

"Thursday?"

"I have to meet with the adoption people and then I

get to see her." Dawn chewed on her bottom lip for a while before saying, "Talk about crazy."

There it was, the sixty-four-thousand-dollar-almost-a-question. The answer, or lack of it, hung in the air between them. Emma couldn't exactly say, "Let me sleep on it."

"I'm taking a six-week leave. Then I'll see," Dawn confided.

"You'll see?" That brought Emma back to reality with a crash and a thud. "See about what?" But Emma knew. "You're thinking of quitting, aren't you? You can't drop this one on me and then fly off to the other side of the world." Emma knew she sounded desperate. She wondered why, and tried being rational. If Dawn left, there might be a new boss who would actually be easy to get along with. In another life, maybe, Emma noted. Her luck didn't run that way, and besides, Dawn was the one she had come back for. Impossible nature aside, she was great at what she did. And Emma knew her quirks.

"Is it so bad to want something for myself? I'm fifty years old, if I don't take the time now, when will I?"

Put this way, Emma felt horrible positing an argument. She looked at Dawn, and tried to see past her own crowded life, past what it would mean to shoulder the burden of Roland Everett, without Dawn to depend on. What she saw was a woman who was desolate. Each day she woke to another Sisyphean effort. Dawn Prescott had spent years trying to save the Roland Everetts of the world, and she wasn't a saint. It was wrong to expect her to act like one.

"Good luck," Emma said, feeling a sudden tenderness well up.

The look on Dawn's face made her more than glad she'd managed to still her own needs, to look past them.

"You mean it?" A little girl's voice, with its tug of hope.

"Of course I do," Emma said. "And don't worry. You'll make a great mom." Before she could be interrogated any further, she added, "Speaking of being a mom, I dumped the kids down the block at Suzanne's. I'd better go get them."

Emma made for the corner, for the safety and security of her own front seat. She revved the motor, pulled out, and hit 1010 to get a traffic update. It wasn't really a lie, she told herself. After all, many women who seemed ill-suited for motherhood flourished in the role, capitalizing on parts of themselves that had long lain dormant.

Of course, others failed in an almost imperial way. Speak of the devil . . .

"Dr. Eleanor Hammond, well-known abortion rights activist, was found early this morning . . ."

Emma felt sadness rub up against her and made an attempt to deflect it. She switched to 95.5. Nirvana playing one of her favorite apocryphal songs. Kurt had had a gun, as it turned out.

4

Laurence Solomon decided the mess in the living room was the ultimate. There were books on top of books, and little pick-me-up, put-me-down objects dressing all the built-in shelves. He exchanged a look with a sad-eyed china bull, then moved on to its co-horts, three African gazelles munching on carved grass, beside them a potbellied clay pig, rolling on its back, a gleeful snout rendered with startling accuracy. One shelf down from the fauna, flora had been cap-tured in a collection of glass paperweights. Underneath that, crammed in, the shelf dipping low from the strain, vases, more than any florist could use.

Decor? That was the wrong word for what the good doctor had rendered in here. Framed posters stacked one on top of the other, up and down the walls. Plenty referred to ending the war, as in Vietnam. One was par-ticularly familiar, since he'd seen it plastered every-where in his youth; a dove gripped a sprig of green in its beak and asked for PEACE IN OUR TIME. Another showed a blown-up photo of protesters linking arms in front of the Pentagon. The next a woodcut of an NLF fighter crouched low in a rice paddy, ammo belts criss-crossing his chest.

On the opposite wall, the theme changed. This one showed an incomplete history of the women's move-ment, posters of lambda symbols and clenched fists, then a line drawing of a woman in a T-shirt with the warning WE OWN OUR BODIES!

Laurence turned back to take in the son. Joshua Hammond was busily tapping something onto his lap-top. Ten minutes ago, Bob, Leslie Hammond's signifi-cant other, had gone in search of the deceased's daughter.

The front door slammed.

"Here I am," she said, an announcement that seemed more than a little redundant.

Leslie Hammond was a tall woman, almost six feet by his reckoning. Her gray hair frizzed out. Her uni-form was country stark, work boots that tracked in some snow, old jeans, a heavy wool jacket. Striding over to the piano bench, she shoved some books off and took a seat. Her look said, "Let's get this over with."

"I thought it would save time if I spoke with both of you together," Laurence offered.

Her brother had watched her progress across the room with a sort of professional cool. Now he clapped his computer shut, and leaned back on the couch, shooting his sibling a derisive look. As for Bob, he was with them, but just barely. He leaned against the door frame, wearing a long-suffering expression.

Yet another happy family, Laurence thought, and went with his instincts, in this case, no sugarcoating necessary. "Mr. Hammond, you told Detective O'Malley that you and your mother weren't close. I wonder if you could elaborate."

"I'll do my best." After this, a self-deprecating smile.

Laurence had noted certain things about Josh Hammond already. Judging from the photos on the walls, he'd grown out, not exactly fat, but thick. He looked prosperous enough. The tan was tasteful, a hint dressing his cheeks, adding a touch of color. Then the suit he wore. It was cut from lightweight wool and fit his body perfectly. Here was a man who knew his tailor. Then that mercilessly thin gold watch, exposed right above his wrist as he tucked the computer into its case.

You couldn't avoid the contrast with his big sister's army-navy attire.

Laurence laid down a bet: like mother, like daughter.

As for the son? He was taking his own sweet time with Laurence's question, making sure to toss a look back at his sister, and offer one to Bob, before finally clearing his throat and turning to meet Laurence's eyes. "We didn't talk regularly."

"How about being a little more specific."

"Well, it had been a few years." Another long, slightly embarrassed pause, then, "Twenty-two, in point of fact."

"You had some sort of falling out?"

"I guess that's one way of putting it."

Twenty-two years without seeing your own mother? Josh Hammond flushed, apparently realizing the impropriety of offering even this low-pitched levity as a response.

"Why don't you tell me about it?"

"I'm not sure how to begin." Hammond's hands were knotting, unknotting. Laurence read his face again and caught the signs of grief. Dark circles under his eyes, and a worn quality, which, with the tan, gave him the unfortunate look of someone with a wasting illness. "I guess Mom and I never really got along," Josh Hammond ventured. "It wasn't that one fight, it was the hundred we'd had before. I got to an age where I could go, so I left."

"You didn't come visit, but you spoke?"

Hammond shook his head.

"That must have been one major blowout."

"I was young. And stupid." The last was thrown out bitterly. "I have this problem with holding a grudge."

The man was the king of understatement. "What prompted the visit?"

"I guess I got tired of sulking." Hammond had apparently regained his composure. There was humor in his tone. "I guess it looks bad for me."

"Now why assume that?"

"A life at the movies, I guess. I've just admitted that there was no love lost between me and my mom. And I found the body."

"We've checked out your alibi. Unless you can shape-shift, I think you're in the clear." Laurence paused to let Hammond release whatever internal sigh he was holding on to, then added, "Of course, you could have hired someone to do the job for you."

"Stop it!"

Laurence had to give her credit. She'd waited longer than he might have predicted. But Leslie Hammond's slow burn had finally ignited. "Josh, the detective doesn't know how you are. My brother thinks he's being funny."

"I'm only being realistic," Josh Hammond countered. "Most people are murdered by their nearest and dearest. Didn't you know, Les?"

"It's sick," she spat out.

"Yes, but true."

"How you can go on like this!"

"Like what?" he posed innocently.

"Pardon me if I don't find having my mother murdered funny."

The glare was official. Hammond seemed chastened, at least for a moment. He brushed his hair away from his forehead, a nervous gesture that must have developed when he had substantially more up top. Dead silence followed. Laurence took a moment to do another survey of the room. Housekeeper wanted, posthaste. The couch needed a good going over, repair of the popped-open seams, plus a stiff dry-cleaning. As for the light, it was stifled in here the same way it had been in the dining room, courtesy of dark blue velvet curtains. In order to see, every lamp had been lit, the murky light they provided symptomatic of the many burned-out bulbs they contained.

"I won't keep you much longer," Laurence said, which was a lie. He was going to keep them as long as he could. What he had were sparks. What he wanted was a conflagration. Josh Hammond might be in the clear, and the *might* was important. The daughter, on the other hand, had not even offered an alibi. At home, alone, was the most Caitlin O'Malley had gotten from her. Laurence took another second to pretend to scan his notes, then said, "Mr. Hammond, you said you arrived a little after three A.M. Stepped out to get your luggage. That was when you noticed there was a light on in the upstairs bedroom."

Hammond nodded.

Back to his notes, then. "You used your own key to open the downstairs door. Twenty-two years of not talking, but you kept the key?"

"Don't ask me why. But then, maybe it's inherited. Look at all this useless shit." Hammond extended his arm, taking in the length and breadth of the room. Then he reached over and unfolded his coat, dug his hand into the pocket, and emerged with a tan leather pouch. He sprang it open and inside there was a flush of keys, enough to make any jailer's belt proud.

"I can't believe you're wasting our time like this." Leslie Hammond threw it out. Threw down the gauntlet. Laurence caught Bob's cautionary look spirited her way, which she pointedly ignored. "This is the Society's work," she said. "They've been stalking Mom for years."

Laurence raised an eyebrow. And she did what he knew she would, rushed in to elucidate, assuming his ignorance.

"The Society for the Protection of the Unborn."

"I see. Your proof?"

"Who else would want my mother dead? Who would gain by murdering her? She was seventy-eight. She wasn't a threat to anyone."

Laurence took her measure with a slow gaze up, then down, and did it long enough to make her uncomfortable. When he saw the flush start on her cheeks, he said, "Popular wisdom aside, I'll ask again, do you have evidence?"

"That's not my job."

"Fair enough. It's mine. And the way I do my job is, I don't jump to conclusions." Point being made, he decided he could throw her a bone. Turning back to Josh, he said, "You think your sister's right? Was your mother's death politically motivated? Was it antiabortionists?"

"How would I know?"

"You've heard what your sister claimed. No one else had a grudge against your mother."

"I don't know. I suppose I'm no expert, but Mom did have a way of pissing people off. It's what comes of being the sort of person who says whatever comes to mind."

"Oh Josh." Leslie gasped. "How can you?"

"Look, Les, she wasn't exactly diplomatic. Remember how Murray put up that sign in his shop, with a photograph of her, WANTED FOR TREASON." Turning back to Laurence, he explained, "Murray ran Kosher Meats on Flatbush."

"If you're thinking of pointing the finger at Murray, he died three years ago," Leslie said.

"You know that's not what I meant," Josh said. And got a derisive snort from his sister. "Murray was a sweet, sweet guy whose political views were a little conservative. He made the mistake of elaborating on what should happen to certain draftees who chose not to serve in the armed forces, and Mom took off after him."

"You would have been one of them if you hadn't gotten that Four F deferment," Leslie pointed out.

"I'm not disputing that. I'm only saying that Mom loved Murray as a butcher, and it would have behooved her to keep silent, considering how she never wanted to buy meat anywhere else. Instead, she pipes up with the very loud description of what courage really is, and goes on to add that if he was a really courageous person he'd know it was better not to believe the pack of lies the government handed out. It got worse after that, something about sheep and being herded along, and then Murray threw her out of the store. Believe me, if it was only that one time, but Les knows how it was with her. By the age of fourteen I was Mom's personal shopper. I'd pick up nylons for her, feel the vegetables, buy bagels from H & H."

"That's quite a list."

"In Mom's view, the more righteous the cause, the more it needed a champion."

"It was only after Dad died," Leslie insisted. "Mom was never difficult before . . ."

"So you admit she was difficult," Josh countered.

"No, I didn't mean it that way. Opinionated," Leslie said.

"Dad did all the errands for her. You think there might have been a reason?"

"I think you always give everything the worst possible spin." His sister's baleful stare was the addendum.

"Always is a big word, considering we haven't seen each other in some time."

"Whose fault is that?"

"Mine," he said quietly.

"In other words, you're hardly the one who should be talking about the family."

Leslie Hammond's nostrils flared. A standoff ensued. Josh finally broke the silence. "My sister knows better than I do about all this. People do mellow with age, I guess." The last was hardly a veiled insult, but it was apparently his way of backing down.

Leslie walked to the window and stared out at the winter wonders. Her back was rigid, quivering with hurt.

Enough for now, Laurence decided, and said to Josh, "It'll only be a few more minutes, if you would come out here in the hall."

Past Bob, still standing sentrylike by the door. The hallway was empty, a piece of furniture there held mail. Above it, a hat rack with two old caps, both of them apparently freebies; one advertised the Bagel Bin, the other Rexall Drugs. Was there even a Rexall anymore?

"You stepped through, set your bags down right there. What next?"

Josh scrutinized the hall, taking in the bags where he'd left them. "Up the stairs," he said.

"To see your mother?"

"Sure, to see her if she was awake."

"You assumed she was because the light was on."

A nod.

Hammond led the way. They passed family photos, big sis astride a pony, offering an elated smile and hoisting a ribbon aloft; posed baby pictures of them both, each cunningly dropped onto a bearskin rug; Eleanor Hammond standing on the Supreme Court steps, arm in arm with a band of women, all of them glowing. By the look of it, taken enough years ago to reflect the *Roe v. Wade* decision. She'd been an attractive woman, elegant, and as strikingly tall as her daughter.

Josh paused by the bedroom door.

"I hope you're not expecting me to reenact the crime," Josh said.

"It would certainly save us both a lot of trouble," Laurence countered, deadpan. Bad jokes were apparently Josh's way of dealing with nerves. Nervous was what he was, Laurence decided, and who wouldn't be? He extended his right arm and Josh stepped into the bedroom, where the bed was still unmade. The entire room had been dusted for prints, a thin layer of white coating the bedside table, the dresser tops. He'd been here once already, second time around he noted her night table reading: at the top, the biography of John Adams by McCullough; directly underneath, the complete works of Shakespeare; then Aristotle's *Ethics*; and finally, in a lighter vein, John Irving's *Cider House Rules*.

He got the reference. "Where did you head next?" he asked, nudging Josh along.

Hammond took a moment more to consider, then walked to the bathroom door, swung it open, and said, "In here."

"Why?"

"I'm not sure."

Laurence waited him out, saw him purse his lips to think it through. He offered, "She was old, I thought she might have fallen."

"Was the door shut?"

"I'm not sure." He closed his eyes, trying for a resurrection. With them still closed he said, "No, open a little, I pushed it back."

Voilà. In they went together, four toothbrushes locked in their holder. Two more on the sink. Three different types of toothpaste, all with the tops off. Craig Martin, a brand so old and so defunct, Solomon remembered it from his youth. The woman must have hoarded it. On the wall opposite the shower there was a daily calendar, another freebie from Ortho, with days marked off with X's. This one was current, and Friday last was checked.

"You have any idea what that's for?" Solomon asked.

"It's a calendar."

"Strange place to put one."

"I don't know, I mean what's strange," Josh countered. "Have you taken in Mom's idea of decor?"

Laurence had to admit he made a valid point.

"Where to next?"

Out, and into the sister's old room. His mother had maintained it as a dual-use unit; half shrine, half garbage pit.

"The light was off, did you put it on?"

"I tried." Josh smiled and Solomon did the honors, testing the overhead, then the lamp on the dresser.

"So you didn't even step in?"

"She wasn't in here, I could make out that much. Who could fit with all those clothes piled up?" Men's suits, a mile high on the bed, and even on the floor. The odor of mothballs filled the room.

"Those were my dad's," Josh said. Laurence had pretty much figured.

"When did you lose him?"

"I like how you put that, tactful. It was thirty-two years ago. I was eleven at the time. Leslie was seventeen."

"What happened? A heart attack?"

"Nothing that benign. A car mowed him down on Flatbush. He died before he got to the hospital."

"That's a hard thing, having your dad die that young."

"For me? Or for him?"

Laurence waited this piece of repartee out. When it passed, he got serious. "It wasn't fun, I'll give you that," Josh admitted. But his expression made it clear how this was none of his business. Protective of the father, Laurence decided; as for Mom, she seemed to be fair game.

Hammond stepped back out into the hall and said, "I tried checking my old room upstairs, but the attic door was locked."

So they went down again, back into the entry hall. Here, Hammond hesitated, because the *where* that was next was the most painful. Then he took a breath, fortified himself, and turned left, heading for the kitchen and offering Laurence the play-by-play. "I came through here." The dining room entered, then exited, as Hammond pushed the swinging door to the kitchen open. And stopped, for good. "She was bent over the table."

"What did you think?" Laurence asked softly.

"What did I think?" Hammond's voice rose. He pushed his hair back, in that reflexive, habitual motion. "I thought she was dead. She had the back of her head

shot off. I mean, who can be prepared. You saw her . . ."
His voice dropped, he stepped back, backed out of the
door and into the dining room, leaning for comfort on
the sideboard.

Laurence saw the shaking in his body, knew he was
holding on and holding back whatever emotion had
come, unbidden.

"What did you think had happened?" Laurence said,
coming closer.

"I don't know!" Joshua Hammond was finally past
deflecting his inquiries with humor; he'd come to the
place where rage took over. Good, Laurence thought.
"You think I assumed she'd fallen and hit her head?"

Laurence refined the question. "Did you feel
afraid?"

"Of what?"

There, there it was. "Of the person who'd done this
to her."

"I don't know." Hammond seemed puzzled, getting
the inference now. "I called the police."

"You waited out by the door?"

Laurence stepped back that way. Hammond followed gratefully.

"Yes."

"You didn't choose to wait outside, then?"

"I don't know. I was in shock."

"But you stayed in the house. Which phone did you
use?"

"That one." He pointed to the hall table, where a ro-
tary phone sat with its veil of white powder.

"Leslie would have helped her," Josh muttered under
his breath.

"What do you mean?"

"Leslie wouldn't have left her alone like that. She would have been in there, trying to do something."

"What would she have accomplished," Laurence said evenly. "And it would only have made our job harder."

"I tell you, I wish I could be that clinical." Hammond stared longingly at his suitcases, waiting by the door.

"After you made the call, while you were waiting, did you do anything else?"

"No."

Laurence pressed on. "People do things out of habit." He pointed to the stack of mail waiting on the hall table. "Did you put the mail up?"

"I don't think so," Josh said. "No. I'm sure I didn't. Why?"

Laurence didn't need to tell him. "Good enough," he said.

Hammond looked as if he might press for more details, but then he shrugged and stepped toward the living room door.

"By the by," Laurence said, "do you think your sister's right about the Society?"

"Leslie's always right, didn't you know?" Josh quipped. Then he returned to the relative safety of the living room. When the door closed, Laurence pulled out an evidence bag and took the top bundle of mail off the teeter-totter mountain, verifying the Friday delivery date by the postmark before dropping it inside and sealing it tight.

5

It was cold, too damn cold. Emma lay on a block of ice, staring down at what was trapped inside, a mastodon in mid-charge, its tusks raised, captured in prehistoric rigor. Her own limbs were stiff. Her breath thin. She was slowly losing sensation in her extremities. She could die, which was a real no-no in your own dream. The only antidote was forcing herself awake.

She did and discovered the truth. "It's fucking freezing," she said, and saw the proof, her expelled breath making a visible cloud. Jumping out from under the covers, Emma pulled a sweater on top of her nightgown of choice, one of Liam's castoffs, a worn-out red T with VOODOO printed in white on a red background. She touched the stone-cold radiator, then made her way down the stairs and into the basement. Switching on the light, she admired her land-based version of an undersea creature, a heating system that most resembled a giant metal octopus. There was no sound coming from its great gas-driven maw.

"Great!" Emma exclaimed. "Just fucking great!" She would have kicked the metal base, but she had done this before, and gotten, in return, a vivid, stabbing pain. Ascending the shaky wooden stairs, she placed an emergency call to Brooklyn Union Gas and waited on the line for fifteen goddamn minutes, with her teeth chattering, listening to elevator music, interrupted by announcements of how this call was being recorded to ensure efficiency. Finally, a human being emerged. He promised to have someone there by noon.

And so begins Sunday, Emma thought, the proverbial day of rest.

Exterior warmth was in short supply. To replace it, Emma heated a kettle of water, then filled the fireplace with the last of the logs she'd dragged back from the corner fruit mart in her shopping cart. A desperate move, since the fireplace was pretty much a decorative affair. It gave off no heat unless you practically threw yourself inside.

Running upstairs, Emma took soft steps, first into Katie's and then into Liam's room to add covers. She returned to the kitchen to drink the cup of tea that she could only stand when it was dosed with plenty of sugar and milk, too early for coffee, not quite six A.M. yet. She felt extremely British, almost ready to queue up. Hearing the thud of the paper against the front door, she went to retrieve it and spread it out in front of the not-quite-raging fire. She contemplated the bad news of the day for an entire minute before Katherine Rose called out.

Emma had long ago dubbed herself the "Multitask Queen." Thus Katherine Rose suckled at her breast while she turned the pages of the newspaper, reading with one part of her brain, juggling what-if's with the rest. What if the heater finally needed replacing? She could take out a loan, except she'd done that two months ago when both the roof and hot water heater developed leaks. There was the possibility of asking a friend to lend her the $4,599 plus tax. But what friend would she feel right being that beholden to? And what friend of hers had that sort of cash to lend? Suzanne, her nearest and dearest, had recently been downsized to part-time status. Suzanne's husband's job was, at best, precarious. Others were in similar tight straits.

All except for Dawn, whose tidy trust fund made salary irrelevant.

Don't go there, Emma told herself. Dump this place. It's worth a cool million. The logical approach, one she had used in getting Will to cede her the property. She'd asked for nothing more than basic child support in return. It had seemed a more than fair arrangement, considering Will's flight into the arms of the lovely, much younger Jolene. At the time, Emma had believed Liam had too much on his plate to cope with moving. She'd thought he'd get used to things, and then they'd see.

Well, she'd be signing the divorce papers on Friday, and as far as she could tell, Liam was getting worse, not better. She pondered the duality; a son who was sweetness and light one moment, harsh and mean-spirited the next. Add to that his near failing grades, his chronic absence from school, and some even more troubling activities. She sighed. There was no choice involved, she would have to patch up this less-than-seaworthy vessel.

Shivering, Emma pressed herself closer to the fire and picked up the Style section. Frivolous, upper-class lifestyles could be diverting. She turned the pages and read the gardening tip of the week, which dealt with forcing narcissi into a perfumed, indoor display to create "the quality of spring in the ruins of winter." Not something she had the time for, what with the piles of laundry lurking in her darkened bedroom. Emma realized that wasn't all. She'd put a load in the washer several days ago and forgotten all about it. By now, it was probably frozen solid. Looking past gardening to the opposite page, she scanned the happy couples. Emma started to turn the page, then stopped, because one of those grinning couples looked a trifle too familiar. Scanning again, she discovered why.

"Adams-Price engagement."

"Jolene Adams announces her engagement to William Price III. Jolene is the daughter of Mariana and Lowell Adams. Her father, Lowell, is the chairman of Empire Industries and serves on the boards of the Metropolitan Museum, Lincoln Center, and the New York Historical Society. Her mother, Mariana, is treasurer of the New York Horticultural Society, and the vice president of the National Junior League."

No need to read on. No need to find out about the groom-to-be's family. She knew every WASPy one intimately. For ten years she had been the object of their mannered disapproval. They had probably been whispering "Jewess" under their breaths, raising their eyebrows at the affront to their dubious purity as soon as she turned her back.

Emma saw that her cell phone was in reach. She wriggled backward across the floor without disturbing Katherine Rose's death grip on her nipple. *There. Got it!* Inching back to get closer to the warmth, she punched in Will's number. No brilliant opening sally came to mind. "Couldn't even wait for the body to get cold?" Or how about, "Do I get to be your maid of honor? I've got the perfect ring." Hers, which he'd claimed was a family heirloom. It was hiding upstairs, at the bottom of her underwear drawer.

Luckily, fate interceded. The phone was sucked out of her hand and into the air, landing with a crash on the wood floor.

"Hey." Emma admired how Katherine had managed to slap the phone away while keeping her mouth suctioned to Emma's breast. Her daughter offered up a self-satisfied smile.

The battery had fallen out. Wires led from it to the plastic casing. Emma took a deep, cleansing breath and decided it was just as well. She was not entirely prepared to do battle.

"Wassup?"

Liam emerged from the doorway wearing a T-shirt and clinging boxer shorts. The goose bumps were apparent from across the room.

"Get over here," Emma said, unhooking Katherine's mouth, which had a film of milk across it, wiping her clean, and buttoning up the front of her shirt, then rolling up the offending newspaper and using it to stoke the fire. Liam came close, bleary-eyed, dazed, and thoroughly a teenager. His hair was tousled with sleep. Pink spots ruled each cheek. Half man and half boy, a stranger who was also an intimate friend. He crowded in close, resting his body against her. Crushing her, in fact, with his full 128 pounds. Liam tugged Katherine onto his lap, and she stared up at her older brother adoringly. Behind him the yellow-tongued flame disgorged chips of blackened paper.

Katherine Rose said, "We um."

Not mama. Not papa. Not dog. Not cat. We um. Latinate in sound. Her first word had been his name.

Emma quietly assessed her two fine children; Katherine was already a talker, the cascade of sounds pouring out of her lips from morning till blessed night. Often enough, Emma actually understood, possibly they shared a telepathic bond. While Liam had talked much later. At one and a half, when words finally emerged, they weren't a cascade of nonsense syllables at all. They were fully formed demands. Liam had always been a watcher, cautious, calculating. Emma knew this about her son, he did not trust easily. But when he did, he offered up his heart.

Emma noted that the cold air seemed to accentuate his tangy smell, the uncorked fragrance known as eau d'homme. Emma nuzzled him. Kissed the top of his head. He didn't push her off but attacked Katherine instead, causing a squeal, and using that as a diversion.

"You want me to stop?"

"Shtop."

He playacted a threatened tickle and Katherine's response was ear-shattering.

"You're freezing," Emma noted.

"I'm not."

"You are. Put on a sweater. And some socks."

"I'm fine."

"There's no heat, Lee."

"It's not cold," he said, stubborn to the last.

"When you leave home, you can be an Arctic explorer. But for now, go."

She flashed her spear-driven eyes his way.

"Fine," he said, with a put-upon sigh. Then got up to do her bidding.

At least he hadn't flipped her the finger to her face, she thought as she heard his bare feet tapping up, his shod ones tapping down. Liam stretched out his now-fully-clothed monumental length in front of her, hogging the fire. His puppy dog gracelessness held its own charm. That hair with its mishmash of color, flecks of gold and red and green, her son's incipient mustache, his brilliant smile.

"Can I put some more newspaper in?" he said.

"Sure."

He stuffed it in. Watched it catch. Leaned in greedily to the flames. "Cool," he said.

"Breakfast?" she asked, knowing that she was putting off the inevitable and grateful to be able to do it for him. And for herself. Avoidance made her feel almost cheerful. "How about pancakes?" she offered.

On the plus side, they had almost enough milk for pancakes. Emma settled into being Mom. Mom in Lapland. Stalactites and stalagmites decorated the kitchen windows. Touching an icicle, Emma found her skin clinging and had to carefully disengage. Turning to the sink, she tried running the water and discovered only a trickle flowed out. The banging from below was ominous. Frozen pipes, all she needed. Emma shut off the tap, then ransacked the closets until she discovered the last surviving space heater. Plugging it in, she directed the flow of warmth to the pipes under the sink, then did the only other thing she could think of, turned on the oven and opened the door.

"There," she said aloud.

Emma cracked an egg, added milk and pancake flour, a dollop of oil, whisked, heated up the griddle, and poured. Watching the batter bubble up, she remembered how her mother had been such a miserable failure in the kitchen. Her breakfast was the ultimate pièce de résistance: pancakes that were either wet in the center or burned on one side; scrambled eggs that her mother dropped back to the mixing bowl to serve, so that the eggs, dry as ordered, betrayed a slippery hint of their former, raw selves; or, on a really bad day, cold cream of wheat with a fully formed tab of butter and a dollop of skim milk. Emma's mild form of protest had been turned to her family's advantage. She rocked at cooking, particularly the morning meal. Today, she loaded up Liam's plate with four perfect pancake circles, golden brown and crowned with a healthy dose of maple syrup.

She should have felt proud of herself.

But didn't. Not at all.

Will, you curious bastard, she thought.

Liam hummed as he chowed down. Katherine Rose had drifted off to sleep in his lap. Emma shut her eyes and leaned back against the fire screen.

"Thanks, Mom," Liam said. Then Emma heard the sound of the plate scrabbling against the hardwood floor. She felt her son lean in against her. He set his legs on top of her own. She held on tight to him, and by proxy to her daughter. Felt suddenly afraid to move, or even breathe, because that might disturb the beautiful symmetry, although her legs were starting to get pins and needles, and he was, in point of fact, cutting off the circulation, pressing down so casually with so much weight, she would have to ask him to move . . . and then, mercifully, the doorbell rang.

"I'll get it," Liam said, setting Katherine Rose down with uncharacteristic care, then leaping to his feet.

Emma attempted to stand and found it hard, due to the lack of feeling in her right leg and the shooting pains in her left. She kneaded her left calf and heard the front door open.

"I'm coming," she called out, making for the hall. And stopped short, because Liam was back, behind him a man who was clearly not your typical Brooklyn Union Gas employee. Another Jehovah's Witness, she decided, then quickly reassessed: the man had on an expensive cashmere full-length coat, and a brown scarf, pulled open at the neck. She dismissed the idea of this man hawking *The Watchtower.*

"Hello, Em," he said. She squinted. He knew her by name, which meant they were at least acquaintances, knew her better than that; he'd said Em, not Emma, not Mrs. Price. The voice, she recognized that voice, but it didn't work with the man who stood before her. She would have to come up with a convenient way to admit defeat, names escaped her so often these days. She'd worked up a file of excuses. "Sorry, I don't have my glasses on," or the entirely honest, if always embarrassing, "I know I know you."

He laughed and that gave him away.

"Josh," Emma said, slapping her hand to her forehead. Then she reached out and gave him a bear hug.

* * *

"Mom checking out all the news that's fit to print. Hell of a way to describe it," Emma said.

"It's my paltry attempt at humor."

"How are you really?"

"Really? You don't want to know."

But she did. Joshua, her almost brother, and best friend for years and years, had emerged through the time portal. She went to him, leaving the half-prepared coffee for the time being, and settled a hand on his shoulder. He looked up, blood draining from his face. "You do this for a living? I don't know how you stand it."

"You learn to divorce yourself," she said. "No one expects that from you, Josh."

"I don't know," he said. "I'm not sure I have the right to feel this bad."

"Why not?"

"You know why not," he countered.

"Don't be silly. You've lost a parent. No one realizes how it feels till it happens."

"You mean all those times when I told her 'I wish you'd die' don't count."

"You didn't really say that?"

"Only once or twice."

"People say horrible things to each other," Emma admitted, stroking his hair gently. It was thinner, but still ample for a man his age.

"You never did," he countered. "You were always generous. Look, you're not even blaming me now."

"It hardly seems appropriate under the circumstances." Emma retreated, busying herself with the espresso pot. She poured in water, stuffed in coffee, set it on the stove, and listened to the burner click once, twice, thrice, then catch.

Liam was down the block at Suzanne's, as was Katherine Rose. Convenient that her best friend was mourning her inability to have a second child and thus in the grip of constant baby lust.

He thinks he can just waltz back in.

It was the mantra she'd repeated as she returned home. And part of her was taking odds on his leaving, but no, he hadn't bolted this time. He'd stayed put in the living room, leafing through an old issue of *Rolling Stone*. In her absence, he'd even done her the service of letting the repairmen in. Their names, he told her, were Sal and Tony. They were downstairs right now, playing a tune on the worn-out plumbing.

"So what does the primary think?" she asked, and seeing his bewilderment amended her question to, "The detective in charge. Who is it anyway?"

"Someone named Solomon."

Oh, Emma thought, and was sure her face gave her away. Then realized there was no reason to expose herself. Especially considering where she and Laurence had left off Friday night. Turning her back, she reined any emotion in tight, then reached up to get them both mugs. Retrieving the last of the sugar and setting it out on the table, Emma took a seat.

"I hear he's very good," she said, satisfied that her tone betrayed no deeper knowledge.

"Leslie's already talking about calling someone she knows at the F.B.I. She's convinced he's not doing his job."

"Why would she think that?"

"Because it's Leslie." Emma knew what he was intimating. She'd run into Leslie several times over the years and always walked away feeling somehow diminished. Leslie had this way of thrusting her back emotionally, to the scared child she used to be, the one who shuddered when Josh's big sister, Leslie, barred her way to the playhouse where she and Emma's sister, Rosa, were thick in conference with a "no brats allowed."

"She should back off," Emma said. Of all people for her to try and mess with. She could easily imagine Laurence's response. It almost made her feel sorry for Leslie.

"You try and tell her," he said. "Even that boyfriend of hers, Bob, is having no luck."

"I met him once," Emma said. "He seemed nice enough."

"What with his infirmity."

"I didn't notice."

"He's mute."

"He is not. Josh, stop it!"

The coffee was burbling away on the stove. She stood, got the pot, and returned to pour them each a healthy dose.

"You know what I do for a living, now what about you?" she asked, changing the subject. "You look altogether too prosperous."

"Only because I am." His smile switched on, full wattage. "I'm a corporate consultant."

"Really? I always wondered, what do corporate consultants actually do?"

"Fix things without getting our hands dirty."

"Ah."

Josh leaned back, sipping on the dregs of his coffee. When he set it down, he dabbed at his mouth with the napkin. Fastidious, still. He'd had the only clean hippie lair in town. Emma looked him over, the body, widened by age and diet, the softness in the cheeks hiding the impossibly high cheekbones. There was gridwork at the corner of his eyes, his hair was graying at the temples. But there were still laugh lines aplenty. He was a man, but possibly still her Josh, that other lovely, daring boy.

"So you live in San Francisco?"

"I keep an apartment there. Most of my time's spent up-country."

"You mean that place you sent me photos of?"

"A new house, actually. But it's the same property. Up in Sebastopol."

"It was beautiful."

"You never came to see."

"You never sent an address."

"Good point," he admitted, and looked like he might say more when there was a crash, bang, boom from below. Then, a burst of heat from the radiator. A fizzing. A bubbling up. Emma felt her body begin to unclench. Heat. A miracle had taken place, here, in her own home in downtown Brooklyn. Things could change for the better, she told herself, then threw in an addendum wrought out of hard-won experience, Right, and cows could spread their gossamer wings and fly.

"Hello?" the repairman's voice boomed out.

"In here," Emma responded, then heard the sound of tramping feet. Sal and his partner stepped into the kitchen. He had the good-natured grin of a working-class savior.

"We got her working," he said, talking to Josh, assuming, of course, that this was the man of the house.

"I'm the owner," Emma said, and saw there was more coming, because Sal's face wore that familiar, funereal expression. She knew, with sinking heart and curdling stomach, what they were about to mourn, together.

"You got yourself a real monster down there," Sal said. "Haven't seen one of those in years. You know when they made them? Back in the forties. Thing is, a boiler . . . it's got a set shelf life. Which you might manage to extend, all things considered. With this one, you've been extending and extending. I look in and what I see is how you got yourself some permanent damage to the motor, plus no way to control the thermostat. Somebody jerry-rigged that thing and got it working, but what they did?" He shrugged, as if to say "beats me." "And that's not the worst piece of news. There's rust showing underneath. Could be holes already. Once you get that, you get a buildup of carbon monoxide. Silent killer. You got to get yourself a new boiler, pronto. Till then, what you got to do is crack the windows. You'll be wanting to once the heat gets going. Now, what I'm saying here is, give us the sign and we'll see what we can do for you. I'm not making no guarantees, mind you." A meaningful look, one that expressed that his only desire was to serve, but he had a predicament, after all. "Still, being as you seem to have kids."

"I do. A baby in fact."

"I figured as much by the stroller." He wasn't only a professional repairman, he was a superspy as well. "You got the holidays coming up, want to have the family over. We might be able to fit you in today."

"But I definitely need a new boiler?"

"That's about the size of it."

"How much is it going to run me?" Emma steeled herself, knowing there would only be an instant's grace between the whoosh of air as the shells discharged and the explosion as they hit their appointed target.

"Four thousand nine hundred, plus tax of course."

"Oh." The word was small. She'd had better offers from other, itinerant repairmen. But none would be able to provide her with a boiler on the Sunday before Christmas.

"We're cutting you a break."

"I'm not sure," she ventured. "I've done a little research . . ." Leaving it hanging in the hopes that he might be moved to pity.

"This here is for a Weil-McLain, top-of-the-line boiler. Gets a five-star efficiency rating. In the end, it saves you money."

Repairmen who touted a new appliance always said that. Emma counted forward, January first the mortgage came due, January tenth, Con Ed. Liam's wish list was not even half done. Look on the bright side, she told herself. It was Sunday, so they couldn't even try to deposit the check till Monday. That was if they accepted personal checks in the first place.

"Do you take personal checks?" she asked, giving herself a final out.

"You got yourself a service contract?"

She nodded.

"Then they got to take yours."

"Go ahead," she said, feeling for a grip on the slippery slope and finding only a handhold. Her fingers curled around the outcropping. She knew better than to look down.

"Good for you." What enthusiasm. As if Emma had made some life-altering move. Did debtor's prison still exist? "Bite the bullet, that's what I say," Sal told her. "Mind if I use the phone?"

"Be my guest," Emma told him.

Josh had gone to the sink, where he was busy washing up.

"Leave it." She knew she sounded less than sincere. Josh scrubbed away, finished, and began to wipe. Of all things!

"That's what the drying rack is for," she said.

Sal was talking heartily into the phone, sealing her fate. Josh ignored her, drying and shelving. So Emma took a seat at the breakfast, lunch, and dinner table and studied the scope of her current dilemma. It was bleak. Complementing that, the way the windows were now fogging up, courtesy of the heat. Here I am, Emma thought, trapped inside an intricately constructed igloo. In ten thousand years, I'll be some paleontologist's stupendous find.

"Well," she said with false heartiness, "it's only money."

"Home owning is overrated," Josh offered.

"Tell me about it."

He was through, and sat down at the table with her.

This time, he changed the subject. "You know, thank God it was me who found her," he said. "I'm saying if it was between me and Leslie, if you had to choose between the two of us . . ."

"Some choice."

"I know." Josh's smile was strangely internal. "It's Leslie," he said sotto voce. "I'm worried about her. Would you talk to her? Maybe she'll listen to you."

"Oh, Josh." Emma found the idea amusing. "Never did, never will."

"But I don't know who else to ask," he said. He did look desperate. Not something she associated with the Josh she'd known back when. Josh. The boy who had found salamanders with her under the backyard rocks at his parents' summer cabin up in Katonah. The boy who had bunked with her on sleepover nights in a pup tent under the stars. Lying under the canvas, they'd pretended to be brave explorers, searching the globe for rubies and buried pirate treasure. Josh had worked on terrifying the both of them, telling stories that were half heard, half confabulated. The sort that always ended with a cliff-hanger, the hook left planted outside the bedroom door, the sound of feet approaching just as the moon slid behind a cloud.

This was a different sort of cliffhanger.

And then there was Solomon to figure into the complex equation. Solomon who had dropped her off at her door Friday night, refusing her invitation to come up, responding with a pointed, "I'll call."

He hadn't.

"I'll see what I can do," she said, knowing that it was a mistake, that she was giving in to her least judicious feelings.

"Emma, thanks. Thanks so much."

"Don't thank me," she cautioned him.

6

Laurence Solomon had knowledge of the abridged history of Ditmas Park, the Brooklyn neighborhood where Dr. Hammond's shabby Victorian was located. Back in the early nineteen hundreds, when most of the borough was farmland, these houses had been built as summer homes for the gentry from upper Fifth. Out here was close enough to the whir of commerce but far enough away for taking a summer respite. In the late forties, when Dr. Hammond and her husband bought, Ditmas Park was solidly middle class. In the fifties, apartment houses on the outskirts were filled up with less well off immigrant families—Jewish, Irish, and some Italian. Then, in the sixties, his people had moved in, and the whites had fled. Pure funk had encroached, apartment houses were trashed and deserted, these old homes taking on burglar alarms and the neighborhood fortifying itself. It had been like that for a long time, really till the mid-nineties, when the housing boom hit with a vengeance. Now, once again, this was a place of privilege, which was the jumping-off point for Dr. Hammond's troubles.

O'Malley reported that the majority of the neighbors

were new, and all of those had a gripe with Hammond. One said her house was an eyesore, which it was, paint chipping off the exterior, and the roof, now freed from its burden of snow, bright green from mold. Another pointed out that garbage piled up in front of her house for weeks before it was evacuated. A third said she'd been the one who started it, complaining about their kitchen reconstruction, halting the project half finished because of possible code violations and the threatening of the neighborhood's landmark status. A fourth talked about continual phone calls, Hammond laying siege to them, saying they were letting their children have wild, late-night parties. The kicker with that one, O'Malley said, was they only had one kid, a five-year-old.

So Hammond had been cantankerous, the son had said as much, no reason to take someone's life. No logical reason, Laurence added, knowing that if logic was king, he'd be without a country.

Laurence had been over most of the house twice. He'd broken the lock on the attic door and considered memory lane, Josh Hammond's old lair where Jimi Hendrix posters ruled. Where he hadn't been yet was down, down to the basement office. But he was headed there now.

Laurence opened the door that led off the kitchen. As he did, he wondered where he'd be at seventy-eight, then reminded himself . . . dead. His family history said as much; his dad, two uncles, and an aunt all heart attack victims.

Flicking the switch by his right hand, Laurence inhaled the odor of mildew, with a subtle overlay of Lysol. Pure funk. A fluorescent light above his head popped and fizzed temperamentally but stayed on. The wall on his left held another portrait gallery. As he descended, he noted a shot of Eleanor Hammond long, long ago, wearing a belted skirt and a radiant smile. Laurence stopped to consider who was next to her, a man with a pipe in his mouth, half turned her way, offering a dreamy look of devotion. Behind them, a backdrop of foliage tipped in autumnal orange and gold. The man wore a tweed suit, duck hunting boots, even a cap. The squire, Laurence thought, and found Josh Hammond in the father; he'd inherited the same almond-shaped eyes, the same chin.

He took the rest of the steps nimbly to the door at the bottom of the staircase and turned the knob, only to discover it was locked. An easy call. He jimmied it open with ease and exposed a ghostly waiting room, shrouded in near darkness. The door to the outside had a window in it, which explained why he could begin to make out color. The chairs were yellow, the coffee table brown, and on it magazines strewn with gay abandon. By the door, apparently able to thrive with minimal light, two potted plants, their green leaves pointing straight up and looking razor sharp.

Laurence fumbled around and felt another light switch. He was about to flick it on when he heard a noise. A small noise, to be sure. It sounded like a scraping, a skittering. Laurence froze, remembering, with an internal lurch, his older brother, Ralph, cutting the light then jumping up on his bed, setting his finger to his lips, the two of them waiting in silence until Ludwig, their cat, got the rat in its sights. Rats big as cats, cats big as houses, all those urban myths coming home to roost up in Sugar Hill, Harlem. Ludwig getting busy, chasing his prey down with a busy scrabble, cornering it and pouncing, then the heart-stopping shriek.

Solomon listened some more. Nothing. But he decided to wait another second and then thought again, better safe than sorry, and pulled the door shut, this time behind him. Because if by chance it was human, not rodent, he was going to have to fool it into thinking he was gone. No rodent would have bought it, but he was good at waiting humans out, and stood there, with his back to the door, in the grayish dark, letting his eyes get accustomed. One minute passed, two minutes, then three, the countdown going in his head until he heard a different sound this time, scratching, no rustling.

Laurence moved quickly. Opening the door to the doctor's private office, he found the intruder. The blind had been half opened so the woman could see. She stood, trapped behind the desk.

"Hello," he said coolly, and tried to figure out what he'd expected; whatever or whoever it might have been, it couldn't have been this. An elderly lady who was a ringer for his aunt Mae. She even had the same coat Mae wore to church on Sundays, fur cuffed and collared, cut from black mourning cloth. She wore a plastic rain kerchief over her steel gray perm and clutched a pocketbook tightly under her left arm. It looked to Laurence like she was getting ready to use it to batter her way past him. Aunt Mae might have. She'd been the one who always surprised him as he was running down the street, smacking him upside the head, saying, "Boy, you'd better watch yourself."

"Yes?" Curious that she didn't seem flustered. But then, she must have heard him coming.

"What are you doing here?"

"And who would be asking?"

The accent made it clear she and Mae were worlds apart. There was a Jamaican lilt to her voice. Laurence felt the internal wince; island women loved to give themselves airs, act holier than thou.

"I would be the police."

"You say that. You could say anything."

She had nerve, he'd give her that much. Laurence lifted out his wallet and thrust his badge her way. She took a long, lingering, contemptuous look, added the "hunh" like an afterthought.

"Your turn," he said.

"I came by to pick up the appointment book."

"You do have a name."

She didn't like that, flared her nostrils, then said coolly, "Bertha Summers."

The nurse, she was on his contact list.

"It's Sunday, supposed to be a day of rest."

"You don't seem to be resting, why should I?"

"You happen to miss the yellow tape right outside the door?" Not to mention Lopez, who was out there in his car, keeping a supposedly watchful eye. More likely taking a nap. Although grandma might have snuck by on looks alone. Who would assume she was trouble?

"There are patients I need to contact."

"About the doctor?"

"Exactly." She sucked on her teeth, island women

did that too. They had twitches, looks, at least a hundred ways to tell you you were beyond their contempt, even while you earned it.

"Seems to me they'd know by now. It's been all over the news for the last day and a half."

"There are things I have to attend to." Vaguer than before. But still pompous.

He didn't buy it. Was he even supposed to? Solomon took a long look around the office, trying to figure out what she'd been into. One thing you could say was that this was a tidier mess than elsewhere in the house. The piles of books were smaller and more logistically placed. On his right stood a tall bookcase, filled to the brim with magazines and medical textbooks. Behind him, the wall of honor, which was de rigueur, he supposed. The doctor's medical degrees were framed and hung in descending order. He did a brief scan, reading the illustrious institutions she'd attended, Hunter College, NYU, Cornell. Past that, a long, lean file drawer. Then a door. He walked over to that and opened it. As he did, she said, "That's the examination room."

So it was. Dark and silent as a crypt. The examining table, with those stirrups hanging off, sat right in the middle. He shut the door and came back to her. "You used your key, I assume?"

"Of course."

He put his hand out. She stared down as if she might spit on it. Then dug into her pocket, took out a key ring, removed the offending object, and dropped it into his palm.

"We have this quaint little rule when we cover a

crime scene. No one except the investigating officers get to cart anything away. So . . ."

"There's nothing for me to show."

Bertha Summers wasn't hefty, but she was imposing. Which was why it was better to get this over with here and now. He didn't need to play the fool, dragging her back down to the precinct, having to listen to O'Malley and the rest ride him. "Next you'll be tossing my grandma."

"Please empty your purse."

She gave him a derisive look, then sucked her teeth again. Your kind is the worst, her look said.

No purse extended. She was going to make him embarrass himself even further. Laurence reached for her bag and tugged. She tugged back, then gave it up. He dumped the contents out on the desk in front of them. As he did, he couldn't help but feel shabby, stupid, a rank amateur, and he caught Bertha Summers turning her head away, as if to press home his smallness of mind.

A rattle of keys.

A spattering of change.

Her MetroCard had been shoved into a side pocket. Laurence retrieved it, then darted his fingers deep into the lining, working to make sure nothing was left, hiding. He unzipped the zippers. Then peered into the empty bag for as long as his self-respect could handle. The desk held the remains; there was a wallet that had her driver's license and two credit cards, plus photographs of many, many children. Grandkids, he had to assume. Beside it, a crumpled lavender handkerchief, a small address book, and an enameled box. The cover had been etched with twined rosebushes, bearing abundantly. He popped it open and found pills, six blue, five yellow, clearly prescription.

"My blood pressure medication," she said.

He set her things back inside the purse, then said, "Your coat, please."

She said nothing, but took it off and handed it to him. Laurence went through the pockets, tugged at the lining, and got, for his trouble, a crumpled receipt from Pathmark, two quarters, and a dime.

"Finished?" she asked as he handed it back.

"I'd like to set up a time to talk."

"Concerning?"

"Your employer. Who might have wanted to hurt her."

"I see." Bertha Summers drew her coat back over her shoulders, slowly, meaningfully. "No one in their right mind would have hurt my doctor."

The catch was the "my." He cribbed that possessive away for later reference and asked, "Even considering how she made her living?"

"What's that supposed to mean? She helped people every day of her life. You don't know a thing about it."

"And you do," he said, careful to offer a neutral tone. "That's why it's important we talk."

"Strange way of making me feel important, treating me like a criminal," she threw out.

"Mrs. Summers, you didn't give me a choice."

"We all have a choice on how we might behave."

He ignored the jab. "You've been working for her a long time?"

"Thirty-nine years come June."

"A very long time."

Summers didn't have to agree. Her expression changed, a shadow crossing her face. When it had fled she looked inconsolable.

Seeing this, he softened his voice even more. Still, he had to ask the question. "In all that time, there was no one who you saw as a threat? Mrs. Summers, I've found out enough about your employer to know she made people angry."

At least the woman took the time to consider his statement. "I don't know how it matters. People get angry over most things," she said quietly, then added, "so you're done?"

Which wasn't really a question. She was lifting her purse and brushing past him.

"You do have to speak with me."

"So you say."

Then he watched her cross the carpet, step out into the anteroom, open the door, step out, and shut it behind her with a soft click.

He began to search, opening the drawers and studying the multilayered mess therein—prescription pads, the doctor's scrawled notes to herself, lists of things to do or buy, samples of spermicide, diaphragms, pills in their pink round boxes. In the well were dozens of unsharpened pencils, and something he knew was an IUD, a piece of contorted plastic with a string hanging off one end. The thought of sticking it up into your body made Laurence blanch, remembering a long ago girlfriend using one called a copper T that had sent her into septic shock.

Damn near killed her, he thought, little thing stuck

up inside her body, ticking away like a time bomb. He
shut that drawer and pulled the top one on the right-
hand side open. There was a far greater mess in here,
unpaid bills, pamphlets from drug companies, informa-
tional publications courtesy of Planned Parenthood.
He shut it and tried the one underneath. This was
crammed with files, each with a different color tab.
They were ordered from AIDS to Amenorrhea, from
Sterility to STDs. He tried the left-hand side and came
up with another bunch of files, these containing personal correspondence. Funny that all that disorder
above managed to right itself when paperwork was involved.

Laurence recognized a lot of the names, most were
politicians, new and old, ranging from the president of
these United States, to senators, congressmen, the local
borough president. Picking up one, he read through and
found pretty much what he'd expected; it contained
several letters that had been written to protest policy
decisions, and she had kept carbon copies of each and
every one, along with whatever response had gotten
sent back.

Then Laurence came to a file labeled "Diehl, Martin." He pulled it up and was amazed by the heft. Opening it, he was even more intrigued by the contents.
Eleanor Hammond had a curious taste in pen pals. She
had apparently kept up a robust ten-year dialogue with
one of the founders and current head of the New York
chapter of the Society for the Protection of the Unborn.

"Dr. Hammond, your attack on me was truly discom-
fiting. More to the point, entirely illegal . . ."

Down the page to the argument Diehl was putting

forward ". . . I can't believe that a woman of your intellect could adopt the philosophy that life only begins when a person becomes fully sentient. This is, of course, the most narrow interpretation . . ."

"A woman of her intellect." Like Diehl had actually been personally acquainted.

In her response, she wrote, "Dear Mr. Diehl, I received your letter of the seventeenth. Your convictions seem genuine, if wrongheaded. Let's take this, point by point . . ."

She did. He read over her graceful deconstruction of the antiabortion argument. Supercilious, even arch at times. But also joyful. She was engaging, and thus engaged. He looked up, took in the room. There is where Dr. Eleanor Hammond had sat, composing her rebuttal. He caught a fleeting glimpse of the woman who had been captured in that photo, the one with her husband's arm tightly around her, the one who stood there, with her skirt billowing out, caught in a fierce wind, she too a genuine force of nature.

This file was a keeper. Riding the surge of elation, he snapped off the light and made for the stairs. Then stopped. He'd almost forgotten. Back at the receptionist's desk, he pulled on the top drawer, and it flew open. There, inside, the leather-bound appointment book.

7

Even all the way up on the third-floor landing, Emma could smell that sweet, familiar odor. Tramping down, she found Joshua Hammond doing what he used to do best, getting stoned. He lay on her living room couch, joint in hand. A stream of smoke trailed up.

"Put it out," Emma said.

"What?" Then, "Why?"

But he saw she was serious, and sat up, doing as requested.

"It's a rule I have," Emma told him, and decided it would be better not to try and explain the rest, how she and Will had fought over this, when she had caught him in the exact same pose. Will's avowal automatically flew to mind, "I'll never light up again. I agree totally. Of course it's a crutch."

Never believe a man when he tells you "I'll take care of it," Emma thought. Will hadn't. Instead he'd lied. When caught he'd start off with the excuse that he didn't do hard drugs, only soft, and there were studies that proved that pot smoking wasn't addictive. "Even if

you have to get stoned every single day of your life?"
she'd countered.

Emma had found his stash so easily, and Will was so
put out he'd accused her of installing a camera to track
his movements. She'd laughed at the idea. And never
told him her history, that would only have weakened
her case. She was clean, and had been for what seemed
like an eternity.

Ten things my ex will never know about me, Emma
thought wryly.

"Ready?" Josh asked.

"As ready as I'll ever be."

"This is just great of you."

No, no it wasn't. Another thing to keep her own
counsel on. She took Flatbush to the park, then through
the split. On their left, a wild tract of land that hid the
combed and curried pastures of the Brooklyn Botanical
Garden from view. On the right, the Prospect Park zoo,
where seals dozed under a splintered cap of ice. Liam's
particular favorite was the prairie dog exhibit, the one-
way glass let the viewers watch them scamper through
the underground tunnels.

Josh was telling her stories of his current life. He'd
been expanding his sphere of influence; in London,
he'd shepherded through a deal between two multina-
tional corporations.

"How much do you get for something like this?" she
asked, and gasped at the six-figure sum.

"Seems like highway robbery, doesn't it?" he offered, then fell silent. Looking his way, she saw him
gazing out at their old stomping ground. This was the
park where they'd spent a good portion of their youth.

It had not changed dramatically. It was cleaner, safer, but there was still that graveyard, hidden away up the steep slope near Windsor Terrace where they'd spent hours, exchanging stories, and yes, getting stoned.

"I don't know how you stand the cold," Josh said, shutting his eyes. Before she could offer a defense or even an acerbic retort about the possible benefits of global warming, he fell asleep. This was a long-standing Joshism. He could nap anywhere, anytime, an ability that certainly had to mesh well with his current frequent-flier lifestyle.

Glancing his way, Emma flashed on Josh's attic room. She was lying on the bed, at right angles to Josh, and he was drumming with his fingers, high, of course, while they listened to Bob Fass on WBAI play Lenny Bruce tapes. What was she doing here, Emma wondered? She could only imagine the look Laurence would offer when Josh introduced her as an old family friend.

Too late, she was cruising down Ditmas. Emma noted the tasteful Christmas decor; twig reindeers on the lawns, frosted lights dripping from the eaves of many of the houses. She spotted the police cars from two blocks away. They made an imperfect barricade in front of the Hammond house. Pulling up, she saw Solomon's late model Volvo V80. She could turn around, Emma thought, all she had to do was pull into the next driveway and back up, or go around the corner and keep on keeping on. Josh was asleep, in fact, tenderly snoring. He wouldn't know, and by the time he did, what of it? But Emma parked instead, giving in to the impish urge that had prompted her to agree to come in the first place. He deserved it, she told herself, not altogether convincingly, remembering her response Friday night in the car, as Laurence Solomon had reached across to flick her door open, bidding her a cold and clinical adieu. "You know, I'm not the enemy," she'd said.

Emma tickled Josh. No response. Clearly, harsher measures were indicated. She offered a sharp nudge of the elbow.

"Sleeping beauty?"

"What? Oh, we're here."

They emerged on a snow-littered street. Emma let Josh take the lead and admired the familiar bounce in his step. Climbing up to the porch, she saw the swing still hanging. Another fond memory, the two of them pumping hard, giddy with pleasure.

The front door opened as Josh stepped forward and there was Caitlin O'Malley.

"Emma," she said, surprised.

"Officer." A curt nod, which seemed to throw Caitlin more. "I'm here on behalf of the family," Emma added, feeling altogether foolish.

"Oh . . ." Caitlin actually stepped back, as if slapped.

Emma pretended not to notice, letting Caitlin regain her composure. When she did, she turned to Josh and said, "Detective Solomon has been asking for you, Mr. Hammond."

"Here I am," Josh ventured amiably.

O'Malley threw her head back, indicating where. Josh opened the living room door, stepped through, and Emma followed. She had to admit the look on Laurence's face was priceless. Take the moment as yours, she decided, striding across the room to greet Leslie and Bob, who were seated on the couch. "I'm so sorry," Emma said, leaning forward, and surprising herself as much as Leslie as she offered an embrace.

Leslie accepted, tilting her body up for one long, awkward moment. Disentangling herself, she said, "Emma, it's so nice of you to come."

The inference was so clearly the opposite. Emma backed up, managing to knock over a pile of books that had been hiding, like a baffle, on the floor. Momentarily losing her footing, she grabbed for the piano, found it, and found her shame growing exponentially. Leave it to Leslie to have such a profound effect. She cursed under her breath and took a look around the room, saw that it was littered with booby traps. The clearest spot was over by the fireplace. In there, no wood, only a Buddha wearing a munificent smile.

"You won't believe what's going on," Leslie said, turning Josh's way. "It's fucking incredible."

"What?" Josh asked. "What's happening now?"

"He's accusing Bertie." Leslie pointed her finger at Laurence. And Laurence Solomon raised his eyes, invoking judgment from a far greater power.

"I'm doing nothing of the sort," Laurence said coolly.

"You are too!" The peevish tone was familiar. Emma had a momentary flash, Leslie stamping her foot, saying, "Mine!"

The rigid quiet that followed gave her the opportunity. "Detective," Emma said, "Josh asked me to come, he wondered if I couldn't be of help. I'm a family friend."

"Really?" He had turned her way, and his eyes were agate hard.

"I know Bertha Summers. I can't believe she'd be involved in anything criminal."

"So you know Bertha Summers too."

"Yes."

"Aren't you a surprise?"

There was no good answer for that. Out of the corner of her eye, Emma detected movement and realized it was Leslie, rocking back and forth on the couch. She gasped and Bob leaned over, then began to rub her back. "Les, stop it," he whispered. A whisper, but hard not to hear.

"What did Bertha do?"

"I'd like to know that myself," Laurence offered, giving no ground.

And why would he? As if this was Gunfight at the OK Corral. It was patently ridiculous. Emma was no sharpshooter.

"Why don't we step outside?" she suggested.

Into the hall, then following him through the dining room and into the kitchen. She recognized he had chosen this route as punishment, saw the dried bloodstains on the tabletop, splatters reaching out along the floor, the outline of Eleanor's body, all this greeting her. Emma felt the immediate shock and did what she always did when she walked in on something visceral, she shut off the part of her mind that felt emotionally connected. It was a neat trick, and one that was essential, given her line of work.

"Family friend! What about giving me a heads up?"

"You said you'd call," she countered.

"Your point being? I've been working."

"You've been working cases before," Emma said. "It never stopped you from picking up the phone."

"This is different."

"This case, or this time?" Part of Emma was observing the argument, and the ludicrousness of where it was taking place. And part of her acknowledged the justice in it. If Eleanor's spirit were hovering, she would more than likely be amused.

"You show up here . . ." he began.

Emma decided there was no point listening to any more. She stepped out, out onto the back porch, then down and into the yard. There were rosebushes that had once been Eleanor's pride, browned by winter and clearly long untended. The huge oak tree was still the centerpiece, but it was naked of leaves and showing signs of age; pieces of the trunk scaled off, a broken branch hung at half-mast. The whole effect was decidedly dismal.

Laurence pursued, stepping behind her, and reaching out to touch her on the shoulder. She turned slowly to confront him and looked up because she had no other choice, he had a good five inches on her. Next time, she'd pick someone a little shorter, she told herself, she was getting a crick in her neck, and besides, it gave him an unfair advantage.

"Look, you'll never understand," he said. His voice was low, strained.

"I can't understand if you don't explain yourself."

"That's the problem, right there," he offered. "I shouldn't have to."

"This is about what that woman said? About mistaking you for Reggie. Or was it because that idiot at the bar thought you worked there and asked for a drink? I get that part, it's insulting. But it happens. People are foolish. You've told me that enough times. If it wasn't racial, believe me, it would be something else."

"Maybe for you, not for me," he said.

"Please!"

"I didn't want to go."

"But I needed you to, so you did." She studied him for a while, trying to assess which mattered more. She'd never know for certain, she decided. "You gave in," she said. "If that's what you're angry about, I've got news for you, you have free will. I can't make you do anything. Nor would I want to. So what if it's not about being insulted, what if it's not what happens when we step out into my world or yours and happen to feel uncomfortable, or feel like we have something to prove. What if that's only the surface part. What if what went wrong here is personal?"

"I don't get what you mean."

"Friday night I told you I needed you, and I think you were looking for a way to punish me for admitting it."

He was shaking his head fiercely.

"Laurence, you have a terrible track record when it comes to relationships. Every time a woman gets close to asking you for a commitment, you break it off. I can go down the list. And you know what I've come to? I'd rather be alone than play hide-and-seek with you."

"What's that supposed to mean? Are you breaking up with me?"

"Only kids in high school call it breaking up," she ventured.

"I see."

"Do you? Do you really see?" Emma wasn't sure she did. The threat had sprung out, unbidden. It was harsh medicine. She was reminded of his kindness. He'd been the one to bundle her into the car when her contractions overwhelmed her, scooting her off to the hospital. He'd held her hand while she screamed, "Fuck, shit, why am I doing this again?" As the ax bent her body in two, she had begged for drugs and the nurse had told her, "Sorry, you're too far along." Laurence was the one who said, "You'll make it. It's almost over," then counted down with her through one brutal stab of pain, and the next.

Katherine Rose had gotten stuck on her way out, her head flopping free, her shoulders trapped. The midwife who was attending had run into the hall to find a doctor and Laurence had talked Emma through. "There's only one thing for it, baby, push like your life depends on it." She had done just that. The nurse and midwife had come running back in to find Katherine Rose lying in her arms, with that creamy white skin and a halo of chestnut hair. The nurse's face had been a study, looking from Laurence, then back down, trying to figure out the genetics.

Emma's gaze was quizzical. Laurence mirrored it, then broke into a slow, honeyed smile.

"What if I don't want us over," he said. And left it, hanging for a nice long while, before adding on, "Nice bunch, this Hammond family, I don't have to wonder why you never mentioned them to me."

*   *   *

"One shot? That's it?"

"Our doer's economical."

They stood very close together on that porch. Emma took in the broken pane, abundantly dusted for prints, then turned and was amazed by the debris Eleanor had collected.

"They're going to need a Dumpster when they clean out this place," Laurence commented.

"So what's the time frame?"

"Carter narrowed it down to a two-hour gap. Between six and eight A.M. Friday. The canvass hasn't turned up much. Ballistics was over, taking a look at the blood trail. They say they're eighty percent convinced the doer used a silencer. As for eyewitnesses coming upon a stranger out and about that time of the morning?" His shrug was eloquent.

"What's this about Bertha?"

"Nurse Summers, you mean? I found her downstairs in the office two hours ago, looked to me like she was digging round for something."

"It's impossible for me to believe anything bad of Bertha," Emma said. "I know Leslie's hard to take, but don't let her in-your-face attitude get in the way of logic."

"Is that what I'm doing?" he asked, offering a sly grin as commentary. "Summers didn't exactly announce her presence. That plus, when I happened onto her, copping an attitude?"

"Bertha Summers would never hurt Eleanor," Emma insisted. "You don't know how it was between them."

"You tell me then."

"They were friends. Eleanor was the one who loaned the money to Bertha for tuition. She encouraged her to get her nursing degree. Bertie gave this speech at the party, thanking Eleanor. Said without her, she wouldn't have had the nerve to apply herself."

"Sounds like a direct quote."

"Well, memory's a funny thing," Emma said. "Little things stick, and big things get totally lost."

"Summers said she'd been working for Hammond for years. You're telling me she wasn't always here as a nurse, so what then? Receptionist?"

"Not exactly," Emma said, and found herself oddly chagrined. "She took care of the house."

"Oh, I see. Maid of honor."

"Don't make it sound that way."

"What way?"

"You make it seem degrading."

"Ah." He reached out, almost touching the shattered pane of glass, then dropping his hand. When he continued, he'd discarded the critical tone. "Tell me about this Eleanor Hammond."

"Eleanor was pretty amazing," Emma said. "One of those outsized people. When I was a kid, I actually wanted to be a doctor because I admired her so much."

"What happened?"

"I didn't exactly have a talent for science." Emma laughed. "It lasted till my first year at college. Then I took bio and we had to breed fruit flies, who was that guy . . . Mendel, right? The one who made the laws about genetics and chance? Well, I screwed up royally. My fruit flies escaped. I had to crib the results."

"That was all it took?"

"If I couldn't pass bio . . ." Emma said. "It's only the tip of the iceberg."

"Hammond seems to have developed a pretty extensive enemies list."

"She spoke her mind. When you do, people hate you for it. But she also had friends, more than most. You should have seen the parties, packed." Emma studied him, then added, "What about the Society?"

"I wish it was that easy," Laurence said, opening the door to the kitchen.

Back inside, Emma studiously avoided addressing the kitchen table. She surveyed the rest of the room instead, and was surprised to find how much of it was unchanged, down to the wallpaper and those depressingly drab cabinets.

"How long since you've been out here?" he asked.

"Years." Keeping it vague on purpose.

"But you did spend a lot of time here?"

"Enough." Half her waking life. There had been family dinners that devolved into heated political debates. She and Josh would ask to be excused and flee, but eventually they'd get drawn back, listening through the door to the adults and their older siblings, both practiced demagogues. They'd dash in to raid the freezer for Eskimo Pies, then retreat.

In later years, they never returned at all. She and Josh would escape to his attic room, burning incense to override the other, more incriminating odor, or leave the house entirely, meeting up with his friends, Erasmus alumni, to tip back beer, or light up a joint.

And once they were both in college, Emma at Barnard, Josh at Columbia, they'd used the kitchen during the daylight hours, when Eleanor was over at the clinic. Josh had set his scales out on that same table. They'd used the poultry shears to snip the buds off the stems, weighing, measuring, and stuffing baggies, cutting up blocks of hash, shoving foil-wrapped tabs of Donald Duck acid into the back of the freezer, which Josh claimed was safer than a vault, so encrusted was it with unchipped ice.

Yes, any real biography of Josh Hammond, entrepreneur, would have to begin here, right here, with those unremarkable cupboards, that old-fashioned double sink, and this breakfast table coated with his mother's blood.

Looking past she saw where the bullet had lodged, where it had been dug from the wall.

"What was the make of the weapon?"

"Forty-five caliber. Now my turn, how did you get here?"

"Josh came by this morning."

"What does he want?" Laurence asked.

"He claimed that Leslie was driving you nuts. He wants me to intercede."

"You told him about your personal connection to me, of course."

"Actually, no. No, I didn't."

"I called the two of them up, after I found that Summers woman downstairs. The sister got here first. Then you and Hammond."

"What's your point?"

"You don't think he knows about the two of us?"

"How would he?"

"People talk."

"What if he does," she countered. "Leslie's going to make it hard for you, Laurence. It's her m.o. Josh says she wants the feds involved."

"So you and Leslie were close?"

"No." Emma couldn't help seeing Leslie, turning her way at the top of the stairs, shoving hard. Emma could feel the whoosh of air, that clutching in her stomach, as the surprise took over. Her body had tumbled head over heels to the very bottom. Then she heard her six-year-old self wail, as the door slammed up above.

"Here's my question for you," he said. "Daughter dear wants me to go with the obvious suspects. My lieutenant feels the same. He's on me, says this is political and we want to make sure we get the collar. Easy enough, because the Society is taking credit for doing her. Easiest way to go is to relent, claim it was them, and let the feds take the rest of it off my hands."

"But there's a problem."

He nodded, then moved to the sink, hooking his finger to request her company. Emma noted what the dust showed, one side was smudged with an abundance of prints, the other was wiped crystal clean.

"The house is a mess, but there's someone who decides to come in and do a pitched cleaning, problem being it's only half done. Half the kitchen tidy as can be, the other half pretty much on a par with the rest of the home environment. You think Mom decided, since her black sheep son was on his way, she'd work on appearances?

"Plus there's the mail. It comes at noon. Friday's got delivered at noon and put up. We collected prints off it, and they don't match any of ours, not her kids' either.

Correct me if you see this some other way, but the way I read it is, Dr. Hammond had a visitor, one with a key. First, I need to know who that was. Second, I want to hear their story. Maybe they didn't happen to step into the kitchen. Or maybe they did and decided to leave things be."

"You think the killer came back, hours later?"

"They might have. Might have forgotten something." He escorted her toward the swinging door, opened it for her, and leaned in close. Drawing her into the dining room, he reached down for the cardboard box on the floor, lifted the lid, and retrieved a piece of paper, covered in plastic housing. He handed it to her and Emma saw it was a letter. "Dear Martin," it began. Emma didn't need to read the signature to recognize Eleanor's hand. Those meticulous curves. Those emphatically dotted I's.

8

Diehl, head of the New York chapter of the Society for the Protection of the Unborn, lived inconspicuously enough, here in the gap between downtown Brooklyn and Fort Greene. Any day now, some realtor would come up with a fancy name for the place and try to sell it to some unsuspecting out of towner as hipper than thou. But for now, it was still no-man's-land, Laurence thought. The housing stock was pretty much a mess, row houses and small tenements in between warehouses and loft manufacturing buildings. On Diehl's street the only sign of the impending Christmas season was a Santa hanging off a fire escape, with a NEW YORK T-shirt pulled over the traditional red fur-trimmed vestments.

As Laurence Solomon stepped out of his car, a chill wind off the river surged up. Only a block away, the Navy Yard. Next to it, white water churning by, heading out to the ocean and freedom.

"You're sure you want me in on this," Emma said. Nice of her to give him another chance for regret.

"Not sure at all." Only he had to be, right? He led the way down the block to seventeen, noting the American flag decals on all the cars, plus a few additions. This one, parked in front of Diehl's place, had an ethnic declaration of pride on the bumper, DOMINICANS MAKE THE BEST LOVERS.

Number seventeen was an eight-story apartment building with a worn-down stoop and a double plate-glass door. Laurence climbed up and pressed 8B, felt Emma move in behind, and then heard a voice asking for an identity.

"Police," Laurence said, and the door buzzed open.

Up, up, up, right to the very top floor where Martin Diehl was awaiting their arrival. Diehl was thin, of average height, with a wedge of dark hair over a moon-white face. He wore a sweater vest atop a pinstriped cotton button-down shirt, a pair of double knits and slippers that emphasized the casualness of this get-together. Diehl's hair was either still wet from showering or gelled to a high gloss. Natty, Laurence thought, flashing his badge.

Diehl said, "Come in," and moved back to let them.

"This is my associate, Emma Price."

The briefer the explanation given, the better later on. If there was a later on with Diehl, Laurence thought. He was betting not, and reminded himself that was the reason he'd invited Emma along. The part he didn't address was how, when it came to dealing with Emma, he too often found himself trading in logic for something akin to instinct.

They took a trip down the length of a long hall, and as they went, Laurence counted five doors, shut tight, on the right-hand side. Five doors meant at least a few bedrooms. He had the sudden, unsettling image of a bunch of Diehl lookalikes, sequestered, pressing their ears against the wood in order to trace their progress.

The hall opened onto a big box of a living room with a threadbare couch that was ringed by three towering piles of cardboard boxes. Posters studded the walls. The most disturbing was of a fetus with a red *X* struck across it, and MURDER in blood-red letters underneath.

Living area slash office, Laurence noted, seeing the computer on a beat-up table, right next to it a fax machine set up on an old milk crate.

"I appreciate you letting us come over," Laurence offered.

"I wasn't aware I had a choice." Diehl's smirk was the exclamation point.

Laurence knew all about Diehl's experience with the ways and means of law enforcement. The man was a regular whirling dervish of disorderly conduct. He'd thrown pig's blood at a clinic worker in New Rochelle. Chained himself to the front doors of a Westport, Connecticut, family planning facility. And done a major sit-in on the steps of the Lincoln Memorial. In fact, in the last few years, he'd gone pretty much everywhere in the tristate area, making himself into a major pest, thirty-seven arrests to his credit, and counting.

"I don't have much time," Diehl said. "I have a meeting to get to by four."

Laurence wasn't overly concerned with Diehl's supposed schedule. Doing another canvass of the room, he spied a Mr. Coffee set up to serve and asked, "Fresh?"

Then, before Diehl answered, added, "Mind if I help myself?"

Diehl pursed his lips, shrewlike. "Be my guest." Laurence did. Then pretended to look around for the milk, moving to the small alcove where he'd spotted the fridge and sink. This was another storage space as well as a kitchen, several bins of posters stacked, one on top of the next. The sink was clean, no dishes waiting in the dish rack. Opening the refrigerator door, Laurence noted the shelves were practically bare, a quart of milk, seven eggs, a half-eaten container of English muffins. Clearly a single man's domain.

He poured himself a dollop and shut the door. Stepping back into the living room, he couldn't help contrast what Diehl's fridge held with Dr. Hammond's remains of the day. Her fridge had been packed tight, a regular food museum as it were, with leftovers crammed into jars and mismatched Tupperware. He and O'Malley had exposed carbon-hard meat, vegetables from some foreign country, salad gone limp and gray. Checking the dates on the condiments, he'd found they'd all expired, most were breeding grounds for penicillin mold.

"How would you characterize your relationship with Eleanor Hammond?"

"My relationship?" Diehl offered an incredulous laugh. "I wasn't aware I had one."

"It seems you might have, reading your letters." He flourished the one he'd brought and sketched in the rest from Diehl's expression, seemingly one of shock.

Diehl took a minute to compose himself, then retrieved a pair of reading glasses out of his sweater pocket and set them on the crown of his nose. He read, silently to himself, then looked back up at Laurence and said, "What of it? We corresponded."

"And?"

"There is no 'and.'"

"A moment ago there was no correspondence between you either," Laurence pointed out. "I see that she kept copies, yours and hers."

"Is there a law against that?"

"The woman was murdered, I'd like to find out what I can about her," Laurence countered. "You wrote to each other for over ten years. That's a long time to keep on disagreeing."

"I'm a very patient person."

"You also seemed to have an honest affection for each other," Laurence said.

"Your call."

"You thought you could change her mind?"

"I thought it was worth making the effort," Diehl said evenly.

"And there are many other people you make this sort of effort with?"

"I can't see how that would be any of your business."

"We both know it is," Laurence said, then put in the bait, "it would seem to me, someone who's a prime suspect would want to clear himself."

"Should I be calling my attorney?"

"Is there a need for one? You said come right over."

"I had no idea," Diehl said, offering a put-upon sigh.

"Could we dispense with the show? You knew what I

was coming here for. Baiting me, or stonewalling me only wastes time. And you with an important appointment to get to."

"Fine, ask away," Diehl said, with a bristling intelligence apparent in his eyes. Thrust, then parry, Laurence thought. Still, it was worth another shot.

"Why did you write to Hammond?"

"Why not?" Diehl grinned, then added, "Would you believe me if I said she dared me to?" There was an elfish twinkle in his eye. Laurence thought of the pot of gold, this lithe, very clean man, leading the way to the base of the tree, pointing down, saying, dig right here.

"She dared you? In what way?"

"You clearly didn't know the woman."

"I did," Emma threw in. Diehl turned her way, took her in.

"So you have a personal interest?"

"Yes."

Time to change the subject. "Where were you Friday morning?" Laurence asked.

"Excuse me?"

"From six to eleven, where?"

"I don't wake until seven. I have breakfast, and go to work."

"Work being that desk in front of the abortion clinic? Protesting is a job?"

"An honorable profession, I might add." Diehl's voice had more than a hint of starch.

"Is there anyone who can confirm your whereabouts?"

"I arrived at eight-thirty, there were other people there."

"Names?"

"I can't go giving out names without their permission. They may not wish to be involved."

"You live here alone?"

"Yes, not that that's your business either."

"This whole big place?"

Diehl didn't rise to the bait.

"Would you like to come down with me to the precinct and continue the conversation?"

"Detective, I offered to speak with you voluntarily. I let you into my home. This is hardly the sort of thing I'd do if I had something to hide. I have no phantom housemates."

Laurence simply put his game face on and waited. Diehl eventually staged an elaborate sigh, then lifted up a leaflet, turned it over, and used it to scrawl down his compatriots' names. Handing it over, he asked, "Anything more?"

The more came from another quarter, Emma. "You didn't like her at first, but you couldn't help being engaged, it felt like cowardice to ignore her," she said. "Maybe you thought you were making a conscious choice at first."

Diehl cast an evaluating look her way and when he did, Emma dug into her pocket and pulled out a piece of paper of her own. "'I wouldn't be able to live with myself knowing what potential had been thwarted,'" she read. "'Who made you think you could have this godlike ability to choose? What sort of hubris does it require?'"

Emma's gaze rose. And Laurence made sure to subdue his own surprise, telling himself this was why he'd brought her along. The woman worked angles he'd never think to notice or, if he did, would dismiss as unimportant; theatrical, maybe, but also telling.

Looking down, Emma tagged the last sentence again, adding a knowing inflection. "'What sort of hubris does it require? There's a question I think you'd want to pose to yourself. You're the one sitting up on a throne, dear Martin, admonishing the smaller, less contemplative souls around you incautiously. Telling us what we must or must not dare to think or do.'" She lifted her eyes and repeated the phrase, as if it might be unclear, "Dear Martin?"

Diehl shrugged.

"You couldn't have thought she'd keep your letters."

Emma seemed to lean in closer, attempting to read the answer in Diehl's inexpressive face. Like Sanskrit, Laurence decided. The dead-on intensity of that look was so familiar, it brought a stab of affection, an unforeseen by-product of her being Emma so completely, so incautiously.

"I went to your website last night," Emma said to Diehl. "Eleanor's name was crossed out with a big red X. It made me feel ill."

"I have nothing to do with the website," Diehl contended, sounding more than a little defensive.

"But I suppose some would argue that you're engaged in wartime activities," Emma said, her voice dropping down to a dangerous pitch. "Hard when you can find things to respect about the enemy. Harder still to know what to do with that respect, when you don't wish to recognize your enemy's right to exist."

Diehl appeared to chew that over. Then gave her a

searching look. Finally, he came to a decision, shifting his body away from her, turning back to Laurence and saying, "I'd like you to go."

They didn't have a choice. They had to comply. Laurence set his cup on top of a pile of posters, put his business card down next to it, and said, "Thanks for the coffee." No tea or sympathy here. Indeed, once Diehl had decided, he began to hurry them out, scurrying down the long hallway, making for the door to throw it open.

Laurence moved more slowly. And he cast out a parting salvo. "This Society of yours is so big on the Bill of Rights, I've got a question for you, seeing as how you must be an expert. Where's it say you have a right to violate these women's privacy?"

"I don't know what you're referring to," Diehl said, by the door now. Laurence heard the click of tumblers and then the door swung back.

"I went on the web myself. I found out you and your friends have been playing Allen Funt, filming women who go into Hammond's clinic, then broadcasting so you can see their faces. That seems to me to be a violation of their basic civil rights."

"I would have thought someone in your line of work would realize the virtue of the approach," Diehl countered. "Crime prevention in its most advanced state. What better deterrent than for a murderer to have their identity captured on film?" The sarcasm had fled. In its place the evenhanded tones that a true believer had to forward. Diehl was one, a man content in the knowledge that those who disagreed were sadly deceived and most certainly foolish. His task was to educate.

Laurence saw what he'd hoped to see then. Dr. Eleanor Hammond made whole out of the parts; not just imperfect parent, irascible neighbor, political activist, but also the correspondent of this particular man, writing to him in an attempt to refine her vision, arguing because it was better to defy and defend than to submit. Pride was a part of her hubris, competition too, most of all she was human to a fault.

From behind Diehl the breeze flooded in. Then Laurence heard Emma clear her throat and that was enough to send a little prickle of warning.

"Would it be possible to use the facilities?"

Nice way to put it. Emma caught his eye and returned the spark of humor, then turned the knob on the door in front of her. Diehl sprang back to attempt to prevent it, but too late. And Laurence took full advantage of the view. Inside the room there were mountains of boxes, and at the very end, a space just large enough to lay out a pallet. Which was what was there, a six-foot length of thin foam, on top of that, a rolled-up sleeping bag.

"Sorry," Emma said as Diehl grabbed the door handle and pulled it firmly shut. Then added, "Here," in a stiff voice, thrusting open the next door down. Emma went in with a submissive "Thank you."

Out on the street, Laurence observed Emma au natural. She looked to him like the cat who had gotten hold of the canary, tail feathers tucked into the corners of its mouth, on its face an expression of tender, sated delight.

"What?" he asked.

"How do you mean?" she countered, doing a little decoy move.

"Clever girl," he said, then reached out to stroke her cheek with a finger. Dropped his hand before he could tempt fate too long.

"You could eat off the floor in that bathroom," Emma said. And she continued down the street, he knew this was her version of punishment, and she was waiting. For an apology he was unwilling or unable to give. That meant he was reduced to following behind her to where she'd parked that near wreck of an old Volvo.

"Emma," he said when she'd managed to get the door open and was about to step in. He could hear the demand in his own voice. It wouldn't do, he knew all about that. She swung around to face him and said, "What am I supposed to do with you, Laurence?"

"Do? How do you mean?" He caught a stray piece of hair the wind had blown free, wrapped it around her earlobe, saw how it would be to kiss her. She sat down instead, not letting him. He held the door, and she tried tugging on it. Then gave up, studied her hands on the wheel for a while, and finally said, "There was an Atra shaver on the sink, and a shaving bowl with soap and a brush. A toothbrush and a half-used tube of Crest. Inside the shower on the soap rack, he had a bottle of Head and Shoulders."

"Drugstore inventory completed, what next?"

She chugged the motor on, then looked up, suddenly juiced. "A pink Lady Bic," she said, and made it clear she expected him to back away. He did, considering the news, Diehl's houseguest quite possibly being of the female persuasion. Emma shut the door with a decisive bang. Laurence waved as she put her car into gear and pulled out. Suddenly he thought to call out and stop her; now when it was too late, he felt the tug on his heart. But she sailed off, down the sloppy winter street, making a right and disappearing from view.

9

Emma's cell phone was beeping. Scrolling back, Emma recognized Dawn's number, then Will's. She was not about to return either call. Better to get home, so she took the Brooklyn Queens Expressway, pulled off at the Atlantic Avenue exit as the sun began to sink into the west.

"Questions, questions, questions," she said aloud, "pouring into the mind of the concerned, middle-aged Emma today."

Zappa coming to mind specifically because of Josh—Josh, whose entry into her life was both unexpected and overly opportune. She'd resisted Laurence's interpretation till now. But alone, it was easier to be clinically critical. Josh certainly could have known about her tie to Solomon. Josh had always been Mr. Expedient, she reminded herself, and spun from there back to Martin Diehl, who had been easy enough to dislike but hard to see as a viable suspect. That is, until she'd happened onto the signs that he was taking in boarders. It made her believe that he hadn't had to wield the weapon himself to be involved. He could have harbored the doer and, in that way, aided and abetted. This isn't your case, she reminded herself, it's Laurence's. His headache, and welcome to it.

Emma drove by the playground that sat right next to the highway. A squad of teenagers huddled around a makeshift campfire that had been set in a wire trash can. This was Liam's favorite hangout spot, these kids, his posse. But, at least today, she'd caught herself a breather. He was hanging with Tony, back at Suzanne's.

How many times over the course of the last few months had he cut class and ended up here? Emma could tick off nine separate instances. She'd found him, often in the middle of a daredevil spin off the makeshift obstacle course. Liam was convinced he'd be the next Tony Hawk.

In front of her house, Emma noted signs of progress in the form of a huge pile of dismembered metal pipes. Running in to check, she yelled out "Hello" but got no response. So Emma opened the basement door and switched on the light, tromped down and there it was, better than frankincense and myrrh any day, an absolutely amazing sight, a brand-new boiler, pumping away.

Back upstairs, Emma went to check the thermostat and discovered another miracle, it was set at sixty-seven and the house was not only warm, it was toasty. She felt the ridge of tension at the top of her neck give way. It was time to retrieve her kids and start dinner, time to forget all the mess she'd gotten herself into, except of course for the one that Roland Everett had created, that paid the bills. Though not this one, she reminded herself, wondering when the check she'd written would bounce. Her shoulders clenched again.

"Oh well," she said aloud, and glanced at the hall table. The bill on top of it had been stamped CASH— PAID IN FULL. Her jaw slackened in amazement.

Who in God's name? The answer came clear to her immediately. Josh had been there, he'd seen her predicament. He had the global resources.

But when, and worse than that, why?

Emma tumbled back along the road to other possibilities, raising up for an instant the concept of Sal feeling tremendous sympathy for her plight, and dismissing that as a delusion sprung out of seasonal folklore. Suzanne? Ridiculous. What about? No, that's not possible, but why not? Will. There you go, a different, more valid explanation, buying his way out of the guilt. Well, if that was the case, she wasn't going to let him get away with it. Or was she?

She sure as hell was. Emma heard her rational self interceding and hated that she would have to take this good advice. Still, it was the price she paid for having an amicable relationship with her ex, done, they both agreed, for the sake of the children. It was so much easier, even tidier, to rage on. So much more natural too. Emma wrinkled her nose, rabbitlike. Then gave up on the idea of fighting against the inevitable, she would do the smart thing and be gracious, adding, because she could, just a little pinch of salt to the pot.

Emma made her way down the street to Suzanne's, and had lifted her finger to the buzzer when, from behind, she heard him call out, "Em, Em, wait up."

If she'd had any doubts before, she had none now.

Here was Will to explain, then rationalize, then beg her forgiveness, her knight in tarnished armor, gallumphing up the steps to greet her. She admired him up close, still handsome in his WASPy way, looking a sterling thirty-nine, which was good, since he was forty-one. Emma noted his mix-and-match look. Instead of the stud, he'd put a Jesus-is-my savior cross in his right earlobe. She decided she missed the days when dress actually meant something about you; for example, an earring on a certain side dictating sexual preference.

"I left you a message," he said.

"I was going to call. I've been swamped."

"I went by the house."

"I know."

No disavowal. More proof she was right. "So Liam's over here?"

Emma nodded. Then added a deliberate, sarcasm-dipped "Thanks."

"Then you do know." Will looked abashed. His expression a perfect replica of Liam's the day she'd opened his latest report card. "How about Lee? Did you tell him?"

"We're talking wedding plans, right?"

He didn't seem capable of breathing out the yes. A flick of the head was given instead.

"Don't worry, I haven't said a word."

"Oh . . . good." The good was a little shaky. "Listen, I know it won't make a difference to you, but it was Jo's idea." His palm was up, pressed flat against the door, in case she tried to escape inside. "She didn't even tell me she was putting the announcement in the paper, then it was too late."

"And I suppose they used your body double for the photograph."

"It's not like that," he began, then blanched. "Look . . . I can understand your anger."

The way he said it sounded so prescribed, Emma had the suspicion that there had been coaching. Will did see a therapist. She imagined the two of them role-playing in advance.

"Can you now?" she countered. "That's very generous of you." An unfortunate choice of words, Emma's view was suddenly obscured by an apparition, her brand-new Weil-McLain boiler. "Forget it," she added inauthentically, then pressed the bell.

There was nothing to add, and nothing said until Suzanne pulled the door back with a jolly "You certainly took your sweet time" and then saw Will, looked stunned, and added a less than fortuitous "Oh lord."

The news was out. Of course it would be. That was why one put those announcements in the paper, Emma reminded herself. It was a way of signifying your own importance, and making damn sure the world was as full of joy as you were when you plighted your troth. In this case, there was another added benefit, the new, nubile bride got to make the retro model squirm.

Suzanne's hard look was great. Emma wanted to hug her tight. And Will clearly wanted to get the hell away, which he did immediately, calling for Liam and taking the stairs before he heard an answer.

"I can't believe he has the nerve to show up," Suzanne said as she helped Emma stuff Katherine Rose into her snowsuit for the trip down the block. There were gleeful sounds from above. Apparently,

Liam still loved his dad. Not for long, Emma thought wickedly, then stopped that thought with a reminder; a boy did need his father.

They were outside, with Liam talking a blue streak and Emma being sure to walk as far ahead as she could. She heard Liam describing this board game he and Tony had spent the morning designing, how it was named Trolls and Treason and it was a strategy game and how there were all these different levels you could play it on and how it was so fucking cool and did he think they could maybe sell it, some kids at school thought so . . . and Will had the nerve to sound so damn enthusiastic. But then, where was the surprise in that, Will was an expert at hiding things, he'd hidden Jolene for months, possibly years. Interesting choice, she told herself, with a wry nod that acknowledged her own complicity. She had liked the distance at first, liked that she'd had to torture his secrets out of him, liked that she'd been able to get him to admit, to break down, to choose her as the one person who would hear his hard-won confession.

Exhausting, Emma thought, but acknowledged there was more to it than that. It hadn't been exhaustion that had wrung her dry, it had been fear, fear of what she might find when she dug down deep. It was a mystery to her, how love dissolved, but it had with them. Emma had known for a while that she was not the right person for Will, not good for him, not capable of shifting enough to make it work.

Back to the present, and Emma heard Will's voice, knew from experience that his overly effusive responses meant disaster was bearing down. Liam was nervous too, he sensed something coming, but chattered away glibly, his way of deflecting the inevitable outcome. Emma wanted to turn right there and send Will packing, instead she handed Katherine off to him, as she fumbled for her keys. Will looked down at his daughter, then lifted her and kissed both cheeks in a benediction. Katherine smiled cheerfully up at him too, so ideal and idealized with that auburn mop of hair, the spray of freckles on her cheeks. She was an innocent Scots Irish lassie full of wide-eyed belief in her dear dad.

Emma took Katherine into the kitchen and heard the sound of pounding feet rising above her head. Liam was so eager to love and be loved. Liam, even in this preternaturally huge state, was still so dependent on both of them. Emma tensed as if the blow was coming her way. She felt the pale shiver invade her. She would do anything to stop this, anything to protect him. Her poor son. Her fists clenched as she tried and, as usual, failed miserably.

Then there was an ominous quiet.

Emma could easily imagine the scene, Will taking the seat next to Liam on the bed, scanning the walls of the room in an attempt to find a diversion, and finding no solace in the photographs of Liam's fallen idols, Mark Messier and Brian Leetch, now hidden behind Eminem and Dr. Dre. Will then offering a "Listen, Lee" and Liam's face getting tight and pinched in the mouth, like an old man's.

"Fuck you both!" Liam was screaming it out. Emma heard his feet pound down the stairs, then the front door slam.

A few minutes later, Will came into the kitchen. He was the shaggy dog that had been kicked and poked, punched and prodded, the dog that didn't have an alternative and so shivered his way back to the land of inhumane treatment.

"That didn't go too well."

An understatement, but he had certainly come to the wrong place for sympathy. Still, Emma cautioned herself to keep quiet, her charity based on the warmth in the kitchen, which was really quite shocking. She'd lived in this house for over ten years, and every winter she or Will had sealed every single window with plastic, caulking the gaps. It was always drafty nonetheless. And now it was temperate. Her body was almost melting in relief, this, a small island of comfort in an unforgiving sea.

"He'll calm down," Emma said.

"You think calming down is going to do it?" Will looked skeptical.

"Kids learn to accept what they can't change."

"That's one of those truisms I never thought I'd hear you utter. And by the way, also entirely wrong. I should know." Will's reference was to his host of errant stepfathers, to the blame he'd heaped on his mother's shoulders for her decision to leave the first, the second, the third, and counting.

"Kids grow up," Emma countered. "They figure out that they're not perfect parents either."

"So you're saying that when he's thirty, he'll forgive me."

"He'll forgive you next week. It's me he won't forgive. I brought him to this pass, remember. I'm his mom."

"This isn't about you." He sounded self-righteous, oddly enough.

"That's where you're wrong." Because everything was, in the end. He knew it too, but he'd offered the white lie, here, in this kitchen with the paint chipping down off the ceiling, and the rattling windowpanes. Her kitchen now, Emma thought, not now, but soon, very soon. The end of the week and it was hers forever, or for as long as she could make the mortgage payments. She darted her eyes around to find the boundaries. The kitchen table, sitting squat in the middle, with its four spindly chairs. Katherine's high chair pulled up, her current feast dressing it, and the floor beneath festooned with applesauce, ground pears, and yams; the girl had de Kooning-esque talent.

Will leaned over, placing a kiss on his daughter's fur-soft hair. Watching him, Emma felt the lurch inside. She should have tried harder, she decided; she'd brought two children into this mess of a world and offered them nothing but her own pathetic attempt at mothering to depend on. What a grandiose vision she must have of her native abilities.

"You're going to go try and find him?" Emma asked pointedly.

"Of course." Which was funny really, there was no of course that existed between them, no assumptions of any known behavior, except that on Friday they'd be cosignatories of several binding legal documents. "Any suggestions when I do find him?"

"Sure, grovel. Kiss his feet. If that doesn't work, try bribery." Emma paused, then added, "That wish list for Christmas. I haven't had time to get him the skateboard. It's yours, if you want it."

"Great. I'll get it for him." Will was knotting his muffler. And Emma? She found she was already regretting her generous impulse. She had a sudden image of her hands, reaching out to tug on the ends, strangling him.

"You know, you've been so great. You should be killing me for this," he added.

Emma didn't comment on his mind-reading ability. "I've seen what the accommodations are like in jail," she noted.

There was a howl from Katherine, then she banged her spoon emphatically against her bowl. The girl was gifted, not just an artist, but a musician as well. What talent might emerge next, Emma wondered?

But enough with diversionary tactics. "About the boiler," she said, "I'll pay you back."

His eyes narrowed. He seemed to be trying to make something out. Was the light too dim in here, it seemed bright enough to her. "I don't get you," he said. "The boiler?"

Shit! Talk about foolish, then she'd been right at the beginning. Strange days, when taking charity from Will was the better alternative. Emma couldn't stop herself from blurting out, "I must have been crazy, thinking it was you."

"What's that supposed to mean?" Will might not have known what she was referring to, but he knew enough to take umbrage.

"Nothing," Emma muttered. "Nothing at all."

Then there was a long, painful silence, finally broken by Will saying, "I guess I'd better try and catch up to him." The shaggy-dog look he offered with the statement did nothing to compel her.

"Try Tony's."

"Suzanne might not even open the door when she sees it's me."

"You'll have to take that chance," Emma said, and saw that Will actually had the nerve to look hurt by the comment. Emma turned her back and only felt herself start to relax when she heard the front door shut. That was when she was left almost alone, to confront a truly unsettling image, Josh Hammond making amends, or else making her beholden. At no cost to the sender, she thought, and realized that wasn't completely fair.

A week before Christmas and all through her house, one creature was stirring and screeching. Miss Katherine Rose was making a typical play for attention, winding herself up for a really big bellow, her face bright pink with effort. She squeezed her eyes tight, until tears popped from the corners. Her fists clenched. Her mouth became an open fishlike *O*, "Maaaaaaa!"

"Oh you," Emma said, tickling her under the chin. Katherine stubbornly batted away her hand, but Emma insisted, until Katherine had to relent, offering a giddy smile. "What a tease," Emma said. She unhooked the safety belt and set Katherine on the floor. The girl who had never bothered to crawl had walked at a tender seven months. She was so steady on her feet that she resembled a truly diminutive adult. Her nature was the opposite of Liam's in so many ways. Where he'd been a relatively mild child, Katherine Rose was opinionated, and aggressive about getting her way. Perhaps birth order accounted for it. Liam called his sister *el exigente* but he still gave in to her slightest whim. In truth, Emma knew, they all did, for who could resist her infectious giggle. At that moment, Katherine's eyes met Emma's, revealing a look of furious, almost desperate intelligence.

"What does he want from me now?" Emma asked, and felt unsettled thinking she might have the answer.

10

Emma had been born and bred in the Bronx. She'd moved to Manhattan for college, roosting at Barnard, then on to Brooklyn later, as a compromised adult. This forced her to acknowledge kinship with three of the five boroughs. Still, New York snobbery required her to draw the line right there. Queens, well it did have Forest Hills to its credit. But it looked too much like what it really was, an extension of Long Island. Still, on Monday morning, sinfully early, Emma was walking past identical row houses, each with its own sacred, rectangular strip of lawn, on her way to meet with her client Roland's wife, Marie.

Emma took care to bypass the slick patches of ice. In the night, the temperature had plunged, turning slush rock hard. Emma's prescription, a pair of shit-kicking blue Timberlands with steel-reinforced toes. Still, even with the extra traction the boots provided, she went plunging forward as she neared Marie's sister's house and saved herself by grabbing onto a picket fence. In the yard behind it, a deflated snowman with a cigarette hanging from its frayed lips seemed to find this more than a little amusing. Behind it in the postage stamp yard, Santa's red sleigh sat, abandoned. No reindeer. No grinning Claus. No presents for the ever-expectant young'uns.

Ninety-one. Emma made her way up to the stoop and buzzed, throwing a quick look over her shoulder at the two news vans across the street.

"Who's out there?"

"Emma Price. Mrs. Everett?" Emma flashed her I.D. at the peephole and she heard locks clicking, then the door pulled back to reveal a heavyset woman in a bathrobe.

"Better get yourself in quick. Those people be on you like vultures." The door closed behind her. "Best you show me that card of yours again."

Emma handed over the folded wallet, a picture I.D. with her name prominently displayed. Apparently this still wasn't enough; she got one more suspicious glance from photo to living, breathing replica, then back.

"I guess that'll do. Marie's in the kitchen."

Emma followed her down a dark hallway that was lit by a ghostly emanation from the living room. In there a coven of girls, ranging in age from early teen to toddler, huddled around the warmth of the TV. One was diligently plaiting cornrows into another's hair. The girl closest to the tube had scooped a spoonful of cereal and now held it aloft, drops of milk dripping down from the metal hull. All seemed to be equally transfixed by the cartoon that was on, which was, of all things, *Scooby Doo*. How retro, Emma thought, as the woman pointed her toward the kitchen, then stepped into the living room, shutting the door in her face.

Marie's sister, Emma assumed, but had her assumption cast into doubt when she saw Marie Everett, in the flesh.

Her hair was one of the first things Emma noticed. It was literally waist length, thick, black, and straight. Then her face, model-high cheekbones, a rich tawny color. She looked a good ten years younger than her ex, and that was an "at least" statement. Where her sister was heavyset, she was voluptuous. Perhaps there had been a different father involved, or else the gene pool had split off on two separate tracks. Whatever the reason, Marie had been the clear winner of this genetic dice roll.

"I appreciate you letting me come by like this," Emma said, immediately extending her hand. The other woman wiped her own off, then shook, barely, looking none too pleased. Not at all surprising, when you considered her present predicament. "May I?" Emma motioned toward one of the kitchen chairs.

"Suit yourself."

Emma took a seat, making a quick study of the room, which was pleasant enough, a frilly lace curtain pulled tight over the window to keep out inquiring eyes. There were spice jars with cute scripted names like Time Before Thyme and Savory Sage on a rack above the stove. The theme of the kitchen seemed to be country bountiful. Under her fingers, a yellow-and-white-checked tablecloth. On the walls, prints of a dairy maid of yore leading her cow to pasture past an orchard overloaded with ripe red apples.

"How's he holding up?" Marie asked, taking the seat opposite Emma. Her voice was low, Emma guessed, so the kids wouldn't overhear. The strain showed in the pallid skin, and the accompanying dark circles under her eyes. Those eyes were as remarkable as the rest of her physique, one was green, the other hazel.

"I've only seen your husband once," Emma said.

"More than me," Marie volunteered. "And let's start off with being clear, he's not mine."

"But you understand what my role is, what the Capital Crimes Office is?"

"Sure, you're the people who want to try and get him off."

"No," Emma said. "We don't get people off. We offer them legal counsel and representation. Your . . . pardon me, Roland is likely to face the death penalty."

"And you don't want him to, right?"

"Exactly."

"There you go, it's like I said, you're looking to get him off."

"So you believe he deserves to be put to death?"

"He went and shot those people. You tell me what else he deserves?" Marie Everett stood, lifting her own half-filled cup of coffee. "I meant to ask if you wanted some."

"Thanks, I would."

"How you take it?"

"A little milk."

Marie Everett poured out a cup and shoved the milk her way. Done with that, she added, "That man's a misery. You spent more than a minute with him, you'd know the truth of what I'm saying."

The coffee was decent enough, but Emma felt it curdle in her stomach, and couldn't tell whether that came because of what she was confronting here or because it was her third cup of the morning.

"Fair enough," she offered. "You left Roland in November."

"That's my point."

"Why?"

"Which why do you mean? Why I left? Or why I waited so damn long?"

"Then you'd been considering a divorce for a while?"

"Sure. Years."

"You have three kids with Roland."

"I do." Marie Everett cradled her own cup in both hands, apparently considering. Then she added, "Look, I don't expect you to understand how it is."

"I'd like to try," Emma offered.

"Fine." The petulance faded. "It gets bad and you tell yourself, it might get better, you've got the kids to consider, don't want to hurt them. You turn stubborn, and stop listening when your friends talk. You make yourself busy, think if you work hard enough, it'll fix itself. Then you get tired, and one day, you see all your kids know is sorrow."

"In other words, you stand it till you can't anymore," Emma said, commiserating.

"There you go." Emma caught Marie checking her hands as they extended across the tabletop. The evidence was there, easily found. She might have removed her wedding ring months ago, but there was still what looked to be a permanent indentation.

"You got your own story?"

"I do."

Marie's look said "Tell me."

"My ex found greener pastures," Emma offered wryly.

"His own little Eden?" Marie countered, giving a hint of a smile back.

"He seems to think so."

"What do you think? Trouble in paradise?"

Emma shrugged. "It takes a while to realize what you don't like," she said. "A while more before it starts to feel like something that should be fixed. After that?"

"I got you."

Emma knew it shouldn't be this easy, but it so often was. If you scratched the surface, nine times out of ten, a woman had a complaint. "Rolly's the kind who likes to blame the world for his troubles. It's never his fault. His thing is always what he's owed, how he's getting cheated. I told him as much when he got hurt, but he wouldn't listen. But then, what else can you expect. Those people are all the same."

"Those people?" Emma felt the internal flinch.

"Hope I'm not stepping on any toes here." Marie fixed her eyes on Emma.

"Not at all," Emma said evenly.

"All I'm saying is those Jewish people, they're clannish. They're always off by themselves. Which is good for them, right? One gets in trouble, the rest pitch in to help. Can't say the same about my people, now can you? A brother's always ready to fight with his best friend over the goddamn table scraps, pardon my English." Marie Everett swung herself up and went to the sink. She rinsed her cup out, then turned around, leaning her back against it.

"Roland was the Ben Dovs' employee for over ten years. He certainly had a right to expect to be treated fairly," Emma said.

"You know, if you can't see what's in front of your face, whose fault is it?" Marie responded. "Ten years of seeing how they were. How they treated other people there. Rolly was supposed to get a raise, supposed to get a promotion, every year it was a different damn excuse. And he was the one they kept on. Someone got up in their face, they got fired. Rolly, he stayed quiet. Kept saying how he had a relationship, how they were different with him. Me, I didn't see it. And come to find out, he was the same as the rest. *Schwartze.* You heard that word?"

Emma nodded. "So you weren't surprised to hear about the shootings?"

"Now why would you say that?" The smirk was truly unpleasant.

"Had Roland threatened the Ben Dovs?"

"Which time? He'd get right up in their faces and ask them, were they ashamed? Or he'd claim that Jehovah was going to smite them, that vengeance was his! Look, they might have their ways, but that's no real excuse. Far as I'm concerned, there's only so much you can do to a man before he wants to get even."

Marie was not going to be much of a character witness, Emma noted. Perhaps they could offer her a long vacation in a foreign country, one that extended through the course of the trial. "I'm curious, what pushed you to leave? What was the last straw?" Emma asked.

"I'm thinking you've already decided on the answer."

"No," Emma declared, trying for innocence. Of course, she'd noted the time frame, the fact that Marie had managed to pick up her things and go only three days after the Ben Dovs disappeared into the black hole of bankruptcy court. Along with their three-million-dollar judgment.

"Fine, you want to know what three million dollars gets you? It gets you plenty. That man owes his girls something. Owes me too." Her eyes glittered. That was honest, Emma decided. A little too honest, in fact.

Marie had moved forward as she spoke, putting her hands around the back of one of the chairs. She seemed to be using it for support, but considering the tenor of their conversation thus far, there was a possibility of her considering its use as a weapon. Emma decided it was more than time to take her leave. "Thanks for the coffee," she said, pushing herself up from the table and drawing her coat around her. "I'll be in touch."

Marie didn't bother to respond. But she followed behind Emma, right up to the front door. Emma assumed this was to ensure her exit. As she touched the handle, she remembered there had been one thing she'd meant to ask. And after all, the money had been spoken of. "The amount, for the damages, I was wondering how the figure was arrived at?"

Marie's face darkened. She'd assumed she was free of me, Emma thought. Marie wasn't going to answer, and that, in itself, seemed curious.

"Did Weinstein come up with the amount?" she pressed.

"What's it to you?"

"Three million. That's an awful lot of money."

Marie reached for the door and Emma stepped back. She imagined being shoved out into the street before receiving her answer, worse, she imagined an embarrassing fall down the three steps up and onto the icy path. "Mr. Weinstein doesn't usually take these sort of cases." Emma saw Marie's mouth set in a thin, negative line. "Did someone recommend him to you?"

"Don't be bothering me with your mess," Marie said. She'd thrust the door open and centered her body, to force Emma out.

"Stewart Weinstein's Jewish." No response to that either.

"Considering Roland's feelings about Jews . . . look, why won't you tell me? Did Roland find him?" Emma tried to assess something from the angry expression she was encountering. "Was it Weinstein, did he come to you?"

"What difference does it make?"

"Probably none, but then, why not explain?" Though Emma knew Marie was right in the larger sense. Roland had renamed himself, from victim to victimizer. In doing so, he'd recast his own life, so that events that once might have loomed large were now virtually inconsequential.

"That man doesn't care what anyone says, he does just as he likes," Marie muttered angrily, then shut the door in Emma's face. Turning, Emma realized she was about to be trapped. A keen-eyed reporter was rushing to get to her. Emma leaped over the steps, sprinted across the icy yard, and managed to high-jump the hedge. Landing on the other side, she felt her knee wrench and then felt utterly silly, but kept going to her car. Inside, she revved the motor, rubbed her knee, and replayed the last thing Marie had said. Only then did she realize that Marie hadn't necessarily meant Roland. Was Stewart Weinstein the man who did as he liked? Now that was interesting!

To Manhattan I will go, Emma thought. And to Mr. Stewart Weinstein.

The last time Emma had encountered Weinstein had been at an ACLU function. She'd spotted him, three tables over, with his mane of white hair. Weinstein had been the keynote speaker, hale and hearty at seventy. On his way to the dais, he'd made quite a stir, glad-handing the natives as he passed. After his speech, Emma had noted that a steady stream of sycophants came by to pay homage.

She had admired him, of course. Everyone did. He'd done the hard thing often enough, railed against the government when it wasn't popular in the sixties and seventies right up to the present minute. In fact, he had been one of the first to speak up against the Ashcroft version of civil rights that had been speedily and thoughtlessly enacted post-9/11.

Emma remembered something else about that night. How many of those who came by for a chat were young, decidedly attractive women. In fact, how one had been seated to his right and how Weinstein had put his arm around her chair, possessively. "Trophy bride?" Emma had asked Dawn. Dawn put her finger to her lips and shook her head. "Nora Pierce, straight from the Ivy League to Stu. She's an associate at his firm." Apparently, Weinstein's wife was sick and had been for years. Some wasting illness. And that was it, the sum of Emma's knowledge.

The phone buzzed and she hit the talk button. "Yes."

"Yes, that's how you answer now? I liked hello."

If it wasn't her almost significant other.

Laurence's voice boomed out, a little too loud. "I'm here by Bertha Summers's house."

"She's still giving you a hard time?" He'd called to ask for help, well of course. Emma thought about talking to Bertie and wasn't sure she could manage. Martin Diehl was one thing, getting Bertha Summers to cooperate? That was a Herculean task.

"It's not that." The catch in his voice gave some warning. "I'm sorry to have to be the one to tell you. Em, are you there?" She knew from the tone of voice, had heard him use it too many times before in his professional capacity.

Emma clicked the phone off. The tone he used was his inheritance. His father, an undertaker, had given him the gift of comfort. All Emma knew of this father were stories about his propriety. As for what he'd looked like, she'd come upon a snapshot in Laurence's desk drawer. In it Laurence was wearing formal attire—a dark suit and shoes, a Clorox-white shirt, a perfectly knotted tie stiffening his neck. His father stood beside him, touching him lightly on the shoulder. Their expressions were identical, and after studying them for a long while, she realized what was wrong. Both their faces were devoid of anything readable, emotional tabula rasae.

Bertha Summers was dead. Emma knew. Knew and couldn't bear to hear him speak the words.

11

Bertha Summers lived at the edge of Bedford Stuyvesant, on a block that had seen better days, not to mention decades. Next door to Bertha's row house, an abandoned building had metal sheets hammered over the windows, tags spray-painted on the brick, and a front yard that doubled as a refuse bin, old tires, an abandoned toaster oven, a worn-out baby carriage rusting, all caressed by the newly frozen drifts of icy snow.

Emma remembered the pride Bertha had taken in home ownership. To her, it had been an emblem of her newfound American roots. She'd told Emma she wasn't like her siblings, she was staying for good. The rest of them were building back in Jamaica, not her. "What I got there?" she'd asked, her eyes as ferocious as ever. Daring me to come up with a point-by-point argument she could rebut, Emma decided. It had been obvious to Emma what Bertha and her employer had in common, ferocious idealism, cutting honesty, and above all a vibrant sense of self.

Back in the sixties, when Bertha had bought this place, she'd taken shots with her Instamatic camera to show all around. After she'd made the down payment and signed off on the mortgage, she'd had a house-warming party. Emma remembered the rooms packed with men in shiny suits, ladies in dresses so colorful they hurt the eyes, all of them dancing hard to a loud reggae beat. Emma had danced, her whiteness over-whelmed in that sea of black.

A few days later, Josh told her that Eleanor had lent Bertha the money for the down payment. "Mom can't stop doing charity work," he'd said. And Emma had countered, "You don't have to hate everything your mom does just because she's the one doing it."

"How about you?" he'd offered. "You're the worst. You buy into all that good doctor, most selfless person on the face of the earth bullshit she puts out."

Walking up the steps now, Emma imagined Josh, seated inside that kitchen, ragging on Bertha. Bertha would sigh, sucking her teeth to add another note of displeasure. She had known he was doing things he shouldn't be doing, but she'd cut Josh slack, something she never did with her own brood. Still, one day Bertha had stopped Josh as he was leaving, grabbing his arm and throwing him a meaningful look, saying, "Boy, you should take better care of yourself. You too, Miss Emma Price," she'd added, chiding them reasonably, not pushing them so far away she couldn't matter.

"I didn't mean you should drop everything and show up here," Laurence told her at the door.

"You don't imagine I could go on about my business after getting that call."

"It's not pretty."

Emma braced herself for the rest. As Laurence stepped aside, Emma realized she was actually crossing her fingers, a totally retro move on her part. Her third-grade classmate Alice, a God-fearing Roman Catholic, had sworn it worked as a talisman, and that you had to do it every time you passed by a cemetery, remembering to chant, "Let the dead stay dead, let those I care about, including myself, keep on with the living." It had worked pretty well for a while, but then she'd grown up and her sister Rosa had dropped out of the sky to her death. After that, Emma had discarded the notion of personal control over one's own destiny.

Not pretty? It was worse than that, although the signs of intrusion didn't start out in the hallway. They began in what had once been known as the parlor. A thin plastic strip had been laid down by the forensics team, to keep all who came and went on one narrow path. To Emma's left a small table had been upended, a vase, split in half on the floor, with paper flowers trailing out.

O'Malley emerged at the top of the stairs off to the right, saw Emma, and turned around, disappearing into what had been Bertha's bedroom. Little red-haired O'Malley exiting stage right on her leather-soled regulation shoes, taking the luck of the Irish with her.

"In here," Laurence said, and held out his arm, like the gentleman he essentially was. They entered the living room, a misnomer for today, Emma thought, letting her eyes take everything in gradually, that same green corduroy couch, still wearing its plastic slipcover, the armchairs to match, still brassy with their doilies in frilly, tacked-on display. Bertha had done lacework as an active hobby, which meant that the arms of sofas and chairs, the length of the coffee table, had lovingly creweled covers.

On the floor in here, another vase thrown on its side, this one apparently wielding fresh carnations. Next to that, a broken flowerpot sporting one of those hideous razor plants, the kind that needed no light at all to thrive. And behind all this, the festive centerpiece, not a burning bush but a tree, real pine with blinking lights, and an abundance of ornamentation, horn-blowing angels, mischievous elves, beaming Santas.

"Over here."

Emma stepped around and found Bertha lying on her back, her eyes open wide. The wound in her chest was bloody, but Emma knew enough about entrance and exit to believe it must have been done from the front, and up close. She turned away, almost immediately, stepping off the track for a second, then putting herself back on, determined to keep going, to breathe evenly, in, then out. She made it into the hallway and felt the anxiety dissipate, out here she was far enough away from the bearer of the contagion. That was what it was, a contagious and terminal illness, passed from one to the next.

Why, she demanded?

Then, who? Who would do this?

It took even longer for her to realize that she was not all right, and that Laurence was with her, that she was using his arm to steady herself, not just holding it, actually digging her nails in. She released her grip, flushing with shame.

"Hey," he said softly.

Emma found she was able to filter out the hum, able to make out phrases, passed from one worker bee to the next. "How'd ya like that?" A query from over by the kitchen. Back to full consciousness, she asked the obvious. "The weapon?"

Saw the answer before the nod. "Forty-five caliber, from the shell casings."

Possibly the same weapon, though not the same m.o. Emma reminded herself that ballistics could hardly file a report this fast, still there were obvious reasons to think there would be a match.

"What else?" she asked.

"Just what you see." Indicating the mess.

"Like this upstairs too?"

A nod, one that gave her clearance to proceed. She did, taking the stairs to the top and encountering O'Malley working hard in the bedroom, sifting through debris. It was as if a tornado had come steaming through, the bedsheets ripped off, dresser drawers pulled out, clothing thrown indiscriminately on top of ripped-up books and magazines.

"My thinking is she might have gotten what she was after at Hammond's and brought it back here. Next thing you know, someone comes and wants it, and she won't give it up."

"Maybe there was nothing to find," Emma countered, still stubbornly clinging to the idea that Bertha had to be, in some way, innocent of the charge. Forget that, she told herself, as her gaze swept over the room again. This search had been too brutally invasive not to be intentional, underwear, bras, full slips, dresses, and shoes all piled up in indiscriminate display. "Have you notified the family?"

"Got hold of one of the daughters. She's down in Kingstown, I have a call out to the other two. And I left a message with the son's wife."

A stab of conscience, which Emma immediately subdued. "How about Josh and Leslie?"

"That's something different," he said.

Turning to confront him, she understood. He'd placed that call to her intentionally. That innocent pose, saying, "I didn't mean for you to drop everything . . ." He hadn't meant it, he'd planned it out, knowing her well enough to know she'd come flying over. "No," she said automatically. "Don't make me do this."

He tugged her out into the hall, then said, "You claim to care about these people."

"You're making it into a threat."

"Emma, you know what I need here. Which way is better for them? Me, coming in and playing hardball. Or you, breaking the news and reporting back."

"Laurence, please . . ." she began, and knew that their voices were being overheard, hardly a discreet distance from Caitlin, whose ears seemed to be twitching, her gaze so purposefully forced away, all making it clear she was hanging on their every word. Emma didn't say another thing, but she took the stairs down, headed for the door, and stepped out, breathing in the quick, cold air gratefully. Laurence arrived a second later. In the distance, Emma heard a siren, wailing its approach.

"What's your better idea?" he demanded.

Sad thing was, she didn't have one. But the thought of being his spy! Telling him how Josh and Leslie looked when she broke the news! It was mortifying.

Her reprieve came in an unexpected way, the siren ear-numbingly loud as the vehicle it was attached to pulled up.

"Jesus, Carter again," Laurence hissed as the M.E. stepped out of the door of the van.

"Detective," Carter said as he climbed up the stairs, brushing past them. He turned her way, doffed a pretend cap, and added, "The lovely Miss Price. So this is one of yours. It really is my lucky day."

Emma kept her disagreement internal. She smiled gracefully, refusing, on principle, to give the bastard the pleasure.

Only a month ago, Dawn had been representing Marcus Dendridge. Marcus, with his I.Q. of 79 and a history of abuse at the hands of both parents, hadn't been smart enough to flip. His friend Lane did. Which was why Lane got life while Marcus got to face the death penalty. True, he'd done something appalling, robbing that 7-Eleven on Flatbush, taking the five patrons and the clerk into the back room and executing them. Yet another sign of his ignorance was the fact that the whole thing had been captured, blow by blow, on direct-feed videotape.

Dr. Carter here had taken special pleasure discussing the entrance and exit wounds for each victim, playing back the video to point out to members of the jury exactly how the bullet had traveled, offering up the autopsy photos to corroborate, and he'd forced the jury into taking two breaks to regain their composure. That, plus the mother of one of the victim's fainting, pretty much sealed Marcus's fate. As far as Emma was concerned, it had been entirely unnecessary, but there was always a point with Carter. He had ended up, yet again, on the courtroom steps, smiling for the cameras.

"Why do I hate that man so?" Laurence said when it was safe.

"Because he's an asshole."

Laurence laughed. "Problem is, there are so many around these days." He was looking back, though, as if he wanted to hear a better explanation. One she was more than willing to provide.

"For Carter, it's all about conquest," she said. "He could really give a shit about the victim."

"Could be."

"Is," she countered. Which made him crack a smile. "Whereas you, you think you shouldn't care so much, but you can't help it. And when someone makes such a show of his abundantly calculating nature, you find it offensive, even, I might add, morally repugnant."

"Now you're giving me too much credit."

"No, I'm not," Emma said. "Don't get me wrong, Laurence, I'm not mistaking you for a saint."

With that, she moved away, out of the yard. Safely inside her car, she looked back. The only person outside was a uniform, spinning out a web of yellow crime-scene tape.

12

E mma told herself there was no way.

"Yes way" was how Liam would have put it, tossing back a retort.

Josh first, who didn't pick up. She left an ambiguous message, asking him to call back. Then Leslie, she made a bargain with herself, worth one attempt. Unfortunately, after two rings, Bob answered.

"Leslie's making the arrangements," he said, not even breathing as he rattled off the where.

Damn.

Leslie Hammond could have picked any funeral home in the tristate area.

Emma was totally unprepared when she got out of her car in the lot of the Parkside Memorial Chapel (so oddly situated next to the Prospect Park Riding Stables) and discovered that the woman walking her way was Leslie, who looked startled, then said, "Emma?"

"I spoke to Bob," Emma explained, adding lamely, "I was nearby."

Leslie opened her mouth, then clamped it shut.

Emma couldn't blame her. What was the appropriate response here? "Nice of you to stop by for a visit, maybe you could help me decide between the velvet interior with the brass fittings or the plywood box?" Tell her, Emma thought. Spit it out and go. Run. Run away, and explain to Laurence how Leslie had always been intimidating, give that as an excuse.

"I . . ." Emma found she couldn't continue down that road. "Leslie, I don't mean to hound you, but I'm worried. I don't think you should push so hard with the police." Instead of offering a confidence and then her condolences, this? Emma gave herself an internal D for effort.

"That boyfriend of yours sent you to find me, didn't he?"

"Boyfriend?" Emma knew she looked completely guilty. What of, she told herself, trying for an adequate defense and failing miserably. She wrapped her arms tightly around her midriff in a suitably protective pose.

"You think I'm that far out of the loop?" Leslie's laugh was brutal. "Is this how you are with men? You screw them, and then do their grunt work for them?"

"Christ!" Emma threw out. She would have preferred a sharp jab to the ribs. But she hadn't taken a self-defense class in years. And she had too much experience with Leslie's ability to physically overpower her.

As luck had it, Leslie's car was parked right next to hers. No escape there. Leslie reached for the handle and Emma decided to act, grabbing Leslie's shoulder. That was all it took for her to turn, acrimoniously spit out, "What now?" and reach out, slapping Emma's hand so hard, it stung. The effect this had was all too familiar. Emma immediately felt herself telescope, she was an ant staring up at this giant boot heel. Hard to stop the impulse to shut one's eyes and pray.

"Dawn Prescott called me this morning and we got to talking," Leslie said. "I thought she might be able to help me get someone competent on this, get the F.B.I. involved, not that I think they're brain surgeons, but at least they'd be looking into the obvious links, so she asks me who's on the case, and I mention Detective Solomon's name. Naturally, talk turns to you."

Dawn, Emma hadn't even thought to warn her off. Of course, the possible permutations of the conversation that might have ensued if Emma had tried were endless. If only she could take all of this back, she thought, admitting finally how complex her own motives had been; Laurence was added to an already lethal brew what with her history with Josh, Leslie, and Eleanor. Not to mention Bertha Summers. It had been tempting to believe she could somehow make amends and revise the past. Tempting, and patently false.

At least there was some good news, she told herself. Clearly, Leslie hadn't known about her involvement with Laurence till this morning, which meant that Josh must not have known either.

Except, of course, if he'd gotten the information from another credible source.

Leslie had opened the car door. If Emma was going to say anything, this was her opportunity.

"Leslie," Emma said, "I'm here about Bertha."

Leslie swung back her way. "Now that really pissed me off, accusing Bertie when there was no one more devoted to Mom."

"Bertha's dead." Emma saw Leslie wasn't quite taking in what she'd said and added, "It's true, I've been to her house." She watched as the defensiveness stripped away, replaced by incredulity. "I'm sorry to be the one to tell you." Emma put her hand on Leslie's arm, attempting to offer some form of comfort.

"God. It was all this stuff with Mom. The detective coming after her. It must have been too hard. I have to say, it's almost too hard for me."

"She's been murdered."

"Murdered?" Leslie's face clouded over. "That's not right," she said, almost to herself, "that really isn't possible." She backed into the door and as it closed, it somehow set off the burglar alarm. Emma started, as did Leslie. The noise was ear-splitting, the car spitting warnings at them, "Burglar. Get Away. Burglar." Leslie went wide-eyed and then bolted. She ran out of the lot and into the street, swerving around the fast-moving vehicles. Emma winced, witnessing three near misses, and was grateful when Leslie made it to the other side, disappearing into the park.

Leslie was certainly fast. And in better shape for a jog. Emma could do a nice Australian crawl, but her knees, her aching knees! Still, Emma decided to pursue, crossing into the park, looking right, then left, and finally making for the frozen pond. She noted how pieces of logs and stray debris were fixed into the top, looking as if a beaver had been madly at work. Standing at another crossroads, Emma tried to put herself into tracker mode. Think like Leslie. Now that was truly ridiculous. Still, she decided to take the wooded path, one that meandered around the park and was surely the best haven for muggers and rapists.

About a quarter mile in, she came upon a solitary dog walker, with a huge albino great Dane loping along beside him.

"Have you seen a woman running by. Really tall, with gray frizzy hair?"

The man scanned her, apparently trying to ascertain her motives in asking, then slowly shook his head.

Emma turned back. She told herself she'd done enough damage for one day and was going to head to her car, but then, scanning the horizon at the corner and a traffic circle that looked virtually impossible to circumnavigate, she decided it was wrong not to make one last attempt, ruefully pointing out in an internal critique that Josh would certainly not regret having her help, after all, she was doing a bang-up job!

Emma took the other path. Walking along, she admitted to herself that it was beautiful in here, as close to nature as one got, living in Brooklyn. There was a thick pine forest to her left, with a coating of white gracing the boughs. She tried to fool herself into believing the sound of the passing cars was the rush of wind. Up ahead, she spotted an anachronistic Japanese pagoda standing sentinel. As she came closer, she realized Leslie was seated inside on the wooden bench.

Emma took the seat directly opposite and was not surprised that Leslie pointedly ignored her presence. Emma noted the lack of gloves on Leslie and how her long, thin fingers were turning pink from exposure. She also saw there was no wedding band, which might put to rest the question of whether there had been marriage vows exchanged between her and her quiet friend Bob.

"You have a lot of nerve," Leslie said. "Coming at me like this."

"I'm so sorry, Les."

"That comes cheap, your sorrow. I haven't seen you in how many years?"

"I realize that."

"Do you? Do you know how it hurt Mom when you disappeared? Now you're sorry. Well, don't waste your apology on me. I didn't miss you."

"You're being unfair." Emma heard the belligerence in her tone and couldn't still it.

"Funny, it doesn't feel that way to me. But go ahead, explain. Explain why you get to walk in and tell me how to act?"

"I'm offering a different perspective," Emma said weakly.

"Is that what it is. I thought you were doing favors. One for your detective friend, another for my long-lost brother. Excuse me for thinking it had nothing to do with me, or with Mom." Leslie nodded, as if agreeing with her own summation. "Telling me what's best! Best for you."

Emma found she couldn't dredge up the energy to disagree.

"I'm not a lucky person," Leslie added mournfully.

"How do you mean?"

"I'd think it would be obvious. But of course, you don't see past yourself, never have, never will. Things come to you, Emma. It's almost obscene."

Emma wanted to laugh. "Come to me, how?"

Leslie had pushed her chin out. Apparently she had some vision of perfection, and looking her over Emma realized, no matter how delusional, there was no way to counter it. "I'm not excusing Josh, but he never got along with your mom."

"And? Who does get along with their parents? Did you?"

Emma shrugged. There had been fights, but she'd never really had the opportunity to withdraw, the burden of both her sister's death and her mother's illness placed squarely on her shoulders.

"What I can't believe is how petty it all is. Josh has a fight with Mom over this girl, and the next thing you know, he disappears off the face of the fucking earth! Never writes. Never calls. As far as she knew, he could have been dead."

"Over a girl?" Such a naive and clueless interpretation, it bore repeating.

"Over you, wasn't it?"

"Me? Who told you that?"

"No one had to tell me." The sly look on Leslie's face was totally disconcerting. She was so proud of being right, and she was so decidedly wrong.

"You never got the full story," Emma began, then realized it wasn't up to her to give it. Eleanor could have done it at any time. And Josh? He had the rest of their lives to consider a way of broaching the subject. It wasn't hers to take on. None of this was, she decided.

"Well, what is it?"

"Nothing," Emma said, then added on the lie, "I don't know myself." A weak defense, at best. One that Leslie clearly didn't buy.

"Josh was her favorite." Leslie thrust it out, like a jab.

Misdirected at best, Emma knew. Leslie was miserable and sinking, heading down past the subbasement and the subterranean tunnels that crisscrossed the city, in a headfirst plunge to the very center of the earth. One woman's hell, Emma thought, and said, "Stop doing this."

"Doing what?"

"Dredging this shit up. Your mother loved you, Leslie."

"I'm not saying she didn't. I'm pointing out the disparity. You have two children, tell me that you don't compare them."

"Making comparisons is different from quantifying your love. Really, Leslie, it doesn't work that way."

"What a condescending tone to use with me. Just because I've never had kids of my own, I wouldn't know?"

Leslie stood, thrust her shoulders back, martinet style, then marched off, disappearing down the slope of a hill. Only then did Emma realize that Leslie's outburst had skillfully sidetracked any further talk of Bertha's demise. Indeed, Leslie had not bothered to ask the most basic questions—the how, and the when, not to mention the why.

"Oh Christ," Emma said aloud.

Weinstein, Levin, and Santiago had its offices in a town house on 76th Street between West End Avenue and Riverside Drive. Twenty minutes late and counting, Emma had to lean into the wind coming up off the river to make any progress at all. The building was impressive, more so when you considered it doubled as his home. A sandstone five-floor edifice that Emma figured had to be worth a cool three million in the currently inflated Manhattan real estate market.

Weinstein's receptionist was casually dressed in the terminally hip manner that dictated all black—stretch pants and a long-sleeved, form-fitting top. What form there was, Emma thought cattily. The woman was flat as a board and sliver thin, perhaps one of those new, ubiquitous size zeros. Emma's own slightly lanky, size-ten physique looked corn-fed in comparison.

"A minute." The woman's finger held up to further clarify.

Emma took a seat and noted that black was the larger motif as well here. The black leather couch and two black leather sling-back chairs in the waiting area were all appropriately worn without being worn through. There was a moderne glass table shaped like a kidney bean. On it an array of reading material had been tastefully strewn: *Paper, The Nation, New York Law Journal.*

"This way," the receptionist said, and curved her finger into an invitation.

Emma followed her to the back of the first floor and up curving stairs that had been planted smack in the middle of an open work area. The air hummed with vitality, which came from the youthful zest of the employees who were coming and going and going and coming. Up they went to the second floor, which was made up of closed-off, glassed-in offices, where more senior staff could be seen working, talking, or, in one case, rubbing a half-grown beard. Up again, to the third, where the great man sat behind a glass door that was not see-through but fogged, so you could make out the outlines within. The receptionist knocked, waited a beat, then opened it and Stewart Weinstein was exposed. The first thing Emma noted, again, was that mane of white hair. Which barely moved as he stepped out from behind his desk to offer her a peremptory handshake.

"Sit," he said genially.

His lean face was tanned. As for the outfit, only subtly formal, worn corduroys held up by a Native American buckle in the shape of a serpent, and a silk shirt in a puce color that didn't make him look in the least washed out. Yes, the effect was undoubtedly as intended. He was comforting in an Aspen, casually chic sort of way.

"I was pleased to find Roland in such capable hands," he said. "Dawn Prescott is an able attorney."

"I'll tell her you said as much," Emma noted, taking her seat, then foraging for her notebook and a sharpened number two pencil. "Sorry about being late," she added.

"There are times when it's unavoidable." Making crystal clear how much he believed she was the one at fault here.

Emma's response was the donning of a sunny smile. She knew better than to rise to the bait, telling herself that Weinstein was of a certain generation, many of his contemporaries were habitually condescending to their juniors.

"At any rate," he added. "I doubt there's much I can offer you'll find of use." He glanced at his watch, underlining the point yet again.

"I'm sure the documentation will provide us with most of what we need," Emma agreed.

"Exactly." He offered a gesture, imperial and sweeping, indicating the two legal-sized cardboard file boxes that sat near the door. Then Weinstein settled in, comfortable in his oversized desk chair. Behind him on the walls, historic photographs of him with famous and infamous clients. Emma knew she had only a few minutes left to work with. "How did you get involved with the Everett case?" she asked.

"Ah yes, the inevitable question." Was it? She supposed. In answer, she received a sturdy silence. Their eyes met and he cleared his throat, then said, "You don't believe a man like Everett deserves the best representation possible?"

"That's not what I asked," she pointed out, still amiable.

"I'm not sure that it matters how he found me, the point is, he did."

"Mr. Weinstein, I'm not sure I understand. Is it that you don't want to tell me. Or that you can't remember?"

"My memory is fine."

And yet, no answer tendered. Curiouser and curiouser. She was plunging down the rabbit hole today, Emma decided. Apparently headfirst. If only she'd known before she left the house, she would have borrowed Liam's helmet.

"The thing is, you specialize in criminal litigation, not civil suits."

"Actually, we do many things here."

No time to dance anymore, Emma decided. "Did the

Ben Dovs' relationship to Moshe Levin have anything to do with your interest in the case?"

"I see." He clucked his tongue, chiding her. For what, Emma wondered?

"See what?"

"If I were to say that it interested me, what would it matter?"

"How can I tell, until I know the history?" Emma countered.

"I can't understand why you're taking this tone with me." Drawing up in his chair, to further express his umbrage. Except he looked more disappointed than outraged. "I knew your father," he added.

An interesting segue.

"Did you?"

"We worked together years ago. A lovely man."

Lovely was one word Emma would never have used to describe Sy Cohen. Her father had had a wry, cynical sense of humor, and a slightly paranoid worldview—blame it on the blacklist, blame it on bad parenting, blame it on whatever you like. Emma had loved him unconditionally, whether he was at his irascible worst or his hysterical best. The way Weinstein was using him here, to sidetrack the question, annoyed her even more than the fancy footwork.

"So when did you realize Roland was going to be a problem for you?" Emma asked.

"Ah." Gravely said, but she saw the pained look disappear and knew she'd gotten some of it right. "It didn't take much time at all, I suppose. On the other hand, I'd like to point out that the judgment was in Roland's favor."

"Yes, the judgment," Emma said. "How did you settle on that amount?"

"I would have thought you'd understand that. A formula is involved."

"Yes, I know about the formula. But it's what you factored in I don't get. At forty thousand a year, for the rest of his working life . . . three million?"

"We factored in the health care costs." He checked his watch again, then said pointedly, "You'll find all the answers you need." A jerk of the head said where. "I trust you're going to examine the issue of mental and physical health. You'll find that Roland was addicted to those painkillers. The bone chips had lodged in the nerve endings, one doctor had an apt metaphor, he compared it to living with shards of glass dug in under the top layer of skin."

He stood, put out his hand, and she took it, feeling even more uneasy than she had stepping in. On his desk, arranged so that the visitors could get equal viewing access, were glowing family portraits; Stewart Weinstein was on display as dad and doting granddad. But Emma remembered his arm slung around his associate's chair back, and it ran counter to the image that caught her eye now, Weinstein and his wife grappling gaily with their three teenage children. His wife had blond hair, a patrician jaw, and steady good looks, the sort that might tantalize but not create much heat.

"I'll call someone to help you," he offered.

Emma leaned down, assessing the heft. "I think I can manage."

"Don't be ridiculous." He lifted the phone, said, "Marion, send Lewis up."

Weinstein came out from behind his desk and reached for his coat.

"So," Emma said gamely, "Mrs. Everett."

He kept his back to her, throwing out a "Yes?"

"I don't know what to make of her," Emma said.

"How do you mean?" He turned slowly, and the look on his face was professionally bland.

"To someone not in the know, it would seem as if she picked the most opportune time to leave Roland. A few days after she found out he'd never be able to collect on the judgment?"

"You're saying her motivation was entirely venal?"

"I'm looking to you for clarification."

"I would think twice before dragging Marie Everett into this mess."

"Why? I would think it would go to his state of mind, having his wife walk out?"

"And I wouldn't like to believe that Dawn Prescott would stoop to smearing a woman like Marie."

There was a knock. Lewis, apparently. "It grieves me to see that I was mistaken, I was under the impression that Dawn had her client's best interests at heart." The rejoinder an addendum to the subtle warning, the one that read, "Back off, Marie."

Weinstein was gone, taking the stairs surprisingly quickly for a man of his years. Emma couldn't help reminding herself of Marie Everett's sensual look and matching it up with Weinstein's possible extramarital predilections. Then there was the personal critique leveled his way by Marie, her passionate dis, "That man does just as he likes."

Lewis proved to be a slightly retarded man in his late

twenties who was garrulous on the walk to the car. He told her how Mr. Weinstein had hired him almost three years ago, and how he lived in the neighborhood and how his mother packed his lunch for him sometimes, but mostly he liked to eat out, did she like Ollie's, they made good food, they had these noodles, did she really like them, proceeding to list his own personal favorites.

Down in the garage, they waited together for her car to pull up and he set the boxes inside the trunk, then headed off, his good mood almost infecting her.

Checking her messages before making her way back to the office, she discovered that Josh had called, said he'd heard about Bertha from Leslie. Emma was glad to be off the hook with that one. Dawn had also phoned in, checking on her progress. Emma's divorce lawyer, Coral Daniels, with an update on the time they'd be appearing at court on Friday and an admonition to "be there or be square." Then, a Lucy Beale from the Shooting Party, asking her to please return the call promptly. Lucy Beale again, sounding more insistent. Beale a third time, saying in a more than aggrieved tone of voice, "Your son Liam gave me this number. We caught him shoplifting and I'd much rather talk to a parent than to the police, but if I don't hear back from you soon, I'll have to call in the cavalry."

13

The bomb had set off a chain reaction, flames slashing out, then a smattering of interior explosions. Laurence had arrived in time to see the coup de grace, the roof of Hammond's clinic falling in with a sharp whoosh. The crowd that had gathered to watch moved back in orchestrated flight. A crack, a sizzle, and a tongue of red-hot flame. Smoke poured out an accompaniment. What had once been a solid brick building, flat and nondescript, was now a pile of rubble, heated past the boiling point.

Laurence counted three ladder companies at work, men running toward what they should have been running away from. Not a profession he'd ever considered, not even when he was a kid. Back then, the skinny was how they'd be unlikely to save your black ass, a rumor that was helped along by the then segregated nature of the New York Fire Department hiring policies.

Things had most definitely changed. Look at the dead lost at the World Trade Center if you wanted multicultural. Laurence crossed over Flatbush Avenue, spotting the office manager, Bettina Gregory, standing at the very edge of the crowd. Was it only this morning he'd been interviewing her? Had to say a yes to that, Laurence remembering how Monday had started, Gregory expressing concern over Summers not showing up at her appointed time.

Here they were now, in the first part of the afternoon. Talk about an event-crammed day. Gregory's skin had ash marks toning her cheeks and forehead. Laurence reached into his pocket, removed a handkerchief and offered it, indicating the need, waited for her to do what she could, knowing it would give her a few seconds more to compose herself. She'd been crying, he could read that in the track marks rendered over the smudges.

"Sorry," she said, handing back the handkerchief, then added, "it's Aurelia. She wouldn't go. I can't believe I didn't drag her out."

He'd heard as much from the dispatcher on his way in.

"She went to find that girl," Bettina said. Her eyes said the rest, gaping, stunned. Not one, but two lost. Another crack, a wheeze, a shot of flame spun into the sky. The crowd shoved back toward what they thought of as safe, but didn't disperse. That was how it went with disaster. There were always greedy onlookers.

"Oh God," Bettina said, and covered her face with her hands. There were shouts from the firemen. Several uniforms were practicing their crowd-control skills, and Laurence decided to take the initiative, tucking an arm around Bettina Gregory's shoulders and guiding her off, down the street to where they were able to manage a little relative privacy. She stared back, hoping, he knew, for a miracle.

"What happened?" he asked.

Bettina shuddered, as if in answer. Streams of water

arced above, having no effect on the flames. She turned back to face him, said, "Who takes these calls seriously. Do you realize how many times we've gotten this sort of call? We go through the drill, but you start to take things for granted. Oh lord." A moan escaped as she looked back again. "Aurelia took care of the clients, she made sure they got out, and then, we were about to leave ourselves, and she said she had to go back and check for the girl. I told her no, but she wouldn't hear me. I said I checked the bathroom; she needed to make sure. Said she'd only be a minute."

"Bettina." A woman had come up the street and opened her arms, they hugged and both of them began sobbing. Laurence decided it was time to fade back toward the building, pulling out his badge and making his way as close as he could. He knew where to head next, knew he wouldn't have much time. That morning, as he'd come by the clinic to interview Gregory, he'd noted the absence of a table in front. No protesters at all and Aurelia, the receptionist, had been the one who had commented to him as he passed, "Those fools park their asses out there most days. You think they actually stayed home out of respect?"

He thought not.

O'Malley was parked out front. They went up to Mr. Diehl's home in the heavens, O'Malley bearing the search warrant in her right breast pocket. When no one answered their knock, he and Dearborn tried muscling the door, then he gave up and shot the lock, deciding there was no need to stand on ceremony.

Inside, no Martin Diehl. No one else either. Pushing

open Diehl's bedroom door, he saw the room held a single bed, made up tight with hospital corners and spanking Tide-white sheets. Little else in residence. The next room down was where he'd seen that bedroll. It was gone, and someone had been at work doing an early spring cleaning. All the boxes were gone too. He saw how, out the back window, down a fire escape that led shakily to the ground and across the winter snow, a tide of tracks led straight to the rear door of another building that looked to be abandoned.

He went the right way around. There were the usual metal sheets on the windows, a stoop that looked to be a dangerous climb, hanging off, as it did, at an extreme angle to the street. The front door had a chain broken in two.

Laurence headed in, with O'Malley and Dearborn as backup. Underfoot, stray crack vials and broken glass off a bottle of Colt. Day-Glo tags glowed in the half-dark. On his right in the defunct living room, a mattress with busted, bulging springs and tufts of cotton dripping out. Over to the left, the seat of a chair, strewn everywhere on what was left of the plank floor, magazines with their pages curling from the wet. No one seemed to be at home to receive visitors, but as he moved through the rooms, he saw that every part of this house had its own story to tell. There were shrines, a mound of empty soda cans, a spray-painted heart with SYLVIO, MI AMOR scripted inside, clothes bunched into a corner, plastic containers bereft of food.

The stairs to the second floor were hard going, the steps gouged out so you had to take two, then three at a time. The handrail swung loose in some places, in others it was gone altogether. Laurence kept his gun drawn, his mind fixed, although he was already skipping back over the territory of what was known, the questions that were going to be his to answer, starting off with who Diehl had been harboring that day and ending with the where and the contents of those missing boxes. In between, Diehl's likely connection with the misery he'd been witness to over on Flatbush, an assault that had most likely been in the planning stages for a long, long while.

He pulled open the first door on his right and found a bathroom or what was left of one, the toilet filled up to the brim with garbage, the sink on the floor, everything coated in grime. Backing out, he turned to the next room down, with O'Malley taking the other side of the hall. They banged open the door at the exact same time, at first he didn't quite register how his door wasn't making it all the way to the wall, but did as soon as the man was on him.

The man, an orange-coated blur, had a knife, and body odor made out of sweat piled up over the months. The knife cut Laurence's hand and he backed up for a second, his senses flooding in. He was able to take a hard kick that connected with his assailant's stomach, then pull out his weapon and use it to hit him upside the head once, twice, and then three times, till the man went down. Laurence felt the adrenaline pump as he knelt over, cuffed the man, then finally took a look at what had been done, a cut that looked deep enough to need stitches.

"Here." O'Malley had come in behind and she pulled out her own handkerchief, seemed he wasn't the only one who carried a spare. She wrapped up his hand, bound it tight enough to stop the bleeding.

Laurence turned to examine what he had. Looked to him to be a homeless man, lying on the floor, moaning, blood making a trail down the side of his head. The man wore his hair in sandy dreads, the color most likely a product of his lack of hygiene. He was scarecrow thin and this room had to be his squat. Laurence took in the mattress with crack vials making a neat pile in the very middle. Homeless here had built himself a little encampment, right down to the signal fire. The miracle was he hadn't set his floor to smoking, except it wasn't so miraculous because, taking a step nearer for a close-in look, Laurence saw there was a piece of metal underneath the pile of charred wood and ash.

"Up," Laurence said, jerking on his assailant from behind, lifting him by the cuffs. Facing him again, he realized the grimmer news. Not a man at all but a kid, maybe twenty at most, more likely years less. The look he thrust back said, man, you be in my crib, get your sorry ass the hell away.

"You got a beef with me about something?" Laurence ventured.

"You come sneaking up, what the hell you be expecting?" His chin stuck out, making the emphatic point.

"I see a padlock that's s'posed to be hanging on the front door, windows sheeted up, a sign out front reads NO TRESPASSING by notice of the government of this city. What's all that say to you? You mayor now?"

"Says how this is private property and you shouldn't be dragging your ass in" was what was thrown back. Laurence had to give him credit for nerve. After all, there was a whole mess of blood coming off the head wound. Laurence thought about the odds that HIV or hepatitis was in residence, and here they both were bleeding. The thought gave him pause.

"You're looking at assaulting a police officer right now."

"Don't try that shit on me. You're no officer."

"Think again," Laurence said. Although it was more than clear he was, and the boy already had. Boy it was, he decided counting down younger, then younger. "How long have you been camping out up here?"

"Why you want to know?"

"'Cause I asked."

A shrug was what he got for his trouble.

"Do you have a name?"

"I might. You?"

"Detective Laurence Solomon."

"I'm Michael Jordan" was what he countered, a glint of humor readily available.

"You look better on the court. Cleaner too."

"Magic of TV."

This little piece of repartee was undoubtedly meant to shore up the boy's lost nerve. What it did for Laurence was set him to wondering how this kid had ended up here, strung out, lonely, and plenty desperate. Worse, starving, that apparent from the lack of flesh on his limbs, the drugs canceling out this basic human need. Don't get involved with this, Laurence told himself, and he heard Emma's voice countering, her maddeningly accurate assessment of his psychic vulnerability. "You were here last night?" he asked.

Mr. Air Homeless was still cracking wise. "Might have been. Might not."

Laurence backed up. Tried to give himself another minute to reason out an approach. As he tried to clarify what he wanted here, he saw the kid, popping up, and back down, tapping, rolling, a crackhead's familiar moves. Got to be patient, he decided, watching as Jordan here tried to keep himself aligned. And failed. A while more and Laurence realized what was going on, he was attempting to be the best sort of decoy, moving himself so that no one would see, his eyes flitting fast from surface to surface, but always returning to one place in particular.

Dearborn had come up and was waiting by the door. Laurence motioned him in, said, "Keep on him." Dearborn was no fool, he had popped on some rubber gloves while he'd been standing there. Grabbing the kid from behind, he held him tight. Then O'Malley helped lift the mattress. The nest underneath was made of old newspapers. Laurence sifted through, filtering out the protests that came out of the kid's mouth, the ones starting with "you don't got no right," going on from there, little drips of water, an annoyance, nothing more. Prospecting like he was, he got lucky, fool's gold in this case the plastic baggie with a lump of rock inside.

Never put yourself in the way of needing something this bad, he thought, badly, he added, hearing his father's voice telling him the correct way to enunciate, the correct grammar to use, saying "talk like they expect you to or else you get what you deserve." Mr. Eloquence himself bragging to all who'd listen how his youngest was over at Columbia Law School getting his degree, doing his father proud.

Not anymore, now Solomon's youngest was inside this derelict piece of housing looking for a ray of light to guide him at least halfway home.

"What's funny?" the kid asked, which was when Laurence realized that he was smiling. The kid's voice was worried and should be; now he wasn't just facing assault, he also had possession on his rap sheet.

"You're thinking you're in trouble. You're wondering what you can do to make it go away, aren't you, Mr. Jordan?"

A nod from him to Dearborn, and the cuffs got tugged up, painfully.

"Sure, okay, what can I do?" the kid said, suddenly eager to please.

"I think you might have had visitors last night."

"Who do you mean?"

"You tell me."

"Tell you. Tell you what?" Back to his one-note defiance.

"Might as well take him down," Laurence said, giving the nod.

Which was what it took for this boy to find clarity—hard to come by, Laurence decided, when you were shaking and shivering, stunning your brain 24/7.

"This little white dude, looks like a pure baby rat?" As much a question as a comment. Laurence figured agreement was due. So he agreed, giving a shorthand nod.

"Came from out of the house back there. I was looking out the window is why I know. Last night, there was this big mothafucka of a moon."

He was indicating the spot that was missing the metal plate, one he'd used to make himself a safer barbecue pit. Laurence cautioned himself against excitement, asking carefully, "All by his lonely?"

The kid licked his lips, scarred and chapped as they were, then said, "Three of them all together."

"Three being?"

"Him and two ladies. Rat face, he's up by the window passing some shit out to the two of them."

The blood on Jordan Jr.'s head had dried, making a curl like a question mark.

"No one camping downstairs last night?" Laurence asked.

The kid shook his head. A second later, he had the presence of mind to realize that he'd just made himself the only witness. "Might have been. Guess there was, sure."

Laurence ignored the afterthought. "You could tell they were ladies? How?"

"Like I said, I could see them clear."

Laurence stepped over to the window and thought back a while, back to the night sky, resurrecting how he'd been making his way home to get a change and two hours or so in bed. It had been late, past one, and he didn't have to pick up a chart of the moons and tides to know what was wrong with the picture.

"Had you seen any of these three before?"

"I knew the white guy from around."

"Around? As in where?"

"Here is where. I don't know one thing more."

"Let's go," Solomon said. Dearborn shoved the kid toward the door.

"Hey," he whined, turning to Laurence, saying, "what you want out of me, man. I told you what I know. You said if I did, you'd help me out."

"Those ladies. What did they look like?"

"I don't know. One was young maybe. About my age."

"Your age being?"

"Eighteen, awright?"

Him saying eighteen made him a few years less. Laurence tried not to think about the waste and couldn't help it, couldn't deny the feelings of sadness stirring.

"You saw all that from up here with the moon gleaming?"

"Yeah, what I said."

"Thing is, I was out last night late. All I saw hanging up in that sky was a sweet little crescent moon."

"That's not right," the boy argued. His body said different. What Laurence was betting was that Jordan Jr. here was going to be his I.D., his little ace in the hole. Only right now, he wasn't going to be any good to him, not until he was relatively clean. The boy's body had taken on a life of its own, shaking so hard it looked ready to spin out of Dearborn's grip and go drilling down, corkscrewlike, through the floor.

Easy to drop him in holding, but easy wasn't going to help, Laurence decided. He ignored the element that was riding along with expedience, the vision of himself as good Samaritan.

Downstairs, Dearborn set Jordan Jr. in the back of a patrol car. Laurence heard sirens coming close, then tilting past, heading a block over; had to be the feds closing in.

"Take him to Kings," Laurence told O'Malley. "Speak with Nathan Kline at the detox ward. Tell him no one gets in to see Jordan here but me."

Caitlin smiled her approval. He knew what it came from, her good Catholic conscience believed he was moved to pity. He didn't dissuade her, it wouldn't matter what he said, not next to the power of her belief— Caitlin kept a portrait of Jesus in white robes tacked up on the bulletin board above her desk, a vial of holy water in her drawer.

His motives weren't anywhere near as pure as she might think. And Laurence Solomon knew the likelihood of a ten-day stay in detox working a miracle. Jordan Jr. had had too many bad things happen, setting him on this course. Getting this boy off crack for a bare bones little while wasn't going to matter, not when the high was the one thing that had sent him soaring up. You get that close to the flaming star, you're bound to get your wings singed, but the view! And life back on earth being what it was . . .

Laurence watched the patrol car pull away from the curb. When it had turned the corner, he set off for Diehl's, making sure to take the long way around.

14

The Shooting Party was one of Emma's favorite stores. It specialized in wind-up toys, goodie bag fillers, cool holiday trinkets of all types and also carried the full range of practical jokes—whoopee cushions, those plastic cubes with the flies neatly inserted, a plastic amputated foot you could stick under the bed.

Today, the in-store special was Liam Price.

Not just Liam but a girl seated beside him, with her own pink-and-green-dyed locks and a cunning eyebrow ring.

Ms. Beale showed her the full array of items they'd tried to cop. "We've been over the drill," she said in a world-weary tone, "but for your benefit, I'll say it again. If he ever sets foot in here again, I'll have him arrested."

"I'm so sorry." For the seven hundredth time because Emma's abasement knew no limits. Luckily Beale had no interest in pressing charges. She might have, if she'd heard that Liam had been in this position three times in the last four months, friendly shopkeepers doing their duty and calling Mom up; each time she'd managed to arrive and circumvent a crueler fate.

Emma assumed that this was only the tip of the iceberg. After all, he had to succeed at this sometimes. Otherwise getting nabbed would have given him pause, or at least chastened him. Then again . . .

Liam and his female accomplice were handcuffed together with fake handcuffs. They found this and everything else amusing. At least once they hit the street. All the way to the car they had wry looks on their faces, marching in lock step. Emma was so angry, she was tempted to go back and have Beale make the call.

Easy to imagine, hard to actually summon the nerve and watch your own son carted off to jail.

She didn't. She opened the door instead and the two of them were giggling as they pulled and pushed themselves into the backseat of the car. Getting in herself, Emma turned, offering a look that managed to shut them down.

"Take those off," Emma said. "Now," she added, when she saw they were making no move to do as she'd asked.

Emma started the car, pulled out, and found herself toting up the catalog of the unnecessary: a package of false mustaches, an interstellar ray gun, a wind-up bucking bronco. This was another example of the lack of forethought Liam exhibited, he shoplifted based on logistics and convenience. Last month, he'd been nabbed in a used CD store where he'd slow-fingered the B bin, claiming for himself the Bangles, the Beach Boys, and the Band, all of which she already owned on vinyl.

Today, it could have been Anything but the Girl. An unpleasant girl at that, Emma decided, noting that a practiced sullen look seemed to have indented the places where dimples might have formed in her cheeks. As for the hair and the piercing? Emma wasn't opposed to them on principle, it was the form they took, in this case rounding out the disagreeable package.

The two of them had started whispering.

"What?" Emma asked pointedly.

"I wasn't talking to you," Liam countered. The formal tone and the sneer together were an unsettling experience. Emma's hand had gone into assault mode, she talked it down like a jumper.

"I'm speaking to you. What do you think you're doing, Liam? If you're thinking of taking up a life of crime, you should reconsider. You're not good at it. And if you think I'm going to let you keep on getting off easy, think again. Next time, I'm having them call the police."

"So what?"

Emma knew nothing would make him happier than a slap upside the head. It would confirm his opinion, prove her to be a completely unoriginal, hydra-headed enemy. Taking a breath to stabilize herself, she vaulted into traffic and let herself go left, go right, play cat and mouse with the Ford truck next to her, get to the red light ahead of it, and, finally, turn back to confront him again.

"Who's your friend?"

"Which friend's that?"

The light changed to green and Emma glanced ahead, then gave up, pulling over to the side of the road with such force the smell of burning rubber rose up off her tires.

"What's your name?" she demanded of the girl, said it ferociously and saw her blink, noting that she had finally had an impact, at least on the secondary target.

"Marcia," the girl offered in a surprisingly shy, unsullen tone of voice. She shrank back into the corner of the seat, not only aware of the threat of physical violence but apparently unnerved at the prospect.

"Where do you live Marcia?"

"On Carroll." She abridged that, "211 Carroll."

"Home phone number."

"No one's home," she said, a little too fast.

"Fine, I'll drive over and wait till your parents arrive."

"She doesn't have parents," Liam said.

Another piece of melodrama. Except that Marcia started to sob and went into retrograde collapse. "My aunt's gonna kill me," she gasped out. "Shit. Oh shit."

Liam glared at Emma, then put his arm around Marcia's shoulder protectively. The way a grown man would, Emma noted, not without a flush of pride.

"She didn't do anything," he said. "This is my fault. You can punish me."

Fat lot of good that's done either one of us, Emma thought.

The drive through the remains of Park Slope, past Third Avenue and the no-man's-land of industrial buildings between, past the Pathmark, the reclaimed auto lot, and into the back end of Carroll Gardens took place in silence, or silence broken by gasps and muffled sobbing.

Whispering recommenced when they were two blocks from their supposed destination.

"Look," Liam said, leaning forward. "I don't see why you're so hot on this, Mom. Marcia didn't do a thing. Not a thing. That woman saw she was with me and forced her to stay. But she didn't even have stuff in her pockets. You can call up and ask, you'll see I'm not lying."

Emma decided not to offer him the "really, that would be a first" comment that sprang immediately to mind. Instead she said, calmly, "I need to speak with Marcia's aunt. I assume that part's true?" She saw by his expression it was. "Liam, I don't know Marcia here. And even if I did, it wouldn't be right to keep this kind of secret from the adult who's responsible for taking care of her."

"You keep plenty of secrets," Liam said bitterly. "You do it all the time. Just 'cause this one time I'm asking."

There's a zinger, Emma thought. She saw the misery etched on his face, and the desperate need. Surprising how much it moved her, out of guilt, she told herself. They were riding down Carroll, crossing onto the appropriate block.

"Her aunt's gonna lose her mind," Liam said. "You don't know."

"She should lose her mind," Emma countered, pulling into the only empty space available, which was, of course, in front of a hydrant.

"My aunt doesn't get home till six-thirty," Marcia said in a timorous voice. Emma knew that the tickets came fast and furious on this block because of the proximity to the local precinct. Besides, it was two-forty, which meant that Liam had cut school. Don't go into that now, Emma told herself. "All right," she said. "We'll go over to our house till your aunt gets home."

"Please, say you won't tell her," Liam urged.

"Fat chance. Marcia can come over and have a nice cup of hot chocolate and you can tell me how the two of you met."

She spun the wheel, pulled out, headed past the expressway overpass and back around toward home. It had gone deathly quiet behind her. Glancing into the rearview mirror again, she saw Liam staring at Marcia, his face flushed with sympathy and concern. Emma felt a heady rush of affection for her son who was capable of this sort of empathy. Perhaps he would manage after all. Perhaps he would turn out fine in the end.

Or possibly not.

Emma surreptitiously tilted the mirror to find that Marcia was whispering to Liam again. He bent toward her and Emma felt a dash of self-pity, knowing that this was his girlfriend, not just a friend, and seeing, through the shorthand of the looks exchanged, that this territory was off limits. This was theirs, would always be theirs and theirs alone. Reassessing, she decided that Marcia wasn't bad-looking, the youthful tender of her face wasn't its only merit. The girl had a generic wholesome look, almost corn-fed if you stripped away the armaments of hair and eyebrow piercing.

Emma parked in the lot, then did a lot of waiting. Waiting for them to get out. Waiting for them to catch up. Waiting for them to leave so that she could lock the gate. Waiting for them to keep pace on the walk home. Waiting for them to make it up to the top of the steps so that she could close the door after them.

She left them in the living room and went to find Theresa, her current disaster of a baby-sitter. Emma fumbled payment, then let Theresa out the door with a terse "see you tomorrow, thanks." Katherine Rose threw her arms out to Liam, who gave her a look that said "not now," then "if I only didn't have a sister." Katherine Rose, thank God, was happy enough to lie on the floor, playing under her baby gym, snapping a hand at Big Bird and going, "Oooha."

Marcia braved a smile and cast it Katherine's way.

"So," Emma said. "Want to give me your side of the story?"

Talk about a significant pause. Marcia looked down at her feet, looked over at the wall, threw her gaze onto Liam, licked her lips, once, twice, thrice, and then said, "Well uh, it's like . . . uh . . . my mom and stepdad, they didn't, you know, they just didn't, like my aunt is my mom's sister so she took me in 'cause she said she would let me stay. My sister, she's with my real dad but she's going to college out where he lives, and I'm like, I'm still in school here."

"Where?" Emma asked.

"Saint Ann's."

Now that was interesting. "Then how did you two meet?"

"Well like . . . uh, we met, through like a friend, you know, when we were both at the like . . ."

"I met her at Roseland," he said. "At the Fountains of Wayne concert."

Last September. Emma had wanted to go but he said there was no way he was going to go if she did. That was a whole three months, and now she had a skeletal backstory. As for Saint Ann's, the tuition was way too rich for her blood.

"You cut school to hang out together?"

"I've got the whole week off," Marcia said.

Emma knew this was more than likely true. Private schools charged you a cool nineteen thousand a year and offered at least a month less time in class, their motto being quality was more important than quantity when it came to contact hours.

"You've been in trouble before." Emma made it a statement.

Marcia shook her head furiously. Desperate to prove and thereby please. Emma turned to Liam. "And you?" She heard her mother's voice as she asked, her mom saying, "What do you have to say for yourself?" She'd always had plenty to say, she thought herself the original purveyor of belligerence. She had plenty of reasons, starting with the unfairness of the system and how she was working to undermine it and needed that alarm clock, the staple gun, the three sirloin steaks, even though she was mostly a vegetarian. Her explanation often ended with a quote from her bible of the time, Abbie Hoffman's amazing resource guide titled STEAL THIS BOOK. He had also attempted to elevate the Pentagon, another idea that hadn't quite come to fruition.

Emma hadn't paid for the book either, she'd tucked it into her waistband at the Strand and sauntered out.

"It was my idea. I went in there to try and cop some stuff. For a joke, you know. She was with me, that's all. And the lady went all buggy on us, grabbed us both. I told her then, I didn't even know Marcia."

"What a brilliant excuse."

"You're being sarcastic."

"So?"

"That doesn't help," he said in an almost uninterested tone of voice.

"You're an expert now? Tell me what does help? I've tried grounding you. I've gotten your father to talk it over with you. I've read up on setting limits. I pretty much wasted the stacks on raising teens at Bookcourt. Tell me, what's going to get you to stop fucking things up? You've got my attention, Liam. Believe me, you've had it for a while."

Unfortunately, he seemed to have no brilliant response to offer. Frankly, she'd run out of options herself. Emma knew she would have to tell the aunt and couldn't help wondering what additional damage would be done there, because Liam would most likely be banned from further contact, which would make subterfuge a viable and intriguing option. Another way for Liam to cloak himself in the outlaw mystique, although only another twelve-year-old would be willing to overlook his obvious ineptness at crime. Not to mention the way he disemboweled his food whenever he sat down to a meal, more like a ravenous wolf than a man of mystery.

You couldn't stop them. Emma knew all about that. The only way was to outwit them. Years ago, she'd thought she'd be able to handle this period so well. After all, who had more firsthand experience with teenage recalcitrance. Well, so much for her arrogantly premature crowning as greatest all-time mom.

"You can go up to your room," Emma said, and saw

the relief flood their faces. "Leave the door open," she added, and didn't hear a sharp word thrown back.

Lying down on the carpet with Katherine, she admired the plastic bodies of her daughter's Sesame Street idols strung up on her baby play gym. Taking out her anger on the only safe target, she knocked Elmo for a loop. He went spinning, once, twice, thrice. Katherine screeched out her pleasure and said, "Mama, gain."

Emma heard the front door open.

"I'm here." Up on one elbow to see. The shoes were the first thing to assess, black leather toes coming to a less than subtle, European point; then the pants, light gray wool with a formal pleat, up to the knees, up to the crotch, a girlish blush exhibited by then, along with a knowing smile.

"Seems like your friend Leslie got her wish after all," he said.

How did she get to be my friend? Emma meant to ask, but she was lost in trying to digest the information he had just ceded her. Emma had kept the car radio off on purpose, not wanting further deflection from Liam and her own parochial troubles. Hearing about the clinic being bombed was a fresh shock.

Laurence was submitting to Katherine Rose's penchant for abuse. She tugged on his nose, then on his eyebrows, then rode her fingers through his tightly curled hair. He winced, extricated himself as kindly as possible, with a tickle, and added, "I was on my way back to the office. I'm supposed to be sharing my files with the feds."

"From Diehl's to the office by way of my house? You're taking a slightly circuitous route."

"Thought I may as well stop by. See what's up."

In other words, what she'd gotten out of Leslie. He had nerve, assuming she'd run off to do his bidding, more annoying still, how right his assumption was.

Laurence picked Katherine Rose up, tossed her lightly into the air, and caught her. An ooh and a clapping of hands, begging for "gain." He complied.

"The feds are going to screw this up," he said.

"You don't know that."

"What I know is what I see. Most times they get their mind wrapped round one doer, they work too hard at making the crime fit the pattern. This one's supposed to be Diehl's handiwork."

"Who says it's not. We both know someone else was living there with him. And he was doing something wrong, running out like that, in the middle of the night."

"Maybe he couldn't foot the bill for the rent," Laurence said.

"Are you sure this isn't personal?"

"Personal?" The spark of humor in his eyes when he added, "I can't really see how."

"You should have gotten the bureau involved from the beginning. You shouldn't have hung back. Now you're trying to save face, because you hate being wrong." She leaned back against the forgiving couch. He'd dropped Katherine onto his chest. "Mo'," she demanded yet again. Nine-month-olds were the queen bees of the repetitive task. Laurence went for X marks the spot, producing gales of laughter.

"It's one thing for Diehl to set off a bomb in that clinic. It's another for him to sneak up behind Hammond, then go by Summers's place, pop her, and excavate the premises."

"Even so, it's hardly impossible. He could have been harboring whoever did it."

"We both read those letters. Do you think the man who wrote them killed your friend Eleanor?"

"I couldn't possibly say."

"And I'm pointing out there are certain gray areas."

"Fine, while I'm telling you this is about you wanting to maintain control."

Emma stood. The music from upstairs had gotten louder, a heavy bass that shook the house.

"You know that family too well to let this go," he said.

"What does that mean? And really, is this mine to let go of?"

"You went over there because you felt a certain allegiance."

"I went over there because I wanted to get your attention," Emma insisted.

"Maybe. But you also thought you could protect them. How are you going to protect them if the feds are the only ones involved? You talked to Leslie, didn't you?"

There, it was out. Emma realized she didn't have an answer prepared. She grabbed up Katherine and headed for the kitchen, buying some time. Setting Katherine in the high chair, Emma went to the cupboard to find her evening meal, Earth's Best baby food, strained, sealed, and delivered.

Laurence was hot on her heels, of course.

"I don't know anything that can help you," she ventured, cautiously avoiding his searching look.

He took a seat at the table and began to fuss. It was what he did when he got nervous, like a child himself, she decided. He took the salt shaker and poured a mound onto the table, attempting to find some precarious balance. When he'd managed to make it stay upright, he actually smiled his pleasure and she had to do it, had to reach over and flick her nail, making contact and causing it to topple.

"Ruining my fun," he said.

"The later you show up, the more you'll piss them off." Emma studied him. "What do you think I'm keeping from you?"

"Up till this minute, nothing." His puzzlement turning into a more pointed question. Then shape-shifting into something she recognized as a need, one that required her to take him into account regardless. Emma reminded herself she had no desire for this, it was a trap. Still, she had to offer him something. "I did speak with Leslie; for the record, she didn't seem to know about Bertha. And she wasn't acting, Leslie's not capable of snowing anyone."

His look was insistent. He expected more.

"That's all she wrote," Emma said. "As for myself, in case you're interested, I've been busy with other things. Just this afternoon, I was over at the Shooting Party, helping Liam avoid prosecution yet again."

"I didn't realize, Em, I'm sorry." He managed to look chastened, at least momentarily. He offered a hug and she most gratefully succumbed. Emma sank into his arms, knowing that this was only a temporary refuge. Back when it had been so easy to pretend that you weren't obligated, Emma saw herself, barely nineteen, escaping from the oppressive summer heat. She and Josh had leaned back to admire Orion's Belt, inside the old Hayden Planetarium. It was Josh who exclaimed, "Damn, don't I feel insignificant."

The feeling never left.

Insignificant, and ineffectual, Emma decided.

"You know, my bro and I used to lift stuff religiously," Laurence said.

"You did?"

"I guess it was to show how I could be evil, like Ralph, because he sure as hell never had to talk me into it. We did finally get our sorry asses caught. The owner of this candy store grabbed us and set us up in the back, waiting on my dad. He knew him from church. That night, Ralph got the shit beaten out of him."

"What did he do to you?"

"He let me punish myself. Said he thought I had a knack for it. He was right too."

"That was all it took? You're telling me you never shoplifted again?"

"I didn't have to. I'd made my point. And he'd made his," Laurence said.

She saw what he was driving at. Children are different, what cures one can be poisonous to the next. But time was running out. If she didn't discover the antidote, the damage could be permanent.

Emma studied her hands, considering the various ways to frame what she had to tell him, and saw the moral was entirely too self evident. There was no way to conceal it from him. She'd have to take that chance.

"It's Josh," she ventured. "When we were in high school, he met this kid in camp who knew someone out in Hawaii. He came back enthused, said we could make a lot of money selling pot."

Emma saw she had his full attention now. And braced herself for the inevitable onslaught. "We did it for fun," she offered, as if that were an excuse. "Then we ended up going to the same college, well, more or less, he was at Columbia and I was at Barnard . . . it didn't seem wrong at the time."

"College? I'll bet you did good business uptown."

"Yes." She met his eyes and told herself there was no reason to feel embarrassed. Then reconfigured that interpretation to meet the burning sensation that was coursing through her system, not embarrassed, mortified. "We sold hash, some acid, peyote buds."

"You're telling me this because . . . ?"

"I thought you should know."

"If it makes you feel any better, I checked your friend Josh out. He's a reputable businessman, not that I understand what he does. And there are no illegal substances involved."

Which was a relief. Still. "Josh lived at home. He got a partial scholarship, but it didn't cover the dorms. He stayed upstairs and he and Eleanor used to fight about everything. When Bertha was the housekeeper, the house was immaculate, but she left when Josh was a teenager, and after that Eleanor claimed she didn't want to have a servant around, it didn't feel right, which was the p.c. attitude to have, except that it didn't take into account her being the world's worst housekeeper. She'd make these stabs at cleaning or hire a

service if she was having people over, other than
that . . . she made it easy for Josh to stash. And keep
our money there too. He said that if we opened an account with this sort of cash, it would be deemed a little
suspicious, us being of such a tender age and all. That
was so Josh, he made everything mysterious. Even
when we were little, we were always in league against
some evil conspirator, always hiding and making our
plans as to how we would be overcoming the villain of
the piece." She couldn't avoid the laugh. "It was usually Leslie," Emma added. "Though most of the time I
think she was blissfully unaware of the arrangement."

"Then he grew up."

"Did he?" Emma offered it as a rhetorical question.
She shifted nervously, moving around the kitchen to
put the washed cutlery away, then cleaning the dirty
surfaces, dropping crumbs and the rest of the mess into
the garbage. Finally, she turned his way again and
knew that in hindsight it did seem sordid, even beneath
her, whereas at the time she had been so swept up.

"He hid his shit everywhere," she said. "Under the
floorboards in the closets in his room, in Leslie's room
too. She was living away by then. He made these
hollowed-out books for the money. Littered the place
with them."

Emma remembered the ingeniousness of the opera-
tion. The bulk of their ill-gotten gains had moved from
one safe house to the next. As for that load of premium
Hawaiian, it ended up in the trunk Eleanor had shipped
him off to camp with, the key placed out back in the
potting shed under the third pot to the right.

Putting it there, the one place his mother actually looked through, meant he wanted it found, wanted her to accuse him. Emma had known, even then. But she'd overlooked the question, or sidestepped it, subduing it with a cloud of pot smoke. Why? The possibility of capture added to the rush.

"Eleanor found out eventually. There was this horrible scene. She threatened to turn us both in, and Josh was so perfectly cold. He said if she did, he'd claim she'd known about it the whole time. He'd implicate her. The way they looked at each other . . . you know when people say they were spitting daggers?"

"I can imagine."

"You know what's horrible in all this," Emma said, "Liam looks at me that way now. I don't know how to help him, Laurence."

"You do your best, that's all he can really expect," Laurence said, then added, "it's a horrible thing, the way we want them to fend for themselves. But they're resilient. You'll see. He'll land on his feet."

"You sound so sure. I wish I could be."

"You know why I'm convinced. Because I know how generous you are, I know what you've given him. Most people spend their whole lives searching for someone to love them that wholeheartedly." Saying it, he moved close to her, pulled her tight, and kissed her, moving his hands down her body, hard and hungry. Emma felt relief in responding in kind. His hand went between her legs possessively, draping inside the crease of her pants.

That was a little too much, considering. "Hey," she said, pulling away. "We've got an audience."

Referring to Katherine Rose, who, as she said it, tossed her half-empty bowl of food onto the floor, where it spun, once, twice, thrice, then settled quietly, covering the spit-out pieces of orange.

15

The drive wasn't long, traffic agreeing to part for him, this once. Usually, even with the siren on, there was a stop-then-start resistance on the part of other motorists. New Yorkers were so blasé, gave no thought to priority vehicles. Hell, he'd seen EMS wagons stuck in traffic so honey thick, every individual was making him or herself into a Checkpoint Charlie.

Laurence drove with a mind on other things. He was listing what he had to deliver by way of an exchange program with the feds, his insight for theirs. First up on the list, the quality of his access to the family, close behind that, Jordan Jr.

Up the stairs, two by two, and straight for Grill's office. A knock and he was invited in.

"You took your own sweet time," the lieutenant told him.

"I had something to check out."

Wiseass response, but put so sweetly, begging for a different interpretation.

"Agent Burton, the long-lost Detective Solomon."

Laurence extended his hand if not his goodwill to the man sitting to the right of Grill's desk. Grill was in his late fifties, a career officer, whose only bow to modesty was what he did to cover the loss of hair, the comb-over that looked even sparser than usual. As for Agent Burton, he was young, in his thirties, Laurence decided, and suited up like a good fed, down to the regulation shoes—a short, squat man with a compact wrestler's body and the thick neck that went along with it.

Burton bent forward, offering a hand. "I used to work homicide myself, up in the Bronx. I know how things come up."

Starting in with a casual comment, one that was meant to make him seem kinder and gentler than his compatriots. Burton offered a little nod in accompaniment, as if to say all is forgiven. Laurence knew better than to be taken in. The words had a well-used ring to them. As did the supposedly empathetic smile.

"I've been looking over your notes from the interview with Diehl," Burton said, gesturing to the empty chair.

Laurence took it. Burton might have the case file, but he had the notes he'd jotted down for his eyes only; they were back in the hard drive of his laptop, locked up tight in the trunk of his car.

"The correspondence is fascinating."

Laurence nodded as dispassionately as possible.

"It serves to remind me how I shouldn't take anyone for granted. I spoke with Hammond once, tough as could be. Diehl? I've been talking to him for years, and the last thing I would have thought was the two of them were having this sort of interaction. The way I saw it, they pretty much despised each other."

"Go figure," Laurence said.

"The part I don't get is why you didn't call us in for help?"

"I didn't think I'd need it."

"Still don't think so either, most probably. Fact is, we have miles of files on Diehl. You could have gotten a little heads up."

"As in?"

"Do I have to spell that out for you too?"

Laurence mouthed the no.

"Just so we understand each other. Now what I see is you weren't looking at Diehl as the principle. Want to explain your thoughts?"

"I'm not sure I understand what you mean?" He did, of course. Keep it together, keep it together repeated in the back of his mind, but he held the smile inside, seeing how Eddie Murphy had looked braving that highway in *Bowfinger*.

"You have two dead old ladies inside three days, plus the bombing, and yet you don't even bring Diehl down for questioning."

"I interviewed him."

"And it went so well, you decided he was free and clear?"

"Looking to blame me or work with me on this?" Laurence asked. Grill was looking pissed himself, although he'd let things come to this.

He cleared his throat, then said, "You boys had your eye on Diehl too. How come you didn't snap him up, seems to me you could have saved the taxpayers a whole lot of time and money. Not to mention a few innocent lives."

Burton grinned. "No need to go off at me, Lieutenant. I'm only doing my job here."

Laurence decided it was time to throw him a bone. "Diehl said he had an alibi. At the time I thought it more expedient to check that out. After all, he seemed to know his rights backwards and forwards. So, where was your man hanging last night when he took off?"

"Three cars down from yours." Burton looked amused. "We all want the same thing," he added.

"Which is?" Laurence asked.

"Catching up with Mr. Diehl and his pals before they get up to more trouble. Detective, you told one of my men on the scene that you thought Diehl had companionship of the female persuasion. Now, I've got to tell you, that was a surprise. Want to explain what you base this theory on?"

Moment of truth, Laurence thought, and took the plunge. "I told him I needed to use the bathroom, opened a door and there was this sleeping bag in there, rolled up. Looked like he had company."

"That's it? A sleeping bag? Was it pink or what?"

"In the bathroom there were certain feminine toiletries." A pause. "That's all I saw."

"Not much for us to go on."

"My apologies," Laurence said. Burton seemed to be trying to decide whether to be pissed or not. Grill cut in with, "That'll be all, detective."

Laurence nodded and stood. He took the door out, closing it softly. As he did, he glanced at Grill and saw the glint of humor. The lieutenant wasn't above taking pleasure in what he knew had been a less than politic retort.

16

It was five thirty-eight. Marcia's aunt was due home at six, which gave Emma twenty-two minutes to come up with a brilliant, life-altering plan. So far she had zip, zero, nada other than the sinking feeling that despite Laurence's vote of confidence, bought at a fairly dear price, it was her fault, all this. Time, she knew, to call up a professional, in other words, a family therapist. This was a solution that had been suggested to her before. Emma had resisted, mostly because she had this horrible image of herself, Will, and Liam seated in a semicircle, verbalizing their very significant rage, while the therapist, always a slightly seedy-looking man with a half beard, who was, by the way, sitting in the most comfortable chair of all, offered all sorts of trite home truths.

Really, she admonished herself, what made her so amazingly special! Why did she need Freud or, better yet, Jung, to talk her down?

"Mom?" Liam was calling out. He'd come down the stairs, Marcia in tow. They were waiting in the hall for her verdict.

"I'm getting ready," she said as she put Katherine

Rose into her snowsuit. Emma didn't utter another word. Carrying her daughter out in her car seat, she could feel the two teens bringing up the rear most reluctantly.

Emma set the car seat between them in the back. Marcia seemed to have been struck dumb with terror, while Liam was taking the high road, looking stoic and veddy veddy British, with that aquiline profile of his. This was the blitz, and Emma was an overeager Luftwaffe pilot, bearing down.

Their journey took place in the almost dark, because her city was never really dark. That was one of its many wonders, Emma noted. The sky tonight was covered in clouds, a mat of glistening gray masking the galaxy from inquiring eyes.

Emma drove down Court, past Thai restaurants, Jim and Andy's vegetable stand, Staubitz, her favorite butcher. She took in the busy travelers returning home from Manhattan. Her city was a soft place in winter, fir garlands banded around the bottom of the streetlights, Christmas greetings hanging in gold trim from above. In Carroll Park, an evergreen tree was covered in lights; red, green, blue, and yellow for the Star of Bethlehem up top. Past it, at the next corner, the church had a crèche with Joseph leaning on his crutch, the three wise men bringing gifts to the swaddling babe.

Around the corner and up to the house. Lights were on on every floor.

"They're home I guess," Marcia said with a catch in her voice.

Emma stepped out and hooked a finger. Marcia exited gingerly and Liam opened his own door. "Stay here with your sister," Emma said, then led the girl up the stoop and jerked her head to say use your key, which Marcia did. Inside, in the hall, she called out in a very soft voice, "It's me, I'm home."

In the living room, a paint job was in progress, light blue and white mixed on the ceiling and the wall nearest the fireplace. Stepping in, Emma saw three children of varying ages lying on the floor, playing Monopoly.

"Is Rain here?" Marcia asked, her voice dropping down to an even more imperceptible octave.

"Mom's upstairs," the older boy said. "I want two more hotels."

A groan came from his companions.

"That's not fair," the girl next to him said. "You always win."

"I don't, Sadie, not always." The boy said it calmly. Sadie glared at him as he started counting out the money. Not my battle, Emma decided. Marcia was back in the hall and then taking the stairs, her head held high, apparently having decided that it was better to face the worst with some sort of dignity.

She knocked on the closed door of the first bedroom. "Rain?"

"Is that you, Marcia? Come in."

So in they went.

"Where were you anyhow?" Rain asked. She was a plump woman in her early thirties. She still had on her workday suit, but she'd kicked off some very high heels that lay directly in Emma's path.

"Emma Price." Stepping over the impediment to extend her hand.

"The lovely Liam's mom?" Rain's eyes flashed with pleasure. "What a great kid you have. So sweet."

"Thanks." Emma deliberately subdued the sarcasm; Liam was certainly permitted admirers, albeit misguided ones.

"Most boys his age won't bother with younger kids. But Liam is such a help. He jumps right in. My three love him. If I didn't have Marcia here to baby-sit, I'd snatch him up. I've given his number to some of my friends. I hope you don't mind. He says he can use the money."

Emma glanced at Marcia and decided she finally understood that expression about quaking in one's boots.

"Liam likes little kids," Emma agreed. And knew this was the moment of reckoning. She cleared her throat and looked at the girl's face, saw the anxiety etched in so deeply, and asked herself what purpose would it serve? Then hoped she wasn't going to appear a complete wimp, offering this last-minute about-face. "My nine-month-old's out in the car with him. I just wanted to say hello. I'm glad to finally meet you."

"Yes, me too." Rain was fervent. In fact, she gave Emma a sudden, entirely unbidden hug. It startled Emma so totally, she had no chance to resist.

"Gosh, it's dinnertime and I haven't even started," Rain said, backing up. "I'm so disorganized."

In the living room, the three kids were still working the game board. Emma noted there was no television in here. There had been none in the bedroom either. She guessed TV was an anathema in this household. Instead there were books and more books, overflowing from the bookcases, piled up in corners. And a plenitude of art projects stuck to the walls and windows. The tools for a new venture into creativity, set out on the coffee table, paints, brushes, pots full of different-colored dyes, next to that a wrapped-up papier-mâché animal that looked like a misshapen cat, half done up in blue and yellow polka dots.

Emma was out on the stoop before Marcia called for her to stop, then came after her, whispering, "Thanks so much. Just so you know, I really didn't take anything."

"Don't thank me," Emma said, interrupting. "And you should know, Liam's going to be grounded for quite a while."

"Well, sure, of course." Sounding chastened enough, Emma admitted, but then, Marcia wasn't her problem.

The boy who was was on his way to his dad's for the evening. Driving over, she laid down the law, grounded for a full month, no phone privileges, no computer access.

"That's fair." A surprisingly mature reaction from her obviously penitent child. She gave him a week of good behavior. What was she thinking, a week? She'd be lucky with a full twenty-four hours. Still, with his friend Marcia gone, Liam seemed to have lost what nerve he possessed. His body sagged and he kept eyeing her. Still, he had apparently realized he was not allowed to inquire about the upshot of the encounter with the oh-so-terrifying Aunt Rain.

When Will opened the door, she said "Take Katie in with you" to Liam and hooked her finger for Will to join her out in the hall. With the door almost closed, she told him a cribbed version of their son's antics and watched the guilt layering his face. Emma laid out her standards of punishment and she saw him open his mouth to begin the discussion. She interrupted and said, "We're going to have to consider therapy."

"Ah," he said sagely.

"Ah? Is that a yes, or a maybe?"

The first time Liam had been brought home by the beat cop, the cop had gone easy because he knew Laurence. Emma hadn't taken it seriously, she'd seen it as a ritual of passage, that early teen thing. And Liam had seemed so shaken, so terrified of reprisals. She'd asked him to swear it wouldn't happen again, and, through tears, he'd raised his right hand up to his breast, lying, as it turned out.

Looking over at her ex, who was apparently still considering her question, Emma realized what might cure Liam for good: a skate at Rockefeller Center, an ice cream sundae afterward, dripping with chocolate sauce and whipped cream, topped with a cherry. Having been sated, they could take a stroll down Fifth, stand in line to enjoy those dummied-up elves in Lord and Taylor's holiday window, watching them bang out presents and thrust them onto a conveyor belt that dropped them into Santa's bottomless sleigh. The topper would be her announcement, how she and Will had decided to dump their respective significant others and retie the knot, would he be his father's best man?

"I guess we have to try everything," Will agreed. "Poor kid," he added a little too dispassionately.

Emma used his disinterest to fuel her mood the entire ride. She parked on the side street and walked through the glass doors into the lobby of the Brooklyn Marriott. The place was a replica of every other Marriott in every other city. Inside, the decor was early-twenty-first-century bland, recessed lighting in the ceiling that was muted enough to make it possible to ignore the drab puce and olive color scheme.

Josh's room was on the seventh floor. He greeted her at the door and motioned her in. She took a seat on a small sofa, decked in paisley print, and noted that a cloud of smoke was emanating from the joint he held in his right hand.

Josh was busy. He was at the laptop, typing furiously, wearing a headset that she hoped linked to a cellular phone.

"When I say it three times, it's not a suggestion anymore. Angry? No, I'm not angry, Bill. I'm disappointed. Right. I'm sure you'll do the best you can."

His petulant tone made her think that working for him might not be too much fun. Josh clicked the phone off, pulled off the headset, and threw it down, in an apparent fit of pique.

But then, turning her way, he beamed. "Em, this is a surprise." He hugged her tight, then stepped back, as if to inspect her. "I'm so glad to see you. So fucking glad."

They sat down together on the couch and Josh sucked in the remains of the joint. She noted three other roaches in the ashtray.

"I can't stop thinking about Bertie," he said. "I keep running it over in my mind. Crazy! That's what I come back to." Josh ventured an inquisitive look, then added, "Em, why didn't you just say you were involved with this guy Solomon?"

"I wasn't sure you didn't know."

"If I had, would I have come running your way?" A pause, then a knowing grin as he made the honest assessment. "Yes, I suppose I would have. Still, I was an innocent, truly. To have to hear it from Leslie? That seems particularly unfair." Josh tucked a sly finger under her chin, gave it a rub. "Buttercup. What was that thing we used to do that my dad taught us? If you saw the shine?"

"You held the flowers underneath. It was supposed to tell how sweet you were."

"You were always sweet," he said. Stoned as could be, she noted.

"Who were you talking to on the phone?"

"Brain-dead Bill, my office manager. If he doesn't screw up once a week, I think I'm dreaming."

"If he's so bad, why not fire him?"

"I'm not good at firing people," Josh admitted. "I keep hoping he'll quit."

"I told Laurence," Emma said.

"Told him what?" The haze, the softness of mood immediately evaporated.

"About the drugs." She caught his glance, kept it, and asked, "Why did you come back, Josh?"

"Do I have to have a reason?"

She nodded.

"I guess you wouldn't believe it, but I actually have a knack for bad timing. Talk to my ex-girlfriends."

"The reason," she insisted.

"Bertha asked me to come," he said.

Not the answer she'd expected. "When did this happen?"

"She called me up in London, last week, said if I didn't come back and make up with Mom, she'd never talk to me again."

"Have you been in touch with Bertha all this time?"

"Of course." Such a matter-of-fact response. As if there weren't even a question.

"Why not with me, then?" Emma exclaimed.

"I don't know. I should have. It's not as if I haven't missed you."

"People who miss each other do something about it. They write. They pick up the phone."

Emma couldn't help but feel aggrieved. Look at him, she told herself, and did, making a clinical assessment. Prosperity seemed to agree with Josh; he looked hale and hearty, and particularly well dressed. Clothes make the man, she decided, noting the cashmere sweater and the pair of fetchingly worn thin-wale corduroys that looked to be impeccably tailored. Then there was his second home; he'd offered a photograph that showed a modern house framed by lush foliage. He'd gone on to describe the rose garden to the east, tall pine trees to the west. From the porch you could admire the gorge through which the Russian River cut an unforgiving swath.

"So what was Bertha looking for in Eleanor's office? You must know."

"Why assume that?"

"Josh, come on!"

"Look, I asked her and she wouldn't say."

"Asked her? When?"

"Yesterday. I went by her house to see her."

"Yesterday?" Emma felt the jangling, raw nerves. "What time?"

"I guess sometime after five."

"You left when?"

"I wasn't keeping track, maybe six, six-thirty."

"Jesus."

"Jesus, what?"

How could anyone so experienced in the ways and means of narcotics trafficking possibly be this naive? Unless he was playacting for her benefit. Even if that was the case, she still knew she had to warn him. "They have your prints, don't they? Tell me you walked in and didn't touch one thing."

"Are you saying I killed Bertie?"

"No, but I'm telling you that when they pick up your prints, they're going to come find you. You need to speak with a lawyer."

"Why? Why would I need a lawyer? I'll tell them when I was there."

"Believe me," Emma said. "It's not that simple, and you don't know who's going to be doing the questioning. The F.B.I. aren't exactly the kinder, gentler alternative. Even if Laurence is still the primary, I can't make any guarantees he'll buy your story."

"You mean because you outed me?" He was standing too, his face moving close to hers belligerently.

"Get a lawyer," Emma said softly. "In fact . . ." She dug down in her pocket and took out her wallet, sifted through until she found Sonia Hart's card and laid it on the table. "Here, she's one of the best, tell her I'm a friend."

"Are you?"

"Am I what?"

"A friend?"

"I'm doing my best for you."

"Really?" The snide way he said it took her aback.

Emma didn't respond, she got up instead and walked out the door, slamming it behind. Emerging from the elevator, she found she was trembling. What nerve he had, calling her out like that! Emma sailed past groups of unsuspecting foreign tourists. Emerging, she spotted a squad car making an illegal U-turn, its siren blaring. Emma crossed, telling herself she'd done her best. There was no need to stick around and see how this played out.

She'd made that mistake before.

In the summer of '78, when the hot nights obliterated the ability to form one cogent thought, she'd stayed on in the city to be with Josh. While all those luckier fled to the Hamptons, to Connecticut, to Maine, they'd wandered the streets. One night at the Summerstage in Central Park, they'd dropped some acid, "test driving" it. By the time the Band launched into the second encore, "The Night They Drove Old Dixie Down," Emma was flying. There were snakes and fire-breathing dragons everywhere.

On the train to South Ferry, Emma memorized the ad for Pond's skin cream, "making you feel silky smooth all over." At the Staten Island ferry terminal, they caught the late boat to St. George.

On the water, she began to crash. All the joy the drug had infused dissipated. Emma realized she was a loser, a misfit, a horrible fucking mistake. Rosa did important things. Rosa went down to Mississippi and put her life on the line, while Emma, what did she do that was for anyone else? She was a greedy, evil person, and who would ever love or admire her?

"I'm so horrible," Emma said, and she began to sob.

Josh had turned her way then and said, "Emma, get a grip." She was shaking uncontrollably and he muttered, "Too much speed," then pulled her close. Hugged her. Stroked her back. "What's wrong?" he asked. She thought about telling him and then did, surprising herself. It came out gasping. How she was a nobody. How no one ever listened, they were all bent on some argument that had been going on before she was born and would go on after she was gone.

"Now that really is ridiculous," he said. "Your parents think you're great. And what about me? What would I do if you weren't around?"

A valid point, surely.

To make it clear how valid, he leaned over and took a kiss. The intensity of that kiss! Emma told herself it was the drugs. Once they docked, Josh had more plans. He commandeered a taxi, and they got out in front of a walled-in place, Emma read the sign, Snug Harbor, liked all it implied.

Josh gave her a leg up over the brick wall. Inside, there were abandoned buildings, and plenty of wooded areas to hide in. A concerto of tree frogs and cicadas played an accompaniment as they made love.

Emma remembered the afterward, the awkward feeling, that this was a friend, not a boyfriend, that they'd known each other pretty much their entire lives. The awkwardness was broken when Josh reached over, tugged back a sprig of hair, and said, "Feeling better?"

It made her assess, and the answer was surprising. "Yes," she agreed.

"Then there's no reason to be sorry."

Back on the boat. Back on the train to Brooklyn. Out

on that late-night street in Flatbush. Four A.M. found them climbing the steps, Josh with his key out, managing to get it into the keyhole, and laughing at his own clumsiness, then shoving the door back with a flourish and saying, "After you, milady." Which was when Emma heard the sound of footsteps and turned to find them. Two pissed-off ghetto boys.

She'd made to slam the door, but then Ari had said, "Hey."

Aristotle Summers, Bertie's son, with his good friend Leroy. Ari with a 'fro and a good three inches on Josh. Ari at sixteen, stepping into Josh's hall, Leroy taking up the rear. The four of them packed into the darkened alcove; Emma thinking Ari probably needed fresh supplies and was here for a nickel bag or two. He'd been dealing some of their weed at a profit.

Except then she saw the knife. Josh said, "Hey, man, what's this?"

"What do you think?" Leroy had said mockingly. It was meant to sound threatening, and did.

Josh saying, "Man, you don't want to do this."

"We sure do," Leroy replied.

It was night down in Eleanor's office. Josh bent over and lifted up the hollowed-out 1965 PDR, opening its top and saying, in a petulant tone, "There."

He had been pissed, watching all his hard work, all his sweat, plus the dangerous idea of who he was, tossed into the flames by the presence of these two cowboys. Leroy had said "Watch him" to Ari and he'd lifted out the first roll of bills, letting out an awestruck whistle, saying, "Damn, hot damn!" It took Leroy a while to realize he couldn't stuff all of what was in there into his pants pockets. He said, "We're gonna need a purse or a bag or something."

Emma had observed Leroy, rangy-looking, with pipe-thin legs and arms. He was slim enough to get caught up in a harsh wind and find himself blown off windmill style. They were both searching the office for a satchel, a travel kit, something that could contain their new fortune.

It was the lights Josh had put on, to descend, that had left the breadcrumb trail. Eleanor was the guilt-ridden parent, searching the woods to retrieve her starving offspring. She had stepped into that room, and when she did, Leroy and Ari both froze. Leroy's hand had been wrapped tightly around the money, Ari's around the knife. But there was something to consider. The weapon she wielded was a good deal bigger and a whole lot meaner-looking; a kitchen knife, honed and sharpened, designed for carving the toughest bird.

"What in hell is going on?"

Surely an appropriate question. Eleanor with her long hair let loose, the nightgown trailing to her ankles. It had reminded Emma of Charlotte, Sweet Charlotte.

"Josh, care to tell me?"

The way she said it meant that she had some inner knowledge that was so profoundly undermining, no question in Eleanor's mind that Josh would turn out to be the root cause, the instigator of this and any other trouble that might befall all therein assembled.

The money fell from Leroy's hand and he dug into his pocket, evidently seeking to retrieve another, hidden weapon.

"No." Ari's voice was firm. There was another

minute to go, and during it, Emma held her breath, hoping Leroy would listen, and seeing that he hadn't fully decided, but then, finally, he did. He bolted past her, and Ari took a close second; Emma could hear them trying to work the bolt on the office door, failing, cursing, taking the stairs.

Emma was the one who went after them to make sure they'd really gone. She double locked the front door, and as she did it had the urge to join them out there, where it could only be safer.

Fast-forward to the day when she'd run into Eleanor on Montague, with Liam in tow. She had burned with shame, what had been a lark to a seventeen-year-old had been redefined through numerous revisitings. She understood her motivations were childish, Josh's even more so. His had been an act of petulant revenge. "See me!" Josh had been crowing. And Eleanor had had no choice.

Emma knew exactly what that felt like.

17

Tuesday morning, dawn came at one minute after seven. The night had been cruel, bringing the temperature down to single digits in the city. As for the outlying suburbs, heat came in the form of special delivery packages. Early-morning explosions rocked Montclair and Tenafly in New Jersey, White Plains and Brewster in New York, and up in the sleeker Connecticut suburbs, Stamford and Westport. The one common denominator was the target: abortion providers.

Laurence Solomon received the news while he was sipping on a triple-tall cappuccino, his second of the morning, not having slept one hour of the night. He watched Joshua Hammond step out of a Lincoln Navigator. The car-service driver pulled away and Laurence noted that Hammond looked fresh, well rested, and wondered how he'd managed, considering the night they'd both spent. True, Hammond had left about midnight, so he'd had a good eight hours to get his beauty rest.

Hammond cleared the front steps with a balletlike leap and pulled off his gloves, stuck them in the pockets of his coat, while Laurence lifted up the crime-scene tape and opened the lock on the front door.

Stepping in, Laurence started his appraisal. On his left the hall closet, holding, for the record, two old hats and seven coats in various stages of disrepair, on the floor, women's galoshes, gardening boots, and three broken umbrellas. On his right, hanging on the wall, that oil painting of a naked woman, quite pregnant, staring balefully at a man who was confronting her with outsized garden shears. What one was supposed to make of this he still hadn't figured out. Were you supposed to wonder what she was doing, standing naked in the middle of that wheat field? Were you supposed to think the man was an abortionist? Behind her the waving wheat was taupe-colored, the sky a crystalline azure.

Hammond took the lead, which jolted Laurence back into the now. They were here at the behest of Hammond's lawyer, Sonia Hart. The deal they'd cut was that Laurence would be led to all the old hiding places. Emma had told him all about it, plus Hammond's admission about Bertie, how she'd been the one to force him to come back. Either not in time, Laurence thought, or at the exact right minute.

If you believed him.

If you believed any of it.

Laurence didn't.

Hammond was passing through the kitchen, avoiding a look at the table as he went. He opened the door to the downstairs, Laurence reached out to tag the light, and down they went. Halfway there, Laurence stopped, pointed, and said, "Your dad?" Which made

Hammond pause in his progress, made him glance back and nod yes.

"This is the only photo she has up of him. Why would that be?"

"I couldn't tell you."

"You could manage a guess."

"Maybe she wasn't a sentimental person," Josh said.

"Maybe?"

"Then again, maybe she just didn't like dear old dad." Hammond moved on briskly, opened the door to the remade basement. He crossed the dull orange carpet, opened his mother's office door, switched on the light, and went to the bookcase, scanned it, then said with a measure of surprise finally in his voice, "It's still here."

Laurence was next to him, reaching out with a gloved hand to lift the *Physicians' Desk Reference*, circa 1965. More of a tome than a book, Laurence thought, noting that this lacked the layer of dust that the companion volumes exhibited. He took the book over to the desk, laid out a sheet of plastic underneath it, then carefully pulled open the false cover, feeling Josh breathing hard right behind him. Inside, no rolled-up bills, a different sort of treasure trove. Laurence lifted out photographs, letters, postcards and heard Josh say, "No fucking way!"

It was Josh Hammond's face he was admiring; the photos ranged from recent to much, much younger. Josh caught in sunlight, in twilight, standing by the ocean, and by some of the world's great monuments: the Eiffel Tower, the Great Wall. A regular travelogue, Laurence thought. The handwriting on the sheets of stationery was remarkably static, Josh's too, he saw, the stationery bearing the marks of various hotels, the Ritz Carlton, the Stanhope, resorts in Monte Carlo and Biarritz. He'd lived well, Laurence gave him that.

"They're Bertie's," Josh said.

That much was evident. Dear Bertie, written as the salutation at the beginning of each missive. He read down one and captured the tone, a little boy boasting of his magnificent progress.

Turning again to Hammond, Laurence found he'd finally been stumped. The emotional payoff was Hammond crumpling into the desk chair, and gazing blankly out. Then he began to shake and finally settled his head in his hands, sobbing.

Laurence gave him space. He went to the window and looked out at the light, bright and bitter, waiting till the sobbing had subsided. Then he turned back and found that irritating smile of Hammond's resurrected.

"It's ridiculous, isn't it? You feel all sorts of things, and why? Simply because the person carried you for nine months and spat you out of her body."

"Seems to me your mother cared for you," Laurence said. "You can't dictate how people act with each other. You can only take them as they come."

"What do you file that under, life lessons?" Hammond asked caustically. But then his tone softened. "Apparently my mom did care, apparently so do I. Wouldn't that seem the biggest joke of all. If you only knew how much I've spent on trying to stop myself, add it up and you could probably fund a small standing army."

"Some things can't be helped."

"I wish you'd been around to tell me that before," Hammond said bitterly. A pause, then in a softer voice he added, "You were asking about my dad? He was a scholar, actually. Worked at NYU as an economics professor. Then the blacklist came along and they fired him. He couldn't get another job teaching. It's not supposed to ruin you, that sort of thing, you're supposed to count on those inner resources, but my dad didn't seem to have any. So he became a drunk. A friendly drunk. A funny drunk. But even so, it was my mother who supported all of us. He made a little money as a tutor, but mostly he went into his study and said he was working in there, writing some amazing text on Locke and Hobbes, and really he was just getting plastered. The day he was killed, he was out picking up some groceries. Mom thought it was because he was drunk and didn't evaluate correctly, we all thought that . . ."

Josh paused, scanned the pile of documents again. He flinched, as if someone had actually lifted a hand. "That was what we thought, but then, about a week after the funeral I came home and there was this man sitting in the living room having a cup of tea with Mom. She introduced him, 'Giuseppe Malo.' He was about thirty, dark hair, not great at English either. Well, later on that night, long after he was gone, Mom called us down. Leslie and I were at the dining room table and she told us what Mr. Malo had said. He'd driven away from the scene, because he was here illegally and he was afraid of being caught, but the poor guy hadn't been able to have a good night's sleep since, he had to come and explain how it wasn't his fault, good Catholics, you know, they seem to need constant expia-

tion. He said he was driving down the street and Dad
was standing in between these two parked cars, and
looked at him and he thought everything was fine, I
mean, the light was in his favor, and then Dad just
stepped out right in front of his car.

"I couldn't believe it. Mom had let this guy Malo
leave, wasn't going to check his story out, didn't even
ask him for a phone number or an address. 'I can't see
the point in dragging this poor man into it.' That was
how she put it."

"You didn't think it was possible, that he might have
intended to take his own life?"

"Even if he had?" Hammond's expression said the
rest. In not even attempting a defense, Eleanor Hammond had apparently committed an unforgivable sin.

"Where else should we look?" Laurence asked.

They mounted the stairs, up to the main floor, the
second, and then to the attic room where psychedelic
black-light posters were still pinned to the walls; Janis,
Jimi, the Who playing *Tommy*. Hammond felt around
and then pulled up some floorboards. All that was revealed, though, was spiders' busywork.

They went down to the second floor and inside his
sister's bedroom. Hammond opened the closet door,
excavated what was inside, piles of clothing and boxes,
and revealed an artfully hidden door that he opened
with a shove. Ducking down, Laurence followed Hammond into a room about the size of a walk-in closet.
The room was empty, and a white layer of mold covered the walls. Laurence felt his eyes itch. They backed
out and emerged into Leslie Hammond's former
boudoir.

"That's it," Hammond claimed, standing next to the bed, which held that obscenely tall pile of outdated men's suits. The rest of the room was a testament to Leslie Hammond, horsewoman. She had shelves full of trophies and ribbons, photos of herself astride various thoroughbreds.

"Girls and their horses," Laurence said. "I've never understood it. Those animals are dangerous. Couldn't get me up on one."

"We get cars, they get horses," Hammond commented. His gaze flicked over the terrain, apparently assessing how quickly he might escape.

"You took off after your mother found out about the dealing," Laurence said, reiterating the story Josh had told the night before. The story that got a whole lot more elaborate after Emma's phone call filled him in on the particulars. "You said you only took that one roll of hundreds you kept upstairs."

Hammond nodded.

"Funny, because only a month later, out in San Francisco, you bought yourself not one but two taxi medallions. Seventy-five thousand dollars is an awful lot of seed money to come up with that fast."

Josh's silence this time was golden.

"You paid your own way through Berkeley, then through grad school. By the time you got out, you owned property all through the Haight and the Mission. Twenty-nine years of age and worth a cool two million."

"You've done your homework."

"I would have thought you'd get my point. You seem intelligent enough."

"If you're asking on Emma's behalf, all I can tell you is, she didn't do it for the money."

"Want to explain what she did it for, then?"

"For the thrill?" Josh ventured.

"Guess again."

"She did it for me, I suppose. Emma's not the venal type."

"And you are?"

"If you like."

"Not just being chivalrous?" Hammond didn't need to reply. And didn't bother. "Even so, I'd think you'd want to tell her about how you had that extra cash all squirreled away, how you were always going to get the hell out and she was never going to be part of it. She deserves to hear about that."

"I don't think she does." Hammond shifted uncomfortably.

"Think it over a little more, then," Laurence said, and held Hammond's gaze for as long as he could manage, before indicating, with a shake of his head, he was done.

Hammond couldn't get out fast enough. Stepping over to the window, Laurence took in his progress. Josh was down the stairs and already had his cell phone out. It was glued to his ear by the time he made it to the curb and crossed the street, heading for an apparently waiting car. He was engrossed, gesticulating urgently to whoever was on the other end, and looking every inch the corporate general, right up until the instant the sheet of ice underfoot gave way, collapsing him and his two-hundred-dollar shoes into a frigid puddle.

18

Emma was trying to read Judith Hochfeldt's statement; Hochfeldt was the eyewitness to Roland Everett's massacre. This was the third time around, her inability to concentrate due to the news reports that she'd heard on her way to work, the ones that told of the orchestrated assault on abortion providers. Emma kept going over the same ground, trying to find what she might have used as hard evidence, because there had to be something she could have done to prevent this, short of a one-woman commando raid on Martin Diehl's apartment.

Ah well, back to the matter at hand. About as pleasant, really.

"This black man opened the door and he came right in without knocking or anything and Uncle Zev, I'm sorry, Mr. Ben Dov, said something to him. He said, I don't know what, Hello maybe, yes, that's right, it was 'Hello, Mr. Everett, what can we do for you?' The man didn't really seem at all upset, he didn't look so crazy. He said, 'You owe me.' That's what he said. That part I remember and then Mr. Zev Ben Dov, he told him it was out of his hands. That's when that man took out his gun and he shot Mordecai first. It's not true, you can't run, you think you can, but you can't. You don't move at all, which is why it's so horrible, I mean, I was telling myself how I should do something but I couldn't. He was the one, that man Everett, he told me to get down under the table, so I did. I did what he wanted. I heard more shots, three, maybe four, and then it was quiet except I heard someone groaning, and I guess I must have had my eyes open, because the next thing I saw was his feet, he was coming close to where I was, and then moving away again and then this sound, I didn't know what it was, but I realize now. He had scissors, he was cutting their payess, grunting while he did it like it was hard work. I saw his feet from under the table moving around again. I kept thinking this is taking too long, you know, and I kept wishing he'd go, would he go? He told me to hide but now what, I was sure he was going to come after me, and then I heard this other sound, which I recognized right away, glug, glug, from the watercooler, and I wondered why he was getting water, I guess, and then he leaned over and I shut my eyes, and started praying again, I guess I was praying by then and he told me to get up and so I did, I got up and he had these pills in one hand, the gun was over on the table, which I guess I must have heard, like a clunk or something, and I should have gone and grabbed it but you see, I didn't think, he said, 'Go on and get them.' The horrible thing is that I did what he wanted each time. I didn't look. I was afraid to look at my uncle even. I ran out of there and got Lucas, he was right at the end of the hall coming up."

Emma had an appointment to vet Hochfeldt at two

that afternoon in her attorney's office in downtown Brooklyn. She had to come up with a strategy for approaching Judith Hochfeldt, who, as the only living eyewitness, was going to be the centerpiece of the prosecution's case. Unfortunately, Emma was all out of bright ideas.

The knock on the door startled her. Undoubtedly Dawn, who was going to ask her if she'd come up with a viable approach.

"Yes," she said glumly.

The door opened. "You don't sound happy," Laurence said.

"Thank God, it's you." Emma meant it in so many different ways.

By the time they'd reached the coffee shop, Laurence had filled her in on Aristotle Summers's airtight alibi. You couldn't ask for a better one and Emma felt that one small layer of guilt had indeed been lifted off her. Ari was apparently a career officer in the air force, and he'd been on duty at the NATO base in Blenheim, Germany, for the past week. Currently airborne, he was on his way to the States. As for Leroy Burnham, he was hardly such an upstanding citizen. His rap sheet revealed a list of B and E's, but all were petty thefts. His last state-sponsored vacation was a three-year stint at Attica, courtesy of his inability to stop himself from trying to make the easy score.

"Heroin," Laurence added. "But his parole officer says he's clean this time round. Apparently he did some sort of new twelve-step program when he was sent up. Plus there's the m.o. No assaults in any of them. He likes it best if no one's around. The last time, he got himself captured because he was too high to do his homework. Thought the place was empty and the owner was there, taking a little late-night catnap. Up and pulled out a shotgun."

They'd commandeered the last booth. From here, Emma could keep her eye on the comings and goings. She scanned the encyclopedic menu. Was it possible that they really made white bean goulash or spinach and mushroom lasagna?

The waitress surged up and said, "Ready?" Then she proceeded to tap her pad, registering impatience.

"Grilled ham and cheddar cheese, side of fries, and what the hell, a chocolate shake." What with breast-feeding, Emma's metabolism had gone into overdrive. Although Katherine Rose had graduated to solids months ago and was down to two feedings, one in the early morning and one late at night, Emma was lucky. She still had to ingest as many calories as a hardwork-ing lumberjack, just to maintain.

"Coffee," Laurence said, shaking his head.

They were alone again, or as alone as they could be, dining in such close proximity to the office. Down near the door, Emma spotted Denny Munoz taking a seat. He was a legal services attorney who was thankfully deeply involved in a discussion with his companion. She looked away quickly, just in case. "So?" she asked.

"Diehl's group has taken full responsibility for the bombings," he said.

"I heard that on the news."

"Three other groups have too, along with assorted individual crazies."

"But you're betting on Diehl."

She didn't get an argument. The waitress stopped by to drop the coffee into his cup with a little-dab-will-certainly-be-about-all-that-we-can-do-for-you attitude. Laurence took a test sip and set it down, grimacing. Emma knew why, the coffee in this place was particularly bad, a rung down from acrid tap water, and about as effective as a stimulant.

"I should have warned you," she said, commiserating.

"That's okay, it's not like I haven't had plenty." He pushed the cup far away, then added, "Six bombings and no one injured. You think they were working on a learning curve?"

"What do you think?"

"They made the calls with plenty of time. And they appear to have done their homework too. One place, the janitor was there, all the rest were empty."

Her order arrived. He immediately grabbed a French fry. "Hey! Hands off!"

"Never saw anyone so proprietary about food."

"You finish things when I'm not looking," she countered amiably enough. "Besides, I didn't say I was ordering for both of us."

"You're not going to eat all that."

"Let's wait and see, shall we?"

"You have this thing about food," he muttered.

"You have this thing about ordering nothing, to fool yourself into thinking you're on a serious diet, then scrounging half my meal."

"I only wanted one."

"Selling me the Brooklyn Bridge next?"

He gave up, threw open his hands, apparently sorely

tested by her derision. She could tell by the humorous gleam in his eyes. "The other news of the morning is that they never found the remains of that girl over by Hammond's clinic."

"Now you're trying to spoil my appetite."

"Only partly."

Emma knew it would take more than this, she was too famished to be denied. Pouring a salt lick into the corner of her plate, she dipped a fry and chewed methodically.

"I guess I didn't mention, when I went by Diehl's to try and catch a look before the feds happened along, I got lucky."

That made her stop chewing and put the rest of her meal on hold.

"How?"

"This homeless kid had his squat right across the way from Diehl's. Looked over on the backyard. That night, when Diehl and his girlfriends took whatever they were carrying out, he was on lookout. And he tells me one of them was pretty young, and blond. So was the girl at the clinic."

"You have a sketch?"

"We're working one up."

"You gave him to the bureau?"

"It's in the works."

"That must have raised you in their estimation."

"We'll see what we see."

Emma knew he hadn't come all this way to drop this dime. Laurence was stalling, obvious since he'd taken up the dull knife in his place setting and was using it to chip away at the Formica tabletop.

"They catch you ruining the priceless decor, they'll make you pay."

Which didn't stop him.

"Not to mention how you're driving me nuts." She stilled his hand, pressing her own on top. "What? What's going on?"

"A whole bunch of things. Starting off with your friend Josh. He took me over the house himself. Pretty clever sort of renovation job he did."

"Ah," she said, feeling his nervousness start to seep in through her natural armor. Emma took a sip of her milk shake, for fortification.

"The joke was on him with that book. Seems his mother kept it filled with photos of him, letters and postcards he'd been sending to Summers." A pause during which he examined her face. "As for Summers, it was her prints on that mail."

"You're saying Bertha was in the house. She was there after Eleanor's murder?" Emma felt the shock pervade her system. "There's no way. Bertha couldn't have . . ."

"Couldn't have what?"

"She'd have called the police."

"Except she didn't."

"She might not have looked in the kitchen."

"That's possible. What was she after, then? And why'd she hurry back?"

"Prints lie," Emma ventured, offering a different sort of defense, but she could see Bertha opening the front door, leaning over to set the mail up. She'd always been the one trying to straighten the ungodly mess in that house. "I grew up with these people," Emma added, faintly. She leaned back and felt the wall of the booth offer an uncomfortable form of resistance.

"It doesn't mean you know them," he countered. "Most especially now."

"Bertha just can't be involved."

"The same weapon used in her murder as in Hammond's. Plus, she let the doer into her house. When I happened on her down in the office, she told me she was there after the appointment book. It does seem odd to me that, having worked there lo these many years, she wouldn't have known the book was kept out in reception, not back in Hammond's office."

Emma shifted uncomfortably, there seemed no point in offering another, ineffectual defense.

"When I went through her purse I got a big load of nothing; her wallet, a pocket-size date book, this little pillbox full of heart medication, her MetroCard." He pursed his lips, then threw in, "You think she got killed over that MetroCard, someone wanted the free fare?"

He had certainly managed to ruin her appetite. Emma shoved her plate away. "All yours," she said, thinking the food might offer enough of a diversion.

"See, that's how it goes, you guard it like a wolf, and then can't finish."

He dug in greedily, his way of diverting anxiety. Emma studied this man whom she apparently loved. "Bertha called me 'Big Eyes,'" she said.

"That much hasn't changed."

"I wasn't like that at home, it was only when she cooked. She could, you know. My mom thought that any resemblance to a life form had to be extinguished before serving."

So much for avoiding the obvious. Emma knew that her presumption of Bertha's innocence was simply wrong. People changed. They grew tired of being in service. Although, she imagined that the anger could have run both ways. After all, Bertha was the one Josh had written to. She alone had mattered. Out of all of us, Emma noted, feeling the surge of anger. It must have driven Eleanor round the bend, and Eleanor had never been the type to pretend, to hide whatever she was feeling for the benefit of anyone else. Emma couldn't imagine the proper scenario for an exchange of documents, but somehow Bertha had given them to Eleanor, and Eleanor had squirreled them away in this significant place. A whole country of misery, there, that had not yet been plumbed.

Laurence was swabbing her plate clean. "There," he said contentedly.

"You know," Emma offered, "you're always nicer when you're full."

He didn't disagree. "Summers told me that those pills were heart medication. I checked that out with Carter, and he said there was no sign of heart disease at all. She filled her prescriptions over by her local pharmacy, and they don't have a record of anything other than a year-old scrip for penicillin."

"What are you getting at? You think she was working with Josh, trafficking in narcotics?"

"I'm not trying to be harsh, there are discrepancies is all I'm saying. And the woman doesn't happen to be around to clarify them for me."

"For us," Emma retorted.

"It was a pretty pillbox, looked to be antique, maybe it was a gift, roses on top, nice gold filigree on the side."

Which was when Emma caught her breath—the vision that came to her was Eleanor, out in the garden, using a pair of savage-looking shears to lop off the stalks and make them ready for their winter hibernation. The names of those flowers, the scent that sprang up from them: Crimson King, Fantasia, Sunset Glory, Vanity Fair.

"Describe it again," Emma said, picturing some obscene exchange.

"The box?" He was serious all of a sudden. "Roses, twined on the top. Gold filigree wrapped around the side."

"It was Eleanor's," Emma said. "Josh bought it for her years ago as a birthday present." She paused, then added feebly, "She could have given it away."

Laurence was kind. He didn't bother countering what they both knew to be wrong. He let her do it for herself. Eleanor had kept that clutch of letters and photographs, none of them intended for her, was it likely that there had been an exchange, would she have ceded one of the few gifts he'd actually given her? Emma saw that birthday—Josh, Leslie, and Emma sitting at the dining room table. Eleanor unwrapping the box that he'd been so elated to find, peering at it and saying, "A pillbox? And here I am, hale and hearty." Then, after a long, frighteningly significant beat, she'd added, "It is lovely, though."

"My treat," Laurence said, reaching into his billfold and dropping a twenty down on top of the now soggy check.

Out on the street, passersby were busy scouring for bargains to fill the Yuletide stocking. From Chambers Street a cacophony of Christmas tunes rang out—"Jingle Bells," "Silent Night," "Santa Claus Is Coming to Town." How about "Dreidel, Dreidel, Dreidel," Emma thought, and then had a sudden savage image of Roland Everett, reaching down to sever those dying men's sideburns. He had meant to shame them, not enough that he'd taken their lives, he wanted them to know that he could do worse. Emma felt a surge of anger at him and tried to set it aside, found she wasn't able to.

People do horrible things to each other, she told herself. Human beings are too damn complicated, who can really understand them? And the older one gets, the harder it becomes.

Suddenly she was grateful, because, turning to Laurence, she felt a stab of longing that seemed astonishingly legitimate. After all, Emma decided, if the universe was tidy, it would be boring. Not to mention she'd be out of a job.

Emma rose up on her tiptoes and kissed Laurence, hard on the mouth. She shut her eyes, doing it, and let the crowd of strangers evaporate.

"You two, get a room."

The tone was meant to be satirical, but envy was more readily apparent. Snapping back to consciousness, Emma opened her eyes to find Dawn, leaning on the glass in front of J & R Music World, sneaking a smoke. Behind her the display of Britney and U2 bore down. Yes, Emma thought with a trace of complacency, the whole world was watching.

19

It turned out Dawn had actually been on the prowl. Evidently, Hochfeldt's lawyer had decided to move up the appointment and so, twenty minutes later, Emma and Dawn were on their way to Brooklyn.

"It seems a shame to go all that way and not tour the city," Dawn was saying. "I'll be there twenty-four hours before my first appointment is scheduled." Then, a plaintive aside. "God, I hope nothing goes wrong."

"Nothing will," Emma assured her.

"You don't know, they could hate me on sight," Dawn said. "Plenty of people do."

"Dawn, this isn't a personality contest." Although Dawn's point was valid. "That's what you've got the interpreter for," Emma added.

"Yes, I've gotten the lecture about staying on their good side," Dawn replied caustically.

"You've done your homework, Dawn. I'm sure you've thought of every eventuality, you're nothing if not meticulous." There, she'd managed to sidestep the personality issue.

"But am I ready? Be honest, Em, do you really think of me as mother material?" Emma thankfully didn't have to answer, as Dawn bolted on, "I don't even really like babies."

"Why do you want one then?"

"I don't quite know." Dawn's eleventh-hour anxiety could put the kibosh on this. Emma thought it might be better for all concerned, but looking over at her friend, she had to reconsider. At least Dawn deserved an honest response, Emma decided, and gave her one. "I didn't like babies either. I still don't—that is, except for mine."

"You're just saying that."

"No, I'm not. You can't be so naive as to think that everyone who has a child adores babies. You think we're all the sort that coo and go soft?"

"I don't know. You always seem so natural around them."

The note of envy was unmistakable. If Dawn only knew the extent of her miserable mothering abilities, Emma thought. "You diaper them enough times, you know what to do. The airplane carry. The basic you-better-not-be-colicky prayer to the gods."

"I don't get you?"

"I was trying to make a joke." Emma looked over and saw Dawn was staring out the window. She caught sight of her reflection and found worry, mixed with longing. Reaching out, she sought to reassure, patting Dawn's knee. Dawn looked down, surprised.

"I'm fine," she said stiffly.

Emma knew better than to insist. She withdrew her hand, put it back on the steering wheel, where it could do some good. "Dawn, there's no definitive test that you can take. You must want this very much, you've gone to such lengths."

"I suppose I have," Dawn agreed wistfully. They rode the rest of the way in silence.

Barry Schwartz's Remsen Street office was poorly lit, the waiting room drab. Inside, two Hasids sat on one couch, joined in a vigorous dialogue. Across the room, two other men wearing yarmulkes were flipping through magazines, one held *Money*, the other *Business Week*. Emma had a surge of true paranoia at the thought of waiting out here with the four of them, and was relieved when they were immediately ushered back into the inner sanctum.

The conference room was small, with one window facing Remsen Street. Seated in one of the six chairs that skirted a round oak table was Judith Hochfeldt. Her given age was twenty-four, but she looked a few years older. Hochfeldt wore a blond wig that had been combed into a fashionable flip. She had on a black dress, long-sleeved and high-necked. When Emma and Dawn entered, she darted a nervous look at her attorney, then stared down at her lap.

"We're very grateful to you for speaking to us at such a trying time," Dawn began.

Hochfeldt didn't even glance at them. Dawn opened her file, then took out a legal pad and began to jot down notes, which Emma knew was a stalling tactic. So, she wasn't the only one who had thought this through, she decided, the realization made her feel even less sanguine.

Dawn cleared her throat, then ventured, "You were employed by the Ben Dovs for two and a half years."

A cursory nod from Hochfeldt, her gaze still leveled at the floor.

"You were hired as a secretary?"

"I'm an administrative assistant." Considering her bashful pose, Hochfeldt's voice was surprisingly sturdy and clear.

"You're attending college at night?"

"Baruch, for business."

"So I assume that part of what you learned was how a business operates?"

"Of course."

"Now, during the time you were employed, my client, Mr. Everett, was the plaintiff in a lawsuit against your uncle's company."

"I wasn't aware of it."

"No?" Dawn sounded more than a tad surprised.

"No," Judith Hochfeldt responded evenly. This time she raised her eyes, met Dawn's look of patent incredulity.

"Then, what did your job entail?"

"I . . ." Hochfeldt looked at Schwartz as she formed the rest, "I was in charge of all the correspondence. I prepared things for Uncle Zev."

"I see," Dawn said, insinuating that she saw an attempt to stonewall. Dawn scanned her documents, then looked back up. "When you were first employed, the company name was BSI textiles. Then Three Cousins Domestics. Then American Funwear. All these changes in two and a half years. Did your employer Mr. Ben

Dov give you any idea as to why they kept renaming the company?"

She looked at Schwartz again, then shook her head firmly.

"You weren't curious?"

"It wasn't my business," she said firmly.

"This is family, you can't expect me to believe you never had one conversation that touched on the subject."

"This is beside the point," Schwartz claimed.

It was, and it wasn't. If Hochfeldt was going to perjure herself about something this trivial, it gave Emma hope. They could surely turn her into an unreliable witness.

Dawn grunted, then made a note. The scraping of her pencil was the only thing heard for a long while. It gave Emma time to study Judith Hochfeldt. She decided that the blond wig was a poor choice, making her appear wan and sickly. When you had olive skin, dark brown was the better way to go. And there were a few other things that belied the mousy mourning attire. Eyeshadow had been layered on too thick, and mascara crested off her lashes. All in all, she seemed a study in contrasts.

"When Mr. Everett walked into that room, who did you think he was?"

Certainly not the question anyone would have expected. But Dawn was like that. Hochfeldt's breathing quickened perceptibly, she looked back at Schwartz who nodded to her, then she said, "I had no idea."

"But your uncle and his cousins recognized him, they greeted him."

"Yes."

"Did you realize who he was, when they said his name?"

"No."

"Ms. Hochfeldt, you expect me to believe that in all the time you worked for the Ben Dovs, they never mentioned my client's name in your presence?" The grin on Dawn's face was lethal.

Schwartz slapped his hand on the table and said, "We're done."

"We've hardly started," Dawn countered.

"It was a nuisance case," Hochfeldt said, and Schwartz looked momentarily nonplussed. He seemed as if he might be about to warn her off, but too late. "If he hadn't gotten that man to represent him . . . that self-hating Jew. That bastard ought to be sorry, he was the one who blew everything out of proportion!"

"You mean Stewart Weinstein?" Dawn asked.

Emma leaned forward and pushed. "Out of proportion, how do you mean?"

"Done!" Schwartz insisted. Only Hochfeldt wasn't. She met Emma's eyes, unashamed. "Zev said they tried to settle years ago. They didn't even have to. Zev said how that man was a drunk, and the accident was his fault to begin with." Schwartz looked as if he wanted to slap a hand over her mouth.

But Hochfeldt couldn't know what she'd just given over, because nowhere in the voluminous documents that Weinstein had ceded was there mention of this original offer to settle the claim.

Of course, Emma thought. The Ben Dovs weren't saints, but they had certainly been businessmen. And the first rule of being successful in business was damage control. They had tried to make Everett go away. Yes, Emma was inclined to believe Hochfeldt's story.

Schwartz was standing. Judith Hochfeldt was leaning down and extricating a pack of cigarettes from her pocketbook, snapping the pack of her Virginia Slims and popping one in her mouth.

"So, there was an offer on the table," Emma said. She had been in hot pursuit all the way down.

Dawn had opened the entry door, was out on the street, exiting. She lurched into the path of a homeless woman dragging a shopping cart full of priceless artifacts. "Fuck you, bitch," the woman threw at Dawn.

Dawn actually apologized. For all the good it did.

"What do you think? We have to go back to Weinstein," Emma said.

"Yes, I suppose." Dawn was peering down the street and Emma realized she was searching for transport.

"Hey, wait, we have to talk about this!"

"I can't. There's so much I've got to do." She flung her arm out and a yellow cab stopped. Hard to find anywhere in Brooklyn, but providence was smiling down on Dawn. Emma grabbed her by the shoulder. "You can't leave me with this," she pled. "You're coming back, right?"

"Em, I'll be back. What am I going to do? Put the baby in a backpack and go traipsing around Nepal with her?"

This wasn't completely reassuring, offering a description of the type of outsized, outback adventure Dawn loved. The door shut. The cab drove away. It took a few more minutes before Emma was able to tell herself there was one thing that would force Dawn back to work. The mournful cries of a needy infant.

Checking back at home, Emma found no messages for her. And breathed a sigh of relief. She tried at Weinstein's, but she was apparently persona non grata. She was told Mr. Weinstein was full up that day and would call her back to schedule an appointment. From the tone, Emma knew this would be around the time hell froze over and elephants sprouted wings.

The traffic back onto the Brooklyn Bridge was backed up all the way down to Atlantic. Emma checked 1010 WINS to discover the problem and was not relieved to hear there were none, none at all. The blaring horns told a different story. She took the back way around, heading for the water, and switched stations, 90.7 was playing "Tangled Up in Blue."

Emma thought about last September when she'd dragged Liam to a Dylan concert. They'd sat in the nosebleed seats, Liam looking studiously cool and bored while she stood, swaying to the music. She was allowed to have fun, she reminded herself, still able to evoke a belligerence in the face of his apparent shame. Up on stage, Dylan at sixty was rocking out. His whole eccentric mien had been inspiring, Emma had concluded that this was the way to be, you simply had to stop giving a shit.

The thing was, you could get away with it if you were Bob Dylan.

The traffic was unreal, even here on the side streets. Emma made a right in an attempt at avoidance and drove down a block of small wooden houses, some of the oldest in the Heights. Halfway down, a crowd had gathered, she thought the worst, of course, then realized the gawkers were not here because of someone else's misery, here on this entirely ordinary block someone had gone mad in a good way.

Emma pulled over in front of a hydrant and admired the yellow wooden house that was adorned with strings of light, rolling currents of green, red, white, and blue. On the roof, a life-size Santa sat in his sled, crackling out a static "Ho ho ho." His reindeer were a full team of Donner and Blitzen look-alikes, and they were working hard to get airborne, their mechanized legs pumping madly. Santa cracked the whip in time to their efforts. Again. And again. And again. The chimney he was heading for was draped in fir, with green and red bulbs winking.

Emma wished for a camera. Wished more for Liam, tucked under her arm. Liam, smaller, ready to admire this and also see the over-the-top humor. She ventured out to get a closer look.

The group of kids crowding in front of her were from a Catholic school. Nuns had them hemmed in on either side. The girls wore regulation-length plaid skirts; the boys, blue slacks and blazers under their winter coats. As for their ages, somewhere in that elementary wasteland. Emma couldn't pinpoint exactly. Eight, nine, ten? The boys were exuberant, acting out despite the chiding of the nuns. They dug into the snow and popped stray snowballs at the girls, who screeched and giggled and lofted a few back in return.

The Christmas spirit didn't end with the roof. Down in the front yard, Joseph stood guard over Mary and her

baby, that significant miracle. Next to them were the
three wise men. All the figures had been hand carved by
a patient sculptor. The yard was done up as a pen with
hay and straw in equal measure. Inside the fence, beasts
of burden; a sheep, a goat, and, my God, a donkey, all
quite alive, all at home here in the heart of Brooklyn,
stretching their necks to reach out and take whatever
was offered them by the children, an assortment of
treats that were certainly not typical barnyard fare.
Emma spotted an Oreo sliding in between the donkey's
yellowed incisors. Quick little hands tapped the animal
on the forehead and tried to avoid getting nipped while
the sisters ordered them to cease and desist.

"Happy holidays," Emma said to the kids crowded in
next to her.

"Happy holidays," they chorused back, as did a nun.

Stepping back in her car, she punched in a number,
got Suzanne's machine, and said, "Suze, about that
family therapist you thought was so great. I'd like the
number. You can leave it on my machine."

It felt good. She had to admit that.

Buzzing her in was the receptionist's first mistake, the
second was saying "I'll be right with you," then going
back to her pressing phone conversation. Emma was
halfway up the stairs before the woman realized.

Stewart Weinstein was taking a meeting with two
young men who were bent over legal pads, scribbling
busily. She assumed they were students, on loan from
NYU law, where he taught several classes and ran a
clinic. Looking up, he did a double take.

"I need to speak with you," Emma said.

"Then make an appointment."

"It's urgent."

"What could be this urgent?" Weinstein shook his head, then heaved a shopworn sigh. "I'll give you five minutes," he said, and raised his hand. More shuffling of papers and then the two men went poof. Emma decided to take a seat. He didn't look happy about that either.

"How much was the Ben Dovs' initial offer?"

"What's this now?" As if he'd spied an unknown life form scurrying across the floor.

"The Ben Dovs tried to make the lawsuit go away. What was the offer they put on the table?"

"It has no bearing on your case."

"Is that why there's no mention of it in the case files you gave us?"

"The offer was insulting," Weinstein said.

"How much is insulting?"

"Thirty-five thousand dollars a year."

"With health care included?"

Weinstein nodded as if to say, You see how negligible!

"Was it insulting to Roland. Or to you?"

"I was convinced we would do better. And events have borne me out."

"Have they really?" The man didn't seem the least bit chastened, despite the insinuation. "Did you ever revisit the question later on with the Everetts?"

"Why would I?"

"We spoke of Roland's obvious deficiencies as a client. Wouldn't it have been easier, all around, to settle?"

"I try to do what's best for my clients, regardless of my personal bias. I assume you must do the same."

A huff, and a puff, Emma thought, and remembered how Hochfeldt had stigmatized him, calling him a "self-hating Jew." Where was the reflexive hate, she wondered, because this man seemed filled with admiration for himself.

"When you took the offer to Roland, how did he respond?"

"You can't expect me to remember verbatim." The sharpness of his tone gave her pause.

"If you'd included it in your notes," she offered, with an accompanying shrug, as if to say, "you see?"

"You did give Roland the option of rejecting it?"

Umbrage was about to be taken. She saw him pull himself up to a great and lethal height. "Are you accusing me of doing something that would, in any way, tarnish my reputation?" An answer that wasn't an answer at all. He hadn't said yes or no, Emma noted. A master of doublespeak, in fact.

"You realize I'm going to ask him?"

"My word would hardly be enough for you. I wish you had gone to see him first, and spared us both the intrusion."

Weinstein was right, she should have gone to Roland first, but she'd done this instead. That this seemed easier did give her pause. And prompted a hard question. Why was she here, ostensibly arguing Roland's cause, when she could have gotten the answer from her client? Because, Emma admitted, she'd have to study how she felt being with him. And it was easier to feel her moral superiority here, where it didn't impact on anyone directly.

"Sorry," she said, apparently surprising them both.

Weinstein's face clouded over. He seemed to be at a loss. Funny, Emma decided, you can assume you know yourself well enough, but then something happens and you realize your own psyche is the ultimate mystery.

"What Roland did, it's horrible," Emma ventured.

"One would think you'd be used to this by now," Weinstein said.

"One would think," she agreed. And knew what had gone wrong this time. When push came to shove, and those cattle car doors slid shut, she'd have been inside. It didn't matter how American she was. After all, they'd believed themselves Germans.

Emma forced herself to refocus. "You never imagined the Ben Dovs would declare bankruptcy to avoid paying? Even though they kept reincorporating on you?"

"I've chased worse deadbeats down and gotten them to deliver. Young lady, your five minutes have been over for quite a while."

Young lady. Emma nodded, inclined to thank him for the appellation, finding that her nerve was gone. She left, feeling more than a little humiliated. What had she gotten for all her bravado?

Out on the street, a crisp wind blew, full in her face. She began to be disgusted at herself. She'd let herself be snowed by him, she decided. It wasn't supposed to be about clans, or tribes, or national character. Look at Israel and Palestine if you wanted to understand the mess that got you into.

Heading for her car, she decided Roland had to be her next stop. The meter where she'd parked had apparently expired. A ticket floated on the windshield. She grabbed it off, stuck it in where it could mate with its fellows in the glove compartment. But as she started the engine, she found herself wondering what had really prompted Marie Everett's cutting assessment of Weinstein's true nature, because it was Weinstein she had been referring to that morning, Emma was certain now. She heard Marie's voice making the summary judgment on him, "That man doesn't care what anyone says, he does just as he likes."

20

Carolina Country Kitchen was the home of the best smoked barbecue in the city. Laurence Solomon had had himself a taste of it, more than once, and even brought home two bottles of their Smokin' Devil's Brew marinade. This made it all the more unfortunate to be venturing into the back of this fine establishment. Posted on the kitchen wall were inspection stickers, all current and up to date, which was remarkable, since what you saw were piles of caked pots, plus nooks and crannies that were most likely home base to vermin armies.

Mr. Leroy Burnham was back here, working hard at his duties. There was a clatter and clash as hot pots hit the sink, then a hiss as they entered the colder water. Steam rose up, temporarily obscuring the object of his search.

Laurence strode on, noting the chefs working on either side of him in a frying assembly line. One cut the chicken up into pieces; another popped the sinewy meat into egg, flour, and breadcrumbs; the third took charge over this huge deep-frying cauldron, setting it in, then pulling it out, piling the thighs and breasts onto separate platters, where the chicken pieces glistened with heart-attack oil.

Laurence lost his footing on the slick floor, grabbed for a hold on the metal counter, and managed to right himself unceremoniously. Apparently, the oil had rendered the place skating-rink slick.

"Leroy?"

They'd said he'd be by the dishes. The man in front of the sink that was full to overflowing turned. Dark-skinned, flat nose that looked like it might have been broken once, and no smile at all extended.

"Yeah." No question, only a comment. Burnham had muscular arms, down the full length of both were matching coiled snake tattoos, with flicking green tongues.

Laurence held up his badge. "Where can we talk?"

"What about nowhere," Leroy retorted.

Laurence waited for that idea to run its course. Which it did. "What's it about?" Leroy's voice was tinged with tired, as in, "This is tired, man, such old news, when is it you people are gonna realize as much?"

"How about we step outside?"

"I got a job to do." Burnham turned his back, making the point. He'd done his time for the crime and now he was working himself up along this straight and narrow path. Laurence set his hand on Burnham's shoulder and got it shoved off for the insult it was, but Burnham wiped his hands off on his apron, threw it off in disgust, and led the way.

Outside, he pulled a cigarette out of the pack, lit it, and said, "You're gonna lose me my job."

"It won't take long. You can say we're old friends."

"Yeah, we go back years, you and me, that's real funny." Leroy pulled in a long, hard, hungry smoke. "Seems I'd have better taste than to be crewing with you."

By the back door of the restaurant, in what passed for fresh air, Laurence saw that his bad impression of the establishment was being confirmed. Garbage bags were stacked hill high, and plenty had been sliced through, exposing the remains of meals mixed with rotting vegetables and gnawed bones, all of it making an unappetizing display.

On the way here, Laurence had been trying to tote up the sum of his discoveries. What if that rose-encrusted pillbox had been the object of Summers's search? Why bother, the pills were clearly prescription, and even if they'd been morphine, there weren't enough to bother over. Laurence was inclined to believe it was something else, but then where was that little antique box? Summers's ransacked house had been turned over, and there had been no sign of it anywhere. Were these two old ladies members of a sinister drug ring? Not likely. What then? What had the good doctor done to get herself killed? The answer was still there, if he wanted it to be. All he had to do was to ignore the politics of the moment, as in capital F, capital B, capital I.

"Last Friday morning, want to tell me where you were?"

"Want to tell me why you're asking?"

"Don't give me trouble with this," Laurence said, offering a look that invited Burnham to make it easy on the both of them.

"I was home in bed," Leroy said. "I sleep late."

"You have someone with you there to confirm?"

"Got to ask you again, what am I up for?"

"Nothing yet," Laurence said.

"I was with my lady." Burnham struck a pose, dipping his cigarette down by his side, leaning against the metal door.

"The lady have a name?"

"That's private."

"You don't get to make that call."

"No?" Sly grin accompanying that.

Laurence decided to switch gears. "How about Sunday night?"

"You got a time frame?"

"Six to eleven?"

"Out. Around," Burnham said.

"No lady with you at the time?"

"Thing is, I don't got to tell you." Burnham threw the cigarette down on the ground, stubbed it out with the heel of his shoe, started off.

Let him go, Laurence told himself. O'Malley was out, as they spoke here, scouring pharmacies. She'd come up empty-handed, more than likely. He'd offered Jordan Jr. to Burton to buy himself a few more hours, and this wasn't the best way to spend it. For all he knew Burton was, at this very instant, giving Grill the required condolence call.

Let it go, he told himself. And found he couldn't.

"Seen Ari Summers lately?" he asked, stopping Burnham's progress with the question.

"Ari? What you want with my boy Ari?"

"I'm investigating his mother's murder."

"You looking at Ari for that?"

"I'm not saying yes," Laurence told him.

"But you're not saying no." Burnham stepped away from the door, obviously interested. "So Ari finally did the bitch in."

"What makes her a bitch?" Laurence asked.

"Not like I'm trying to bring down my boy Ari, all I'm saying is, no love lost there."

"You and Ari used to be friendly enough."

"Like this," Burnham said, crossing his fingers tight and displaying them.

"Do you think he could have killed his mother?"

"Sure, he could have popped her." Burnham stopped then, fronted an anxious look that darted to the left, then right.

"When was the last time you and Ari saw each other?"

"Ancient history."

"How ancient?"

"Five years maybe?" Burnham adjusted his stance, shoulders even, eyes level.

"You were upstate back then."

"Must have been some other time. I saw him over in the hood. He was in for a flyby visit."

"He called you up?"

"No, man, we happened on each other. I can't say where. Who remembers that shit?" Burnham was uneasy, but what ex-con wouldn't be, considering. A capital crime, the police stepping around to your door. Still, one thing stuck with Laurence. He'd been circumspect, kept the details of the murder from the news media. "Popped?" The casual way Burnham had offered it . . . don't go grasping at straws, he reminded himself.

"So Ari went off about his mom when he saw you?"

"No. I was only speaking about, you know, how it

was." Truly uncomfortable now, looking for an escape, his hand on the door, working the knob. "I guess he said shit about what he was up to. His mom was the one spirited him off to that military academy, you know? I mean, that was his beef with her, how she always wanted him to operate on some superior level. I asked him was it true, what I heard?" Burnham rolling up and back on the balls of his feet, his body twitching. "He said, it might be at first, started in by making it mysterious and shit, but then he said, sure, maybe it was. Turns out he's one of those trained killers, you know, the kind they send in under cover of darkness and such, he ended up telling me all sorts of crazy shit."

"Crazy shit? As in?"

"How he snuck up on people with his squad, cut their throats and left them laying there. Or popped them with silencers. All sorts of wacked-out spy shit. But hey, he was probably fronting this shit, 'cause he wanted me to think he was doing something devious. You know how it is, he knows how I've been upstate and all, wants to prove himself. I mean, how's it look, here I am, doing time by the numbers and he's some squeaky-clean mama's boy." Burnham nodded after, concurring with this ingenious psychological profile. "Got to go," he added, and had the door open.

"That's fine," Laurence said, feeling the crunch of nervous energy in his stomach. "Still, what I don't get is how Summers goes and takes out his mom, where's the reason for it. Why wait all these years?"

"How do I know? Could be he was making up the plan, looking to make it the best he could." Burnham threw this off a little too eagerly.

There was no way to hold on to him any longer. But an idea was definitely forming. Desperate, certainly, but no one had forced Burnham to go with this story of his. He could have done it out of habit, or out of spite. Whatever the motive, it gave Laurence a way to proceed, and one where the feds couldn't horn their way in.

"Appreciate your time."

Laurence followed Burnham inside and watched as he retrieved the apron from the corner where he'd dumped it. Filthy as it was, he proceeded to slip it over his head, wrap the strings twice around, and tie it behind. Without visual aids, his fingers worked adroitly, producing a perfect bow.

21

"**P**rice."
Josh looked so woeful, there at the bottom of her stoop. She wanted to tell him to go away, explain that her troubles were more singular, more remarkable, principally because they were hers to own. Emma wanted to go in and shut the door tight against him. But she took pity on him instead, letting him escort her across the street for a drink at the Brooklyn Inn.

Glenda, the barmaid, with her stunning white-girl dreads, offered her usual "Howdy." She had clearly wanted to be a cowgirl in a former life. Now she was a performance artist. Emma had sat through three of her pieces. The one that always came to mind was the one where Glenda outfitted herself as a nineteenth-century virgin and played the lute, while the slide projector coated the room in photographs of world disaster sites.

"The usual?" she asked, and Emma agreed. Josh preferred a rum and Coke to Emma's draft pint of Guinness.

At the other end of the oak bar, a group of twenty-somethings were laughing at their own private joke; two men and a woman, all in the ever-popular black-is-hip uniform. Both men also had sprung for those clunky nerd glasses.

"Out-of-work techies," Josh said, pigeonholing them. Then he turned back. Eager, Emma decided. Wanting more, as always. Didn't everyone? She thought about opening her hands palms up and saying, "I'm all done," then fleeing.

Instead she said, "What's up?"

"I took your advice and called that lawyer. She was amazing."

"I heard you worked out a deal."

"So you know." An even more expectant look offered up.

"Know that you're sitting here, and not down in a holding cell."

"What could they arrest me for?" Innocence was apparently his crowning achievement. "I remember this place when it was Kings Pawn Tavern," he added.

"There was a restaurant phase in between."

"Didn't Washington take a room here?"

"From what I can tell, Washington got around," Emma said.

"Don't hate me." Josh sounded as if he were actually begging. "I won't be able to stand it if you do."

"I don't hate you," Emma retorted, feeling unaccountably annoyed with the direction of the conversation. "Josh, I don't know you well enough to hate you. I'm disappointed in you," she added. Then decided that wasn't right either. She would have to be completely honest. "Spurned," she added. "Why I would feel that way, shit, I don't know. I mean, you haven't even crossed my mind in years. Not to say that I didn't wonder about you for a good while, but I told myself I'd be hearing from you, you'd write, or call when you got things worked out, or maybe come back, or if not, then you'd send for me."

"I meant to," he ventured. "I guess life interceded." A lame excuse, lamely offered.

"What was it you meant to do?" Emma countered. "Life interceded. You must have known all about how that happened with me. Bertha must have mentioned how I got orphaned, bit by bit. I kept telling myself, every time, he doesn't know; wherever he is, he doesn't realize. Because if he did, he'd come. Come back and help me get through this."

"I don't have any excuse that works," he said.

"Why does that sound like a first for you?" Emma drained her glass. She'd had enough of him. She went to pay and he put his hand out.

"Hold on," he said. "I need to tell you something. It's about Bertie."

No, Emma thought. He was going to confess here, in this public place, and then walk away. Or maybe he wants me to force him to stay, force him into accountability.

"She was scared when she called me up," he said. "She said Mom was being threatened and I had to come back and help her fix things."

"What?" Not at all what she'd expected. Emma shoved her empty glass a little away as if it were, in some way, culpable. After another moment's thought, she said, "Tell Laurence about it, don't . . . please . . . don't leave this with me."

"He won't believe me. Why should he?"

"You're wrong, of course he'll believe this."

"I doubt it. You filled him in on my dubious past."

"Mine too," she noted, and felt her curiosity nibbling around the edges. "What else did Bertha say?"

"Only one other thing I can remember. She told me she and Mom had had this horrible fight. That Mom wouldn't listen and was going her own way. She was desperate. She wanted me to talk to Mom, make her see reason."

"About what?"

"She wouldn't tell me that, said we'd talk when I got here."

"So didn't you?"

Josh shook his head. "I guess it was too late."

"You didn't ask her what the argument was about?" Emma narrowed her eyes. "That's beyond unlikely. You must have asked, Josh."

"She was too upset. I couldn't. But of course you don't believe me. And if you don't, imagine what your friend Solomon will think."

"You didn't find her asking you to come back, insisting on it, not the least bit strange?"

"No," he said, with more than a trace of regret. "Bertha had been hocking me for years, telling me I was an ingrate, how much Mom missed me and longed to see me. I'd say, if she cared so damn much, she could write. Finally she did. And I never even wrote her back."

"God!"

"Exactly. I'm the ultimate asshole."

Emma found herself seconding that assessment. "Tell Detective Solomon, have Sonia Hart call him up if you want. Just leave me out of this."

Josh tugged on his chin with one hand. So clean-shaven, so boyish, she decided, not even a hint of five o'clock shadow. "You didn't ever care about the money," he insisted.

"What?" Then realized he was talking about the boiler. In all that had gone since, it had completely slipped her mind. Or else, she decided, she'd nudged it out. Convenient. "You shouldn't have done that for me," she said. "But I'm not saying I don't appreciate the effort. I'll write you a check." Which would bounce. There was a certain innate humor therein. His arm was thrust out and she couldn't help thinking, that watch alone . . .

"I don't care about that. I don't need the money," he said. "I was sure your boyfriend explained this to you."

"Ah." Emma saw where they were headed. "*That* money. Do you really take me for a fool? I might have been stoned much of the time, but I was never brain-dead. How much had you squirreled away, Josh? I've always been curious."

He didn't pause. "One hundred and forty-six thousand, nine hundred and seventy-three dollars."

"Fuck!"

"No kidding."

Another drink was going to be required.

Emma returned to that night, remembered how she had attempted to meld with that baroque kitchen wall-paper as Eleanor and Josh raged on, and on. Eleanor threatened, Josh responded in kind. Finally, he'd been the one to storm out and leave Emma with his mother. Eleanor had settled herself into a kitchen chair, the blood drained from her face. They'd both winced when the door slammed upstairs. It had taken a long time for Eleanor to register Emma's presence, but she did, looking at her with such sadness, it was torturous.

"Emma Price, you, of all people! It breaks my heart."

This is why she couldn't listen to him confess, Emma decided. He was right, she'd never cared about the money, she'd done it for him.

Emma pulled her coat on, slammed a twenty down.

"I'll take care of it," Josh said.

"No, you won't. Not this time."

Then she got the hell out of there.

It's amazing how people flatter themselves, Emma thought, taking stairs and rushing through the door. Josh had made an investment, and he'd gotten the hoped-for return, she told herself. Her sacrifice had been factored in, and only now, when he needed her, was he even attempting to reevaluate.

Emma dispensed with her outer garments, then reached for the phone. Laurence wasn't answering, so she left him a message. At least her house was deliciously warm. She'd gotten the furnace out of all this, she thought. After all, she could have taken that seventy thousand plus and ended up investing it all in tech stocks.

"Mom?"

Liam was watching her from midway down the stairs.

"What's up?" she asked.

"Nothing."

He came down. Followed her into the kitchen. Katherine was using the chopped-up fruit in her plate as a missile defense, raining them down on the invisible troops who were apparently attempting to scale the legs of her high chair. There were dishes piled up in the sink. Theresa, her baby-sitter of the hour, was at the table, head down on her arms, snoring.

"This is grand," Emma said, which didn't wake her. "Theresa!" Not effective either. Emma jammed a finger into her shoulder and Theresa sprung up, spitfire that she was. "Get the hell away from me, you little creep!"

"Which one of my little creeps would you be referring to?" Emma asked.

Ten minutes later, she had listened to every excuse in the book, noted the smell of alcohol on Theresa's breath, and gotten rid of her, managing with some effort to retrieve her house key. Emma wondered if it would be paranoid of her to change the lock. Newly baby-sitter-lite, she returned to the kitchen, reminding herself it was better not to attempt to survey her predicament until all had been fed. With that in mind, she ordered a pizza, then took the chair so recently vacated by Theresa and settled her head in her hands.

"I never liked her," Liam said, standing next to her and slinging his arm around her shoulder. "She was obtuse."

Not to mention a tippler. Emma laughed. True, a legion of others had not been. They had quit in rapid succession, an army of noncombatants who had been aghast at Liam's attitude, his refined mixture of sullenness and contentiousness, he'd tried their patience and found it lacking, and thus they'd ended on this sour note, Theresa.

* * *

Emma paid off the delivery man and gave Katherine Rose a whole plate of her favorite, clementines sectioned into bite-size pieces, then dug in. Liam offered to bathe his sister, then helped by reading her a story while Emma got to take a hot bath and shut her eyes for an entire five minutes, sliding almost completely under the water and thinking that perhaps she might escape, via the drain, to the paradise of Atlantis. Fat chance! Shrinking to pint size meant no great adventure; riding south on that tornado of water, she'd end her days as rat food.

Emma called the service that existed to provide her with temporary help at outrageous cost. The woman on the other end of the phone assured her that someone would be there at eight o'clock Wednesday morning, and all she'd have to do was pay this perfect gem fifteen dollars an hour for an eight-hour shift, and time and a half for any overtime.

"Ah," Emma said, thinking seventy-six thousand at an even three percent interest over twenty-two years.

Liam got himself to bed. And Emma stepped out onto the deck off the kitchen for a long moment of peace, her feet shoved into wool socks and slide-'em, slip-'em moccasins. Above the bare branches of the maple, the stars were woven into the fabric of the night sky, with a sliver of moon tacked underneath. She trailed her fingers across Orion's Belt and listened to the siren, running, like a current, up the street next to the Gowanus Houses, then wailing off, and finally disappearing.

Back inside, she headed past her bedroom and up to

her study. Emma switched on the light and opened up the voluminous Everett file, hoping that in here was an answer that would help her avoid the inevitable trip to see Everett in person. Great, how was she going to represent the man if she couldn't even sit down and talk to him, she wondered. And didn't have an answer, or even an excuse. Halfway through the first page of her notes, she heard Liam calling for her.

Down one flight of stairs, to his bedroom.

"Could you rub my back?" he asked.

"Sure." Emma lay down beside him and began, tucking her hand around the curves of his shoulders, smelling the tart difference between this boy-man and the small creature she had nursed and nurtured.

"Mom?"

"Yes?"

"I hate Dad," he said.

Charity begins at home, she reminded herself. "You don't hate him, not really," she said.

"Yes I do. He's stupid."

Stupid. The word could as easily be applied to her. After all, she'd been the one who'd hired Miss Theresa, even though she hadn't particularly liked her during the interview. Those recommendations had carried too much weight, her own misgivings too little. How could that be, when her own children were involved, when there was nothing more precious to her than these two? A certain recklessness was clearly attached. "Your dad's lots of things, but he's not stupid. I don't find stupid men attractive."

"You're wrong," Liam said, using his pathetic voice,

the one he'd used to wheedle an extra pack of Marvel cards, or a banned soda. "She's not going to want us hanging around."

"She?" Emma gazed curiously at him. "You mean Jolene? You always say how much she likes hanging out with you, Liam." Not adding the salient point, how, after all, he was almost her contemporary.

"You don't understand." Liam had pulled away, he was in the corner, with his knees tight to his chest.

"Maybe not, maybe I'm dense as they come, but I love you, Liam, you own me, kiddo."

"Do not."

"Do so."

She reached in to tickle him. He pulled away, scowling.

"Don't," he said.

"What if I can't help myself."

"Mom, stop!"

His voice was stern. Dramatic. "I see how you are. You don't even see me half the time when Katie's yelling. I'm only good for taking care of her. For doing things with her."

This complaint was certainly valid, but then, how did one avoid making the older child bear the younger one's weight. I'm alone here, Emma wanted to point out, could you cut me some slack.

"Jo'll be the same. She's already acting weird, the same way you did. Getting pissed at me for nothing. Last time I was over she yelled at me for hogging the bathroom. Dad says it's going to pass but I know how it is. She'll have her own kid soon and then it'll be the same there as here."

"She's twenty-nine. I'm sure Dad and Jolene will wait a while," Emma said. "He's got plenty to deal with with you and Katie."

"She's thirty," Liam said. He had pulled himself up to a sitting position, and he was rocking. The look on his face said the rest.

My God, he's right. She was as dense as they came, Emma thought. The hasty engagement, it made sense that it had been spurred on by the imminent arrival of Will and Jolene's little bundle of joy.

"Good night," she said numbly, then kissed him on the top of the head, adding, "Go to sleep."

Out in the hall, Emma leaned against the wall for support and wondered that it didn't give way. How long had Liam been keeping this secret? How hard had he tried to protect her? And didn't anyone believe in using birth control anymore? Emma had to laugh at herself. After all, Katherine Rose's existence didn't exactly give her grounds for righteous indignation on this front.

When the receptionist had asked for a name, Emma had come up with Missy Gordon. Then she'd requested the white-haired doctor. And Eleanor had done a double take when she'd opened the door to the examining room and found Emma, her best friend's daughter, waiting, nude under the cloth gown. Odd, then, that she'd played along, staring down at her chart, then saying, "Missy, what can I help you with today."

"I'd like some advice about birth control?"

"I see."

The nurse was there, which explained part of her reticence. It was the nurse who had fitted the heels of

Emma's feet into the stirrups. "Try to relax," Eleanor said, and shoved that piece of cold metal inside. Did some invasive work, a few swabs here, another "hmm" there, then released the clasp, removing it, and saying, "Get dressed and step into my office. We'll talk there."

Emma had pulled on her underwear, then her faded blue jeans and a Russian peasant blouse. She'd crossed the hall and knocked, although the door was already open a crack, and Eleanor had said, "Come in." Emma had taken the seat directly in front of Eleanor's desk, not crossing her legs on purpose, the way she did on the subway to make sure no one squeezed in too close.

"Missy," Eleanor said. "You don't look like a Missy to me." A sly smile, as she took a pink circular plastic case out of her drawer and set it atop the desk, between them. "That's your first month's supply. I'll write you a prescription for the next three. If you want the pills to be effective, it's wise to let the cycle kick in, so give yourself at least a full month before you consummate. After you're no longer a virgin, you can consider other methods." Then Eleanor leaned back in her chair, folding her arms and giving an exacting look, and Emma saw it wasn't going to be this easy. "Emma, I consider you a supremely intelligent young lady."

The lecture was on its way. Emma immediately shut down all hearing functions, nodding and offering her most placating smile. Her interior monologue questioned her good sense. She could easily have dropped by her local Planned Parenthood office instead of taking the subway here, to Brooklyn and ignominy.

"Don't get that look on your face. Don't worry, I'm

not about to give you the usual lecture. I applaud your desire to be fully prepared. And I'm certainly not going to pretend that sexual intercourse isn't something to be taken lightly, when everyone does. I'm not a Puritan, and it would be foolish to imagine that every boy you sleep with is a special somebody. Besides, nothing I say is going to stop you from doing whatever it is you want to do, which is part of growing up, am I right?"

Emma nodded. This was why she'd come to Eleanor. Because Eleanor did understand. Even applauded who she was. And did it without blinking, did it when her parents never, ever would. Emma was relieved there would be no prying. She wouldn't have to tender a description of her boy of choice, the one who she'd be offering the supreme sacrifice to. This was particularly good, since she didn't think Eleanor would altogether approve of Brando, who was a half Cheyenne, half French Adonis. He was also a member of a street gang and had been a heroin addict for a while. Brando had a talent for hot-wiring cars and driving them to his second cousin's chop shop. This was the great choice she'd made, the one who would rid her of her virginity, this thing that hung albatrosslike around her neck.

"I am going to keep this visit totally confidential. And believe me, it matters that you trust me for this, Emma. But I have to ask, it's not Joshua, is it?"

Emma burst out laughing. Of all things for her to imagine! Her response should have been enough to lay the question to rest, but she saw that it was only causing agitation. Feeling how much she held the upper hand, Emma had asked caustically, "Why would you think that? And anyhow, if it was, is there a problem?"

"Once again, I can't tell you what to do," Eleanor said firmly. "But I have to conclude from your response you might be considering him. I understand you're good friends. Still, Josh has certain issues. He doesn't take things seriously."

"Well, who does?"

"You do," Eleanor replied. "I've always known that about you. You're worth three of him, Emma."

How could she have said that, Emma wondered now? How could any parent, even in jest? There had been not a jot of humor in Eleanor's assessment of her son's worth. Emma had never reported the conversation to Josh, why bother, when he already understood his mother's sentiments so completely.

The phone was ringing. Once, twice, thrice, and it was too late at night to be anything but bad news. Emma recognized Dawn's number. What now, she wondered, hesitating for long enough. Her machine picked up and she had to grab the phone and say, "I'm here."

"It's Dawn."

"I know."

"Oh?" Caller I.D. was one of the many modern conveniences that Dawn resisted comprehending. She also took call waiting personally. Whenever the beep sounded and Emma had to explain that she would be putting her on hold, Dawn said, "I suppose you have to!"

"Penelope," Dawn said.

"Yes?" Not getting where they were heading at all.

"It's Homeric."

"I realize that."

"The baby's name, Em, don't you love it?"

She saw this was comic relief. "I like it fine," Emma offered.

Dawn thankfully didn't comment on her less-than-ardent response. "I can't sleep. I know I should. I mean, I have all these Xanax to take on the plane, but you know me, I'm always sure the wings will drop off or something, the damn thing bobs around and all I can think is now we're done for, so I should sleep tonight and tomorrow night, but I can't . . . everyone tells me I'd better rest up now, that the baby will make sure I don't for the next three years. Em, I'm asking you straight out and you have to tell me, is this the biggest mistake of my life?"

Again, Emma sighed. "Why would it be?" she asked weakly.

"I can hardly manage the cats. How am I going to take care of a baby?"

Emma wondered if it was truly only nerves, or if Dawn was actually doubting her motives. Perhaps the light was dawning at the end of the long, solipsistic tunnel. If so, Emma knew she had a duty.

"You don't have to do this," Emma said, cautiously.

"So you think I should back out? That's not what you said this afternoon!"

Immediately on the defensive, how like Dawn. Still, Emma nudged a little more. "Better now than later. It's not a test of your virtue."

"Oh." One small word that said volumes.

"Dawn?"

"One second I think I'm going to be fine, the next I'm sure I'm incapable. I'm afraid I'll fuck up the kid, what if she turns out like me, Emma? She'll hate me for that."

Yes and no, Emma thought. "Sometimes you have to do what your best self would do. Sometimes you have to leap before you look. You'd tell me the same."

"Would I?"

"I think you might."

"Perhaps." There was a little more spirit in her voice. There, Emma thought, service has been rendered. Now maybe she could finally get to sleep. Glancing at the clock, she saw it was already after twelve. "That's not even why I called," Dawn said. "Did you hear about the demo?"

"No."

"There was this impromptu march, pro abortion rights, demanding that the police solve Hammond's case, pronto. Over three hundred arrests and still counting. Leslie's one of them."

"I'm hardly surprised," Emma ventured. And wasn't all this meant was that the pressure on Laurence was going to be intensified. Undoubtedly, the Bureau was already busy wresting control.

"So, they take Leslie down to Central Booking, and she won't let them have her handbag." Dawn's gleeful tone was unnerving. "Guess why?"

Emma prayed it wasn't because Leslie was carrying a forty-five-caliber handgun around with her.

"I can't," Emma said, mustering her last bit of courage.

"An urn." The pause was more than significant. "Em, do you get it? Eleanor was there, at the demo with her. They shipped Leslie off to Bellevue for an evaluation." Dawn giggled, adding, "I only wish I could have been there to see their faces when they unscrewed the cap."

22

"It's me."

Emma heard his voice but didn't quite manage to force herself awake. She was drifting, drifting, and as she did, she felt hands, Laurence's hands, it had been his voice, scalloping her body, greedy, touching everywhere, curling up to nest in her hair, then too busy to stop, moving up to roll lightly over her nipple, the current singeing her.

"It's okay?" Wherever he touched, he exposed her need for him to do more. Laurence rolled her on top and ran his hands down along the sides of her legs. Emma moaned, heard herself and misplaced any embarrassment she might otherwise have felt. It was late at night, no, it was morning, and Laurence kissed her hard, pushed inside of her, as the last piece of her poorly constructed dream world collapsed.

Afterward, he went to shower, came back, his hair kinky and damp, and got in beside her, shutting his eyes immediately.

She was, of course, wide awake.

"You got my message and decided it was easier to drop by." Emma was offering it as a prelude. The grunt he gave in response was meant as assent. Reading the clock, she saw it was after two, and Laurence dragged a pillow up, already almost unconscious, preparing his habitual battlements. It perched between his stomach and knees, he had managed to sequester two more under his head, leaving her one in toto.

Emma got up on an elbow to view him.

"Josh waylaid me," she said.

His eyes were shut, a snore rippled through him.

"I think he meant to apologize," she continued.

Laurence had his back to her. She moved in tight, her arms wrapped round.

"Mmmm," he said.

"Listen up," she told him.

"I'm listening." He barely managed to get the words out.

"Really? What did I say?"

"Josh came by." His voice sounded stupefied. "Emma, I haven't slept in days."

"I'm sorry." However, this took precedent. She nudged him awake.

"What?" He turned her way, blinked, and then said, "I could have gone home."

"Maybe you should have, but you came here."

"Emma . . ."

"Josh told me Bertha called and said there had been a threat."

"I see." Patiently done, as if she were the child, he was the reasonable adult.

"You knew about this?"

"Threat as in . . . ?"

"Threat as in, Eleanor had started something she couldn't stop."

He finally seemed to be paying attention. His eyes didn't need to be propped open anymore. He had even gone so far as to hoist himself up on one elbow and turn in her direction.

"You think he's telling the truth?"

"What reason would he have to lie to me about this?"

"If I knew that . . ." Laurence sighed grimly. "What else did he say?"

"Not a whole hell of a lot."

"Ah." She saw him reach for comfort, the pillow that had slid out of place subtly reconfigured.

"There's something else," Emma said. "Josh had quite a mother lode when he left."

"Really?" The way he said "really" made it clear this part wasn't news. "Did he write you a check, with interest?"

"I didn't think of asking for one. Should I?" Mischief in her tone. "I don't think I'm going to pay him back for the boiler. Would that be very bad of me?"

His eyes bore sharply down on her and worry broke over his features. "What's this about?"

"The boiler broke for good Sunday. And I'm cash poor. Josh did me a favor."

"That's how it went down?"

"More or less." Emma added a stubborn, hapless laugh at her own expense.

"I'll give you the money."

"Why?"

"I don't want you beholden to him."

"I don't think you get to make that call," Emma retorted. "Sunday, by the way, was two days after you went stalking off into the night."

He studied her, and Emma felt chilled by it. Then he got up out of bed and began to gather his clothing.

"You're being ridiculous," she said.

"I don't believe I am." Laurence pulled on his underwear, then his pants.

"Would you stop. You're acting like a baby, Laurence."

Not the right tack to take. He had his shirt on, was buttoning it from bottom to top. Emma got up and shoved her face pugnaciously into his. She saw that stubborn pride, and a desire to protect, but more important she saw what was lying beneath the disguise he'd assumed, a man who was inclined to care too deeply, so fragile, so decent. He was meticulously sparing in the way he showed his feelings; how else could he be, if he expected to construct an adequate defense against this sort of injury?

"I'll think about your offer," she said. "And I apologize that I didn't consider you as an option, but I think I had reason not to. Still, you know I'm not the most trusting soul. If you walk out now, and leave me here like this, I'm going to ask you not to come back. Don't confuse the issue. Don't give me the idea that the two of us can make something together. If you decide to let me go I promise to do the same for you."

He studied her for a long while. Emma found she was holding her breath and found nothing of any consequence passing through her mind. She was aware of how frightened she was, the tip of her heart pumping blood determinedly, but the rest of it fragile, even imperiled. She saw he was about to take her up on her kind offer and leave, she had tempted fate one time too often.

And then, he sat down next to her. A little while later, he ceded his hand. Their naked feet splayed out together on the floor. She held on to it, on to him, and they both lay back down on the bed, Laurence with his trousers on, his shirt half buttoned. He fell asleep, deeply and immediately.

Only three hours later, Emma woke with a start. It was almost six A.M. and daylight was beginning to edge into the room, bands of it teasing along the floor. She realized Laurence was holding her tight, smiled, drifted off again, for a long, delicious minute, then extricated herself and got up to go to the bathroom. In the mirror she saw what no sleep wrought, her pallid complexion and puffy eyes.

"You gorgeous girl," she said.

Unfortunately, the glow didn't last. By the time the sitter arrived at eight, she was in the throes of pitiful exhaustion. Laurence meanwhile was deep into his beauty rest. Emma got Marisa, a cheerful twenty-something who described herself as a novelist/techie, situated and then shut the bedroom door, padded over and whispered a sweet nothing into his ear. When that didn't work, she shot him an elbow.

"What?" he demanded, springing to life.

"It's eight."

"Your point being?" He was already burrowing back in.

"You have to get to work, don't you?"

"Did I get beeped?" Something they both knew he would have heard.

"No, but I had this idea," she ventured.

"Oh lord," he said, and dragged a pillow over his head, to no avail.

Forty-eight minutes later, at the Hammond manse, Laurence unlocked the office door, pulled on his gloves, offered her a pair, and reached for the light. It blinked on fitfully, whirring and crackling before catching for good.

"Same as you remember?" he asked.

"Pretty much." Emma had realized, on the drive over, that the last time she'd ventured into this office was that night. She'd been in the house several times since, but you couldn't have paid her enough to step back into the room where she had, so forcefully, encountered her own mortality. There had been plenty of time, while Ari and Leroy did their search-and-discovery mission, to construct a scene. In the morning, Eleanor would tramp down to open her office and discover them, bloodied and savaged.

Instead, years later, it had been Josh who had made the gruesome discovery. That night, Eleanor had managed to save them from their own stupidity.

It was time to return the favor.

Emma opened the office door, found the light switch without even glancing for it, then asked, "Where was Bertha standing?"

"Behind the desk." Emma went around, then did what one naturally would, opened the top drawer and rifled through.

"I've done a complete search," he said.

Still, she scrutinized the contents of the open drawer; spare birth control parts, an outdated IUD piled in with the paper clips, brochures, notes on torn-off sheets of paper. Lifting one out, Emma recognized the sloping, hard-to-decipher handwriting. It was a list of reminders. Call Phyllis. Antonia Wilder. Telephone Jerry. Trash out.

Inside the next, another nest of notes and a huge pile of unopened bills. More lists, one an apparent genealogical history, "Great-aunt Marilyn. Mother— Sadie Ruth Levitt. Father—Milton Joshua Levitt. Daughter—Leslie Anne. Joshua Moses—son." At the bottom a tag with three words in bold print—TURNIPS, CARROTS, CELERY—then in a script at odd angles to the rest, the name *Londren*.

Emma dug down a little deeper, past the brochures for Ortho, and came up with a rendering of a giraffe, its long neck beating against the sky. Eleanor had written GIRAFFE next to it. A child had clearly rendered the simple lines. Emma thought of the many Eleanor had delivered, coming back to visit in this very office with their moms.

He was right, there was nothing of importance in the drawers. Or at least, nothing other than the Diehl file.

Emma took a tour of the room, scanning the bookcase. Laurence had carted off the hollowed-out *Physicians' Desk Reference*. Too bad. She would have liked to have had a chance to see Josh age slowly. It was disconcerting to imagine him young, then old, sprung from the Hydra's head as his prosperous, middle-aged self.

On one wall, a long rack held patients' files. On the other, Emma saw the door to the inner sanctum. She opened it and went in. They had spent hours as kids playing down here, and this had been their favorite spot. Josh had dubbed it "the dungeon." Popping the light on, she saw "the rack." Those cold metal stirrups hung down at crazy angles, its leather top had worn out in too many places. No paper sheet had been rolled on top to hide its faults. Behind the examining table, the ceiling-to-floor cabinets were still painted white, though chips exposed the steel innards. Emma knew which tools were likely tucked away. She and Josh had used them imaginatively, as prods to confessions, one the interrogator, the other the victim of the alien mind probe device. Probably the first and last time a speculum had ever been used for that particular purpose.

"We used to sneak in here with her medical texts. I was the only kid in my school who knew what elephantiasis of the testicles was," Emma confided.

"That must have really raised your stock considerably."

"It did. We're talking elementary school," Emma said. "The grosser the better."

"It sounds pretty damn uncomfortable."

"Your worst nightmare and then some."

Opening the door to the cabinet, Emma saw change had arrived in some form. The medical instruments were sealed in plastic bags. She recalled the metal sterilizer that had let that hiss of steam escape whenever you pumped the pedal that pushed up the lid.

"He really pissed you off but good," Laurence said.

"You mean Josh? I guess he did, yes."

"Why?"

"Do you think it's because we're more generous when we're young?" she asked.

"You mean the way we assume everyone's capable of living up to his potential?"

"Yes."

"How much did he say he walked away with?"

"One hundred and forty-six thousand. I calculate that over twenty-two years, my share would have done pretty well."

"But it isn't about the money."

"No." But she knew to leave it at that was to put a better spin on it than she deserved. "It would have been nice to have it, all the same."

"You'd have kept it?"

"I've never been selfless," Emma said.

"No. But you still manage to give more of yourself than most do."

Emma saw how wrong he was. Roland Everett's needs stabbed into her consciousness. Get this over with, she told herself.

"When did you realize there might be someone else down here?"

"What warned me?" He appeared to be pondering the question seriously. "I heard something."

"A cough? A door closing?"

"No, nothing like that, I was on my way down the stairs off the kitchen."

"You didn't come in off the street?" For some reason Emma hadn't figured that in. And there it was, the punishing moment of clarity. "Go upstairs and come down," she said, with a fervor that made him give her a keen look.

"Why?"

"Just do it, please."

He went, begging the question with a kiss.

Emma heard Elvis Costello telling her "history repeats the old conceits." It did. Josh was huddled down here beside her, the flashlight scouring the pages of the book. And then they'd heard it. The creak of the third step, then the eighth. Plenty of time to hide the evidence before that voice cracked the whip. "If you two are down here, you better show yourselves, and I mean now!"

The telltale creaking as he came down. Then Laurence was back.

"That noise you heard, what did it sound like?"

"Sounded like a cornered rodent."

"As in?"

"Skittering, then this high-pitched sort of shriek."

"Something like this?" Emma opened the double doors that hid the mechanism and reached in, turning the lever counterclockwise. The noise was fiercer in here, and the table rose like Frankenstein's own. As the gears turned, they released their burden, two sheets of crumpled paper came fluttering down.

23

The first page had the name and address; the second the briefest of medical histories. Don't get ahead of yourself yet, Laurence admonished, his cautionary interior voice suppressing that first rush of elation. By the time he was standing at the door to 175 Sterling Place, he was perfectly calm, which was more than could be said for Emma. He noted the way she moved, up a step, then back, her eyes glancing off him, nerves ringing from her.

The house was one of a matching row of grand, turn-of-the century brownstones. Laurence knew the difference between here and two blocks away, on the other side of Flatbush. Over there it was pure Park Slope; might as well be on the Upper West Side of Manhattan as Brooklyn, what with the strollers and the nannies, and the various mixed-race, mixed-gender couples. Across to this side, you still got a little taste of what used to be. Right around the corner was an establishment that boasted some of the best Jamaican meat patties in the area, and pretty decent jerk pork besides.

He pressed down on the buzzer. No answer. Dug his finger in again. Emma was doing a nervous two-step, staring hard at the door as if her eyes could actually see through the hard wood. "Relax," he said, touching his hand to her head.

"You are?"

"Sure."

As relaxed as he could be, considering. Laurence was studiously manufacturing a humming noise in his head, driving away whatever thoughts might be springing up, quite naturally, to undo him. God had a way of teaching you about presumption, Laurence reminded himself. Then heard the cylinders click. The door pulled back a few inches and a girl poked her head out.

"Gina Collins?" Laurence asked.

"Yeah." They'd clearly roused her from sleep. His acute detecting skills discovered this by the way her hair was matted down on one side. Plus she wore a pair of blue and white cloud-print pj's.

Laurence flashed his badge. She blinked a few more times and then said, slowly, "My parents already called you guys."

"I'd still like to come in and talk."

"But they're not home."

"Talk to you, Gina." Better than he'd hoped, this one girl trying to vie with the two of them. Gina started to close the door in their faces, and he stuck his foot in, leveled his body weight against it.

"Hey!"

"Let's talk," he insisted.

"I'm not letting you in without them being here," she countered, plenty of worry inscribed on her face.

"You are, though," Laurence told her.

"How do I know you're even who you say you are."

"Call the precinct, I'll wait out here till you confirm. But the door stays open."

"You aren't police at all," she began.

"Why would you even assume that?" Laurence had his badge pressed up in her face. He flipped it close so even a nearsighted person could read the number and see the authenticity of the shield.

"You don't got a uniform on."

"I'm a detective. Plainclothes? It won't take long, Gina. A few quick questions and Ms. Price and myself will be gone."

Gina Collins looked at Emma, possibly noticing her for the very first time. Laurence saw her finding reassurance, skinny little bit of a teen, seeing this kindly, well-dressed, middle-aged white woman standing on her doorstep. Not someone who looked to be even remotely terrifying.

"It really will be only five minutes out of your day," Emma said soothingly.

Gina backed up. In they went, into the hallway that could only be described as gaudy. A Tiffany chandelier hung down close enough to scrape the top of his head. On the wall, a Victorian side table made out of dark wood, with carved lion's heads for feet. Gina headed into the living room and in here, heavy velvet curtains were held back with gold braid, a sofa and two side chairs wore plum velvet. Laurence tagged it as the worst in opulent discomfort. Taking a seat in one of the chairs, his opinion was confirmed. He sat rigid and motioned for Gina to join him. She did, on the sofa, her bare, toe-ringed feet settled on the coffee table. The soles, thus exposed, were crusted with dirt.

And no, it had not escaped his attention. Gina Collins was pregnant, just as her chart had signified.

Where to start? Then Laurence saw that there was something, right underfoot, so to speak, that might work as an opening. He reached over and found Emma there, before him. They each lifted one off the pile. Posters showing a younger, better-scrubbed Gina. And right above her photograph, the word in thirty-point block print: MISSING. Then her particulars—Height: five feet, six inches. Hair: dirty blond. Age: sixteen. Last seen wearing an orange goose-down jacket, blue jeans, and Nike sneakers. Last known location: Flatbush Avenue and Ditmas, October 29, 11:30 A.M." Please contact 718-555-2210 with any information.

"They're taking the rest down," Gina said, watching as Emma set the poster back down on top of the pile.

"So when did you come back?" Emma asked.

"They told you. Last night."

"You were gone a long time."

"I guess."

"Your parents must have been frantic. How'd they take it when you showed up back here?"

"They were thrilled," Gina said, rolling her eyes.

"You're in eleventh grade, Gina?"

"Tenth," Gina said.

"Attending . . . ?"

"Packer."

Laurence knew that the last thing the very preppy Packer Collegiate School wanted was a pregnant tenth-grader roaming their hallways. Plus, she'd missed most of the year. A good twenty grand, basically, flushed. Yes, her parents must be thrilled, he decided.

"The thing is, with runaway situations, we are pretty much required to alert social services, that is unless there's some special reason not to. Which is why we're here, Gina. We want to speak with you about your situation, vis-à-vis your parents. Are they cool with you being pregnant?"

"Cool with it?" Gina's laugh said the rest. "You're kidding, right? What are you saying? You want some social worker coming round to talk to us?"

"It's part of the process." Emma's tone was perfect, Laurence decided. Even, unemotional, a professional doubter would most likely believe her. And Gina was an amateur. A scared amateur.

"The last thing I need is some social worker messing up things. Look, my parents have me in therapy, I mean they did. With Dr. Goodwin, he can fill you in on everything. I can't fucking believe this."

"I'm looking for a way to help here," Emma said.

"Help? You're talking about helping? Look, it was all just a stupid misunderstanding," Gina muttered. "I mean, I thought my mom was trying something with me, she does that sometimes, you know, but I was wrong."

"Trying something? Be more specific, Gina," Emma coaxed.

"It's how she is. She tells you one thing and then you find out she's been not exactly lying, only not telling you the whole truth."

"So this misunderstanding was about having the baby?"

Gina nodded.

"Explain it to me. If it makes sense, I'll do my very best to see you're left alone," Emma said.

Laurence watched Gina's face, saw indecision rest there for a long, fluttering while, and he set about making his look do the rest when she turned his way. He was calm, unconcerned, all up to her and only her. Gina shuddered, then said, "Look, it was only when I told my mom about the baby, she wouldn't hear me, she said I had to get rid of it, you know? She didn't care that I hadn't decided."

Emma translated. "You left because you had to think it through?"

"Yeah," Gina said. "My mom gets really wacked out, you know. She acts all ferocious, like she's not ever going to change her mind about this shit, but then she does. Last year, she was all hot on sending me off to this place out in Arizona to retrain me, and then some kid died out there in the desert. That got her to thinking. Maybe she didn't want me quite that dead." Gina cracked a smile.

It seemed that Gina had a sense of humor, at least. She'd need one, Laurence noted. "Last seen on the corner of Ditmas and Flatbush, what about that?" he asked, breaking into their little friendly repartee.

"What about what? That was where I was."

"Yes, but why were you there? And who was the last one who saw you?"

"My mom. Don't you guys write any of this shit down?"

"We want your version," he explained.

"Fine, she dragged me over to see this doctor," Gina said. "They were gonna make me have an abortion."

"No one can force you to abort your child," Emma said. "I find it hard to believe that a doctor would have given you the idea that she or he was going to perform this procedure without getting your permission."

"Pretty Goth, right? My mom says the same, I guess. She tells me I was hysterical and stupid and I got the whole thing wrong, which I guess I must have."

"So?" Laurence's turn. He kept his voice level, his eyes centered on Gina.

"It was that old lady that got killed."

"Hammond?"

"Yeah, her. She was my mom's doctor. Guess she delivered me even. Plus, got my mom pregnant when she'd pretty much given up hope. What do you think, you think she's sorry?"

Laurence didn't venture a guess.

"Anyhow, my mom didn't know how I'd been to see her over by that clinic on Flatbush. The doctor acted fine when she was over there, said how I should take my time about deciding what to do and who to tell."

"She didn't notify your mother?" Laurence asked.

"I told her I was eighteen," Gina told him. "Look, I didn't exactly give her my right name. Far as I could see, it wasn't really her business."

"So you went to the office," Emma said, nudging her toward the point. "What was different?"

"Well, first off, she pretended how she'd never met me before, which I thought maybe was her way of being cool. But then, when the two of us were alone, I started to say stuff to her and she didn't get it. I mean, like, hellooo! what am I supposed to think? Then I realize they're in on this together, her and my mom, and the last thing she wants my mom to know is how she let me off the hook that first time. She has me in her office by then, and she starts lecturing me about how serious it is for a girl my age to be having a baby, and I see she's pissed that I didn't tell her my right age all along, and she's going to fix it for my mom, 'cause they're all cozy with each other, and then she has us go over by the clinic to get some tests. Well, I know what that means. I'm not stupid, right? My mom's big with the euphemisms too. First time we went to Dr. Goody Goodwin's office she said we were meeting this old friend who hadn't seen me in years and was only in town for the day. Next thing you know she's ushering me inside and shutting the door, and there he is, my shrink-to-be."

"I see you decided to keep the baby," Emma said.

"Yeah," then a little more tentatively, "I guess."

"Where'd you stay all this time?" Laurence asked.

"My friend Trudy's house."

"And your parents didn't track down your friend Trudy, didn't speak with her parents? Or did her parents cover for you?"

"No, Trudy's in college, she has her own place. When they phoned up, she just lied."

"I'll need her address and phone number," Laurence said.

"Sure." Gina was suddenly cheerful. Laurence knew why. She thought her story washed. He reached for the poster, examined it again. "When was the photograph taken?"

"Last year sometime," Gina said nonchalantly. "Here, I'll write it up on the back if you want. You can keep it for a memento or something."

Handing it over, he added casually, "That orange down jacket of yours? Have it around?"

"I lost it," she said quickly, and jerked her gaze back up to meet his.

"Where'd you lose it?"

"I don't know, I left it in a bar maybe, downtown."

"Alcohol and pregnancy doesn't mix," he chided. "Not great for the baby."

"I was hanging with Trude," she said. "I wouldn't drink. I want my baby healthy."

"Good for you."

Gina shoved the poster toward him and said, "My parents are gonna be back any minute. You want to talk to them, you're welcome." She got up, did a patently artificial yawn, and stretched her arms overhead.

"There's this homeless kid I know, he's got a squat over near the Navy Yard. Has himself this fine-looking orange jacket. Come to think of it, his arms are too long for the thing. Looks brand-new. Maybe it's yours? I can check for you?"

"I don't get you."

"Then again we might go and get a subpoena and get some of your DNA, the jacket checks as yours, the kid I.D.'s you, and we find out where you really were these last three months."

Right on time, the front door opened, Laurence felt them at his back and didn't turn, hearing a worried voice say, "Gina, who are these people? What the hell is going on?"

24

Roland Everett was put on hold again. He would keep, Emma decided, at least till later this afternoon. She headed up the West Side Highway, past the piers that jutted out into the Hudson, past the sewage treatment plant and Riverbank State Park, which had been built as a sop to the Harlem residents for having to endure these pungent fumes the plant excreted. Beyond this the toll plaza, which she EZ Pass'd through, and onto her old stomping grounds in Riverdale, where she'd sprouted up, gone from zero to seventeen. Here was where she'd spent time, hanging by the freight train tracks with Rosa, spying on royalty, the *Queen Mary* and her twin sister *Queen Liz* steaming past.

Farther north still, into Westchester, then Putnam where the suburbs became more like country. The reservoir was stippled with ice. Emma disliked the Taconic at night, a curved two-lane road where you could be blinded by oncoming headlights, but during daylight it was easy to hug the road. She almost missed the turnoff and took it with a gut-wrenching squeal of tires, decelerating to a full stop and catching her breath. Proceeding on, Emma passed an empty fairgrounds that had been transformed into Christmas tree heaven. The sign read $15 MAX. As for the housing stock, it was a mix of residential homes, farms, and Edwardian mansions.

A flock of crows flew up, making a vivid black line in the sky. Emma took a right and drove down a narrower road; here, the foliage was thicker and tall firs and pines stretched out their greedy branches. And the holiday decorations were tasteful: icicles sloping off the eaves, red bows punctuating the doors and windows, wicker reindeer munching at the snow, and artful tapered candles beckoning to the weary, passing traveler.

No one seemed to be in at Leslie's. But Emma had phoned ahead and knew she was expected. Checking the garage, she found it shut tight. It occurred to her that Leslie might have decided to punish her, but then she spotted a path through the woods and followed it down, through a windswept pasture to a picturesque, tumbledown barn. She threw out "Hello?" as she stepped in.

"Back here," Leslie responded.

There were four equine residents. As Emma passed their stalls, each stuck its curious head out. The last was a chestnut with a white blaze; the horse whinnied, and then, as she came a little closer, bared its teeth.

"Ruffian, stop!" Leslie appeared from the next stall and banged on the side with her pitchfork. "She's a real bitch," Leslie said.

"I loved her namesake," Emma noted.

"That's right. You used to ride, didn't you?"

"I was never all that good at it."

"All it takes is practice."

And money, something that was in short supply when Emma was growing up. She'd paid her own way, scrimping and saving, doing chores to get the money for the lessons over at Van Cortlandt Park while Leslie had had a country house with a stable nearby. She had a pony first that Emma admired. Then a hunter that she showed. Once, when Emma asked if she could ride that pony, Leslie had laughed and said, "He'd run away with you, I can't be responsible."

A different Leslie here, with her mane of hair pulled back, her cheeks holding pinches of red. Great rubber boots that were stained with mud. In the light cast by the hanging bulb, she looked almost farmer's-daughter wholesome.

In Leslie's tiny kitchen, Emma dubbed the lack of decor left-wing ascetic. Tacked-up posters were frayed at the edges, Che, brandishing his fist, vied for wall space with the Sandinistas and the National Liberation Front.

"What can I get for you?"

"Coffee, if you have some made."

"It's not rocket science," Leslie said. She went to work, grinding the beans, setting the pot on the stove. When it was stoked, she took the seat opposite Emma.

"Bob's working?"

"He's at his place," Leslie said tersely.

Oops, Emma thought. "I'm sorry."

"Don't be. He's not." Leslie grimaced. "He does the right thing by me. Got me out of Bellevue, for one thing. It pleases him to pretend he's selfless. And I'm willing to go along, if the need arises."

"Yes, I heard about that," Emma said.

"You and the rest of the greater metropolitan area." Leslie did manage to smile. "Well, better to be an original fruitcake then a tendentious bore."

Could it be? Was Leslie actually making a joke at her own expense? Had she finally developed a sense of humor?

The pot on the stove bubbled up and Leslie grabbed it, poured the coffee. "Milk?"

"No thanks."

"So you came by to apologize for making me crazy that day, right?"

Emma stayed silent.

"What then?" Leslie demanded. "What was so important you drove this far? Doing more of your boyfriend's legwork for him?"

"No."

"I'm curious, why do you hate me so much, Emma?"

"I could ask you the same thing."

"What?" Leslie looked completely shocked. "I don't hate you."

"You were always horrible to me."

"I was not."

There you go, Emma thought, here's why eyewitness testimony is so unreliable. No two people see the world the same way. "You pushed me down the stairs and broke my arm," she offered.

"I did not push you, you fell."

"No, you pushed me. Then you told your parents I fell, and made Rosa swear to back you up. She apologized to me later on, and begged me for forgiveness."

"You were only five," Leslie said. "You wouldn't remember."

"Actually I do. Five-year-olds remember being terrified. I was. But I didn't come out here to revisit the good old days." Emma set her cup down, shoved it away, and added, "Was it senility, or was it Alzheimer's?"

Leslie's turn to choose silence as a tactical weapon.

"Your mother was forgetting things. There were notes to herself in her desk. Masses of unpaid bills that went back almost a year. And there was the thing with that girl Gina Collins. It wasn't a conspiracy at all. She forgot. Forgot she'd ever seen the girl before. I'm thinking she'd been doing that a lot."

"Mom was old. You get old, you get absentminded," Leslie said defensively.

"Then you rushed to have her cremated. You needn't have bothered. Who was going to be looking for that sort of evidence? And what were they going to find? She'd been shot through the back of the head, after all?"

"Stop it!" Leslie looked sick. "Mom told me she wanted to be cremated."

"When was that?"

"I don't know specifically, old people talk about those kinds of things. They try and make sure they're not going to be a burden."

"You did know about Gina Collins, though?"

"I knew something had happened," Leslie admitted.

"You knew Gina had run away. That her parents were concerned?"

Leslie nodded.

"She was with Martin Diehl."

"What?" That stunned her. Leslie backed up, leaned on the counter to gain support.

"It's part of what he does, he provides sanctuary. It's

part of the m.o. They try to talk the woman out of getting an abortion, and if she vacillates, they offer her a safe place to think. He saw Gina running off and scooped her up."

"Sanctuary! A travesty to call it that," Leslie said. "Anyhow, what was the girl thinking? Mom would never have forced anyone to do anything. I'm sure it was the Collins's girl's own mother's hysteria that set her off. They didn't get along."

The pot speaking of the kettle? Emma kept that less-than-gracious thought to herself.

"Was it your idea to get Bertha to call Josh?"

"Right, I'd want Josh around," Leslie said.

"I'm not so sure you wouldn't. Sure, it was a relief to have him out of the picture and have her all to yourself at first, but when Eleanor started failing, you must have felt it was less than fair to have to bear the entire burden yourself."

"Mom was never a burden," Leslie declared.

"But she was sick."

"She was old. She forgot things. And all right, I did ask her to go to a doctor, but she claimed she'd spoken with her friends, that all of this was a natural part of aging."

"You didn't believe her, Leslie. Come on, all those fights with the neighbors, the incessant calls to the police. She claimed they had teenagers, wild parties that went on all night? They had a five-year- old. It was the people who lived there before who had the teenagers, but Leslie, they'd moved years ago."

"I know all that. Look, when I tried speaking with the people over at the clinic, they claimed she was fine, just fine. I don't know if they were covering for her or what. Maybe Mom kept it together at work, or at least I guess she did, till that day with the Collins girl."

"Bertha told her to retire?"

"Yes," Leslie said. "I said to Mom, she was free to come and live with me. She laughed. Said, 'I couldn't think of it. Living up there with you, that's a recipe for disaster.' I suppose she was right. Neither one of us is exactly easygoing. It's why Bob has his own place, actually. He says no one could live with me." Leslie added a knowing smile. The second time she'd dissed herself, it was almost charming, Emma decided. "As for phoning up my brother, believe me, I was not in the loop. Josh is the very last person on earth I'd turn to in a crisis."

A van had rolled over on the Henry Hudson Parkway, disgorging its load of frozen turkeys. Traffic was backed up for a good ten miles. Idling over the Spuyten Duyvil, Emma tried Laurence. He answered on the very first ring. "Where'd you fly off to?" he demanded.

"I have a day job," she countered. "What happened after I left?"

"Joy all around. The Bureau, the federal prosecutor's office, and me. Seems they thought there might be a problem with so many cooks. So I took my stockpot and came back home."

"Didn't your lieutenant fight for you?"

"Grill's making some calls. Now you."

"Actually, I've been with Leslie," Emma said.

"They let you into the lockdown ward?"

"Very funny. They released her. I had a hunch."

"As in?"

"Gina's story didn't make sense to me. First, I thought Eleanor might have been acting circumspect, you know, in front of the mother, then I wondered if she'd somehow forgotten, if she'd seen so many patients, but no, that hardly made sense, unless . . . and I started putting everything together, those notes, the way her house looked, so much worse than it had been, which is saying a lot, believe me. Eleanor was losing her memory, acting even odder than usual. At her age, it could have been a host of things, but Bertha wanted Eleanor to retire. She refused. Anyhow, that was what the two of them fought over. And that was why Bertha begged Josh to come back. She wanted him to talk to his mother, to get her to see reason."

"It was all she had, work," Laurence said. "Without it, what would she have done with her time? Old people are stubborn."

"Which doesn't bode well for those of us who already have that personality flaw. Does this help?" she asked.

"It might. I'll have to think it through." He paused, then added, "I've been having some other ideas. You know, now that I've been given free time to ruminate and all. There was this story Leroy Burnham gave me about Aristotle Summers, I didn't get a chance to tell you. How he was some sort of lean, mean crazy-ass fighting machine. I had a notion to try and set them in a room together, run it through, see what came of it."

"You're kidding, right? You told me Ari was clean."

"He is. It's Burnham. His parole officer phoned while we were over by the Collins place. Asked what

I'd said to Burnham during our little confab. He was due in for his meeting today and didn't call, didn't show. First time he's ever missed."

The cars in front suddenly surged forward.

"Sounds interesting," she said.

"Desperate more like," he ventured. "Love you." And hung up, without hearing how she'd respond.

The man made caution into a science, she decided. The pleasant surprise was how the traffic was finally moving. Glancing at the clock, she saw she could make it in to see Roland after all.

Except . . . Emma was cleared and vetted, passing through the weapons detectors, letting the guards pat her down, only when she asked for Everett, they directed her to the infirmary. The nurse came out and told her he'd taken sick at lunch and right now was bent over the toilet. They couldn't tell whether it was food poisoning or a virus, but he was in no shape to confer with anyone.

25

At seven-forty the next morning Emma returned to find Roland Everett no longer in residence. He had not escaped boldly during the night. Instead, sometime after midnight, they'd taken him, via ambulance, to Long Island College Hospital and given him an emergency appendectomy.

The fates were conspiring, Emma decided, forcing her to choose the one even less agreeable option.

Half an hour later, Emma was in Queens. There were no news vans in sight, Roland Everett's crime already superseded by others that were equally horrific, and more timely. A young girl wearing a pink nightgown answered the door. Her hair had been plaited into stylish cornrows.

"Mom, it's for you," she called out, without asking who she was or what she wanted.

A far cry from the battened-down feeling of a few days before. Or so she thought, because as soon as Emma stepped inside, she heard Marie screaming, "What are you doing, precious! Rene, you're supposed to watch your sister, and I told you not to answer the damn door!"

Marie emerged, apparently ready to do battle, and Emma braced herself.

"Just you?"

"As far as I know. Thanks for saying I could stop by."

"Well, you're here now. Make it quick."

Marie was fully dressed and Emma had no reason to ask where she was off to, the uniform gave it away. White, crisp, and the script above her breast stating her full name, along with her degree, Marie Everett, R.N.

She didn't offer coffee or a seat. They were apparently going to have this conversation as close to the front door as possible, the better to eject her through, Emma noted.

"They called you about Roland?" Emma asked. Something she had purposely avoided mentioning during the thirty-second phone call.

"Who? Called about what?"

Marie made the obvious connection, more bad news, and hooked her finger, made her way quickly past the living room and into the kitchen. This time closing the door behind them both.

"What?" she demanded, hands on hips.

"He had surgery last night."

"My lord, what now?"

"An appendectomy. He should be fine."

"I'm supposed to be grateful?" A rhetorical question. Marie glanced down at the table, then sat. "I'm finishing up," she said, and stabbed a piece of uneaten waffle. Chewed on it, chasing it with some coffee.

"It's about Mr. Weinstein," Emma said.

Stark silence, then another careful jab. And another

piece stuffed into her mouth. That's me in there, Emma thought. I'm being ground into little edible bits.

"I've learned about the original offer the Ben Dovs made."

That got Marie's attention. "Heard it from Weinstein?" she asked.

"No, from someone else."

"So? That's old business." Marie had at least stopped chewing. In fact, she lifted the plate, stood and scraped the remains into the garbage, then dropped the plate and the coffee cup into the sink.

"When did you hear about the offer?"

"When I heard."

"In time to reject it?"

Marie offered her a look that dripped with contempt and Emma couldn't figure out how she'd earned it.

"You haven't answered me directly," Emma said. "Did he tell Roland and let Roland decide whether or not to share the information with you?"

Marie shrugged.

"That's a yes, or a no?"

"That's an I don't care to tell you. And as far as I can see, it wasn't Mr. Stewart Weinstein holding the damn gun. That's my very last word to you on the subject. Now get!" Marie added the hiss, to make it clear how much she meant this.

And Emma "got" out the door and into her car. But once there, she was unable to let it go. Marie's anger raised her hackles too high. A grim sort of determination gripped her, after the responding pissed-off mood abated, and she slid down in the seat, eyeing the front door for a long while. No one appeared. But Emma saw the blinds poke up a little. Marie would go, but only if she left first. Then I'll oblige, Emma decided, and spun the car out, took a right, then another as fast as she could and pulled up to the end of the block, hoping she hadn't missed her opportunity. Ten, then fifteen minutes passed and she was almost out of patience, her temper now completely cool, but her curiosity inflamed more. Finally the garage door lifted and a car backed out.

Marie was coming her way. Emma ducked down and hoped that Marie had given up watching for her car after she'd spun off. She heard the whoosh as the other car passed and waited as long as she dared, then got up, made a U-turn, and gave chase.

When Emma told people what she did for a living, they seemed to have this quaint notion that she was like a P.I. in the movies. She never bothered to enlighten them, even though real-life P.I.'s hardly did glamorous work. As for tailing suspects, that was not routine; in fact, the only other time she'd done it had been on a bet with Will. She'd almost killed the two of them in the process.

Yet here she was, playing Bullitt again. Stay back, Emma reminded herself. But also stick close. It was not exactly a cakewalk. Marie took the most indirect way to the expressway, apparently only for those in the know, because suddenly they were there, and she was rolling up an on-ramp. Emma let another car pull in between, then pursued.

Clicking on NPR, Emma listened to the latest international and local news while she kept an eye on her prey, who was weaving in and out like this was the Daytona 500. In the holy land, they were celebrating the birth of Jesus in the usual manner; seven Palestinians had been shot by Israeli troops and a car bomb had exploded outside a busy Tel Aviv supermarket.

It was a day of surprises, though, because Emma was able to keep up the game of cat and mouse all the way into downtown Brooklyn, passing the Heights, then back around onto the bridge. As they made it off, Marie got the left turn signal in her favor and Emma was stranded, here, where every light had a camera attached to it, waiting to catch you making a turn on red.

"Fuck," Emma said aloud, pumping the gas to squeak through the fading yellow and nearly bowling over an eager pedestrian.

Marie was three cars up, her turquoise old-model Chevy luckily easy to keep track of. Emma trailed her up Chambers Street, and then made the right behind her onto the West Side Highway. Here they settled into a rapid, stop-start pace until they got up on the ramp again and sailed past the new Trump complex, to the first exit, 72nd Street.

Marie drove up to Broadway, passing Fairway shoppers as they wheeled their abundantly full carts. Then she turned into a garage. Emma took a meter up the block and hid inside the front door of Ollie's, closed and sealed for the morning, because even inveterate New Yorkers were not inclined to order Chinese food for breakfast. She caught sight of Marie emerging and watched that switch of dark hair, amazed at its length.

Marie headed for Weinstein's building.

And Emma, watching from across the street, saw

which door she walked through. She stepped in and pressed the buzzer that read, "The Weinsteins—Private Residence."

Marie's voice on the intercom said, "Yes."

"Delivery."

"One minute please. I'll be down."

And so she was.

Stewart Weinstein's living room was a work in progress. The couches had been pushed back against the walls, and a hospital bed was in residence. In it, his wife lay, attached to various machines that pumped out information that only a trained medical professional could interpret. It didn't take a genius to figure out that she was dying. The woman in the bed reminded Emma of a husk, her body had stayed behind, but the person had been excavated long before. The smell in here was familiar, Emma recognized it from her mother's hospital stay; antiseptic did nothing to hide the more pervasive scent, decaying flesh, departing bodily functions.

"She's been like this all week," Marie told her. "Every night I go home expecting by the morning there's gonna be a call. But she hangs on."

"Marie, how long have you been working for Mr. Weinstein?"

A humph was the response to that, then, "I don't work for him."

"Of course," Emma said, finally seeing Marie for who she was. The concern etched on her face gave her a gravity and a humanity that had been missing. "You work for her, for Mrs. Weinstein."

"Hilda," Marie said. "It's been nine years now." Unbidden, she went on. Perhaps it was a relief to be caught out, and this was the moment she must have been dreading as soon as Roland unleashed his fury. "In the beginning, she didn't need much. There were months when she'd be well enough. But that's how MS is, you see. It flares up, subsides, you never know when it'll strike you down for good." Marie had taken the seat next to her patient. Marie was stroking the blanket, half without thinking, and then she took Hilda Weinstein's jaundiced hand. "I met her at the hospital and she and I, we hit it off. She told me, if I ever decided to do day work, to call."

"Then it was through his wife, the connection to Weinstein?"

Marie Everett released her grip and fussed. She straightened the bedding, moved a piece of hair out of the woman's face, then leaned over and whispered something to her. "Over here," Marie said, pointing to the alcove. "I like to keep an eye on her."

Out there, she did keep good watch.

"She saw our trouble," Marie said. "She was the one who asked Mr. Weinstein to find it in his heart to help us. She was the one who insisted on me getting us a lawyer, and then when I was afraid of what they might charge, she made him do it."

"What did happen with that offer?" Emma asked.

"Roland is what happened. Nothing was good enough, he got himself up on his high horse and claimed it was an insult."

"And Mr. Weinstein?"

"You know how that man is. He was the one set Roland to thinking it. And you and I both know why.

Thought there'd be something in it for him, bringing the case, you should have seen when he found out who the cousin was. Before he was doing his poor sick wife a favor, halfhearted at best, but as soon as he heard about Mr. Levin, he was the one meeting with us, talking up all these outrageous possibilities. You want to know why? 'Cause what's good for him is good for the world. You should see how he's treated her, all these years, parading around with his women right under her nose."

"Perhaps they had an arrangement. Some couples do."

"Please!" A derisive laugh followed. "What arrangement is it, that man walks around like cock of the roost. Her, she sits home, smiling and patient, and saying he does what he needs to do. Propping him up every step of the way, down to the bitter end."

"How do you mean?"

"She begged him to help her when it got this bad. I heard the two of them talk it over. She told me even, what he'd agreed. Had the pills put away. Did it all, planned it all. But when it comes to it, he doesn't even have the nerve. Says he can't bear to lose her. Lose her? Some days I think I should do it for her. But if I did? I don't know, he might come after me, crazy as he is. I can't take the chance on it."

"You're saying Mrs. Weinstein asked her husband to help her commit suicide?"

Marie nodded.

"You know, I think you say you can do something," Emma noted. "But when it comes down to actually making the choice. It's not that easy."

"You promise something like that, you best do it," Marie said.

"Not everyone is courageous," Emma said. "It's an awful lot to expect."

"You say you love someone, you better honor that statement," Marie insisted.

"What about you, Marie? You and Roland? You must have loved him once."

"Me and Rolly?" Marie added a hearty, derisive laugh.

"You say Weinstein influenced his decision. That goes to your husband's state of mind. It could help. Roland was vulnerable."

"Vulnerable, Roland? His state of mind? Don't come to me on that one. You don't know what I might say, if you ask me to swear the whole truth and nothing but."

"I understand your anger," Emma started to say, and then realized what a petty remark that was; no, she didn't understand. Luckily, she couldn't.

Marie bore down on her mistake with a vengeance. "He's got three girls. You think I want them visiting that man, ever? You come round, imagining it's me, I'm worrying over. Think again! I got to live with knowing I picked that man, then added to the mess, had three children by him who bear his name."

"You think it's better for them if he dies." She didn't bother to add that putting him on death row was hardly a quick and final solution, what with the appeals process. It would be years before Roland was executed.

"Now you get it."

"I'm sorry, but I don't think they'd be better served, losing their father that way."

"Well, that's your job, to think that. I've got my own job to do."

This time she didn't have to add in the "get." Emma said a polite "Thank you for listening at least" and was out the door.

Emma stepped out onto the street. A hard wind blew off the river, nearly bowling her over. Emma knew she would work hard for Roland. Despite her reservations, she would do her best because she believed that life had value. Although, perversely, she knew Martin Diehl would say he believed the same.

As she moved up the street, Emma found herself trying to order events, and in that way make sense of them. She remembered how, only a few days ago, the snow had come down, obliterating what lay beneath, the dirt, the grit and grime, the aching heart of a great city. What was left from that storm now scarred the sidewalk, the pristine white had melted into misshapen ashen mounds. That morning she had awakened to an almost silent city. But not for long. Its devoted inhabitants had brought it to life again, out on the street the pulse, the frantic hum. Devotion, Emma thought, and saw Marie taking her elderly patient's hand, stroking it lovingly. Then saw her righteous anger, her flush of pain at Stewart Weinstein's cowardice, his multiple betrayals. Stopping at her car, she turned and looked back toward the river. The wind shoved her hair back, chilled her lips, and then Emma realized what Bertha must have done for *her* doctor.

*   *   *

Noon found Emma hard at work. A few things were better than Emma might have expected. Roland had done fine in surgery. And back on Bergen Street, her son was smitten with his new, outrageously expensive sitter.

"We're making brownies from scratch," Liam told Emma gleefully when she called.

She trusted no hashish was involved.

Meanwhile, Laurence had phoned to tell her Leroy Burnham had not shown up for work, and he was busy getting a warrant. She didn't go into what he'd base it on. "Grasping at straws," she ventured.

"You know it," he admitted.

She would have added something about him doing good work, but he clicked off without saying good-bye. When it rang again, a second later, she assumed he was calling back to correct the mistake.

"Love you," she said automatically, giving him the option of repeating it back to her.

"Love you too," Josh's voice rang out.

"Josh." She felt actually cheated. "I thought you were someone else."

"I'll bet you did," he said. "Em, could you do me one last favor? If you could take me to the airport?"

Take a cab, she wanted to say. Still, she did have a few questions of her own. And Josh rattled on, how he had to get back to the coast, things were blowing up out there, it was important. Anyhow, he'd cleared it with her boyfriend. "That was who you thought I was, right?" he asked, and Emma didn't dissuade him. She agreed to give him a ride, and decided that on her way back, she'd stop in at the hospital, see how Roland Everett was.

Josh was waiting downstairs at the Marriott. He loaded up her trunk with suitcases, got in on the passenger side, and looked like he might venture to kiss her in greeting. But her demeanor must have given him pause, instead he said, "Thanks for coming."

"Not a problem."

Josh lit up as soon as they hit Atlantic Avenue.

"At least vent, open a window," she said.

"Sorry." He did as ordered. "So, how was your day?" Like this was routine, they always saw each other, always spent this sort of quality time together.

"Amazing, yours?"

"Brilliant."

"Brilliant?"

"That's a Brit phrase."

"What's going on that's so pressing?" Emma asked.

"There's this deal I'm working on, and it looks like it might fall through if I don't get back and give some people hell." His eyes narrowed, apparently in response to the thoughts of losing out, losing money, she decided. He certainly didn't look like someone you'd want to mess with, though. And an uneasy feeling stirred inside of her. Ridiculous, she told herself. Josh wasn't scary. Josh didn't fight, he ran.

"What did Bertha really say to you?" Emma demanded.

"How do you mean?" But his face showed it, the flicker of certain knowledge.

"Josh, you could have taken a cab, after all. You wanted to see me, don't make me suck it out of you too."

"I wanted to see you because I couldn't leave it the way it was."

Emma found that abundantly amusing. "No? You did for twenty-plus years."

"Not now, though." But he went quiet again. The joint was done, he stabbed it out in her ashtray. Then picked up the end and flicked it out the window. "Wouldn't want your kid to find that, right?"

"Right," Emma agreed. "Bertha called you because your mother was sick, isn't that right? Did Bertha really think you could stop her?"

"Stop her. Stop her from doing what?" he asked.

"From killing herself." Emma offered it slyly.

The response was an incredulous, "You know?"

"I do now."

"Shit," he muttered. "How did you figure it out?"

"Things came together," Emma said. To explain how would have taken too much time. Still, thinking back to what Marie Everett had said that morning, that plus her understanding of who Eleanor was, and what sort of control she would demand, added on to Leslie's avowal, the knowledge that Eleanor would have hated losing her independence. "How was she going to do it?" Emma asked.

"How was she going to do it?" Josh said, and this time the laugh was convivial. "Emma, darling, she did do it."

Which was when she saw the scope of what she'd stumbled onto. And realized that she'd known. Known even as she'd confronted him, and wanted to deny it, all the same. Because knowing meant judging, and she didn't want to judge Eleanor Hammond. "Your mother hired Leroy Burnham," Emma said. "She wanted to make it look like she'd been martyred."

"I like how you put it."

"But what happened with Bertha . . . what went wrong there?" Emma asked, only now piecing this together. "Was Leroy afraid she'd talk?"

"I don't think it was only that, but it probably came into play."

"That morning, Bertha came to the house, your mom was already dead, why didn't she make the call, why did she wait for you to come and find her?"

"Bertie told me she was afraid to," Josh said. "Afraid that if the police spoke with her, she'd give something away. She thought it better, since I didn't know what had gone on, to leave it to me. I'd really be naive about it, you see. And I was, for the most part. All she'd demanded was my presence. She'd been vague about the rest. But of all people to choose, why Leroy? He's such a wild card."

The way he said it, the prickle of discomfort extending down. "Have you seen Leroy?"

"I might have." Josh was reaching into his pocket for another happy smoke.

"Stop," she said, putting her hand up and touching his. "You didn't do something to him?"

"Do something? How do you mean?" But he knew. "I'm incapable of causing physical pain," Josh said. A statement she would have disagreed with, but Emma decided it was better to keep her own counsel. "I come equipped with rolling papers and a cell phone," Josh explained. "Leroy Burnham carries a different sort of arsenal around."

"He came to you? What was he after?"

"Pretty much the same thing he wanted the last time he and I met up."

"A payoff? To keep his own counsel? And you gave him the money?"

"You have a better idea?"

"Why not turn him in?"

"I didn't think that was wise, since he was armed and apparently dangerous."

"Where is he going?" Emma asked. A bit of a rhetorical question, considering. Josh complied, though, with an answer that was fairly persuasive.

"Wherever the ten grand can take him."

"Josh," Emma said, "there are options. Why are you running? We should tell Laurence. We can get Leroy, bring him back. He's not going to get very far with that money."

"I think he thought he'd hit the jackpot. Mom only paid him a thousand."

"That's double the going rate," Emma said, not able to avoid the privileged aside. "Look, Josh, if he killed Bertha, and you don't go in and talk, you're going to be in more trouble. Not to mention that he'll be eager enough to take care of you."

"I don't think so, my guess is he sees me as a cash cow."

"You'd rather he keep on bleeding you?"

"Don't worry about me," Josh said. "I can actually take care of myself."

"What, you're going to hire a bodyguard?"

He didn't answer, but the expression on his face made it clear the concept wasn't new. Or at all original. "Go to Laurence," she begged.

"And tell him that my mother isn't a martyr to the cause. That she got her best friend killed because she was out of her mind, and couldn't stop herself from buying a little extra piece of glory. Couldn't do what most of us have to do. Die ugly. Die pathetic. She had it all figured out, except for a few missteps. Mom claimed that she couldn't understand me, I was so selfish, you see. Isn't it ironic, it turns out she wasn't any different."

"She was different," Emma argued. "There's her whole life that says as much."

"That was the thing, she had you snowed too," Josh said. "Look at the evidence, Em. See what she really was like."

"She was old," Emma said. "She'd done wonderful things."

"So you excuse her, then? You'll be happy to explain that to Ari and his sisters, I'm sure. I'm not going to. And I'm also not about to break my sister's heart. Mom being great is pretty much all she has left."

Emma arched an eyebrow. "Josh, you don't care that much for Leslie."

"Yes, believe it or not, I do. And I'm more shocked to realize it than you. I've been with her these last few days, on and off, and find I feel deeply sorry for Leslie."

Emma shook her head.

"You don't buy that as the only reason, though, do you?"

"No."

"Then why don't we call it guilt," he said. "Better yet, why not think of it as doing penance."

They had come quite far. The road dipped and

curved and suddenly there were signs for the airport. Terminal A. Terminal B. They were going to C.

"You can drop me there," he said, pointing. He actually expected her to leave him. After this?

"Josh, what's the point of telling me when you're not going to do what's right?"

He turned to confront her. "So you claim to know what's right? Then go ahead, you do it," he said, adding, "You always were my moral compass. You expect the best of everyone, don't you, Em?"

They had pulled up to the gate. She was going to let him go after all. He was stepping out. She got out with him, ostensibly to help him get out his bag from the back, in reality to somehow stall him.

"We have to accept responsibility," she insisted.

"For what? For Leroy Burnham? He came after us that day, remember?"

She did, all too well. Intersections in a life, the mess made thereof, the road quite possibly not taken.

"He was looking," Josh said. "We were available. You can't tell me Leroy hasn't happened to plenty of other innocent people between then and now."

"But it was you and me, we started this off. And we were hardly innocent," she argued. "That day, it changed our lives."

"Not ours, maybe Ari's. That day was his wake-up call. Look, Em, you deal with it all the time, how life is a messy business. You can't fix this," he added.

"Better to run?"

The airport security guard was requesting his tickets and Josh reached into his jacket but emerged with an envelope. He handed it to Emma.

He'd written it down after all. She would have this to cede to Laurence.

"Are you sure?" she asked.

"Positive."

Then this had been some sort of perverse test. Josh was always testing, wasn't he? He kissed her, then hooked her in, held her close for a long second, and whispered, "Don't forget about me."

Like she ever could. He left her standing, envelope in hand. Back in the car, she stared at it balefully. Whistled out of the spot, she drove on and got trapped once, followed the signs back around again, this time getting on the highway. Emma glanced at the envelope lying on his vacated seat until she could stand it no longer. She imagined Josh with X-ray vision, honing in on her, through paint and metal, captured here, in a critical instant of indecision.

Thinking that, she tore it open. "I owe you so much more," he'd jotted on a Post-it attached to pages of legalese. The very last was a deed. The house at 1730 Ditmas and a document indicating that she was now the owner of record.

26

Friday morning dawned with a blast of arctic air sweeping in from the north. As she made her way up the courthouse steps, Emma was almost whipped off her feet by a particularly violent gust.

The courthouse had been refurbished recently, and grand architectural details from the Boss Tweed era had been lovingly restored. The result was overwhelmingly formal and outsized; an outrageous marble staircase that circled up to the second floor dwarfed the tiny humans tramping up and down. It made it clear to Emma, particularly today, how petty their needs were, the perfect spot to put an end to a marriage.

The wedding had taken place in a much less formal setting. It had been a hot June day, Emma and Will exchanging vows on the sloping front yard of his mother's country house in Rhinebeck. The assembled guests had listened as the minister, a woman in a suit, spoke of a nebulous god, the sort Unitarians seemed to specialize in. Then Will slid the ring onto Emma's finger. She remembered her heart pounding hard, the sound had seemed so loud, it had obscured the words, which she luckily had memorized. She had managed, in that way, to agree.

"I do."

Then they'd kissed to sustained applause. Hardly a passionate kiss, more a release of nervous tension. They'd had a wedding cake with three tiers, and before they'd sliced it open, the happy bride and groom had been removed from the top, later spirited away by someone and never found again.

Late that night, in the rustic suite at the local bed-and-breakfast, rented for the occasion, they'd gone into giddy delight, opening the wedding presents, drunk as could be by then, celebrating Christmas in June. There were piles and piles of wrapping paper, red, blue, green ribbons snaking down the king-size bed, and then they'd made urgent love.

"I'm here." Coral, her lawyer, announcing her arrival and breaking Emma's reverie. "You okay?"

A nod.

"We're in B one seventeen," she said. Up those intimidating stairs, down the hall, and into the courtroom. Coral held the door for her and they took their seats in the back. In time, Will arrived with his attorney. Two men on his side, versus the two women seated across the aisle.

Nothing significant in that, Emma decided, only everything seemed so significant today.

"Next case."

Their names were called. They stepped to the front of the courtroom. The judge asked the pertinent questions, and then it was her turn to answer. She glanced at Will and discovered, to her amazement, he was crying.

* * *

On the steps outside, Emma caught up to him and tapped his shoulder. "Honey." She hadn't called him that in a long, long while, and hadn't done the next for a while either, leaning toward him, kissing his cheek, then whispering into his ear, "I'm so sorry."

"What have you got to be sorry for?" he asked. His smile was soft, affectionate.

He took her hand. And held on to it.

"Good luck," she said, and felt a wave of relief course over her.

"You too."

"With everything," she added. "Really, I mean it."

"That was magnanimous. That was so amazingly adult." The voice was Laurence's, emerging from his car, flagging her down.

"Fancy meeting you here," she said, and turned back to find Will, hesitating at the corner, his demeanor one of potent misery.

Then he turned it and disappeared from view.

Emma got into Laurence's car. He leaned toward her, plucked himself a kiss.

"Leroy?"

"No sign still. But I have the word out."

"You happened by to check on whether I'd emerged unscathed?"

"I wouldn't expect that," he said quietly. "I thought I'd just show up. You'd take it as a good thing."

She did. What she wanted, though, was more. She was hungry for reassurance and knew it was pointless. The need inside her a historical piece of the puzzle of Emma. Why did he care about her? She was not overly gifted in the looks category, pretty enough, but not drop-dead gorgeous. As for intelligence, she had more than her share, but hardly enough to send anyone into rapturous frenzies. She was only herself and that was an odd mix at best.

"You love me?" she asked, trying to temper her voice.

"I believe so."

"But why?"

"You can't honestly expect me to answer."

"No, but I'd like you to anyhow. It's been a bad week." Emma knew it was absurd. Still, she needed this from him and couldn't even say why. Don't hide, she begged silently. Don't pretend to be cooler than thou. Don't be that boyfriend who only liked me after his best friend was hot on my trail. Let it all go. Stop playing games with me. Stop seeing what's hard between us as adversity. I'm willing to go there, if you are.

"You never bore me," he said.

"That's your criteria?"

"That's what comes to mind. What do you want out of me, woman?"

"I thought at least you'd say I have a wry sense of humor. Or a nice ass."

"That bony thing?"

Then he kissed her again, harder this time, and after a while it was better than enough. They could have their own small miracle, Emma told herself. It was Christmas. What better time to turn vice into virtue, to subdue love and turn it to their own advantage?

27

On the following Monday, Emma found herself in a small, exclusive crowd, traipsing through the woods behind Leslie's house. They hiked silently as befitted the solemnity of the occasion. Emerging from a stand of sweet-smelling pine, they arrived at a vista. Below them, the swathe of the forest and then clearings marking farms and country homes. Down below, trails of smoke emerged from the working chimneys. But up here, they stood unprotected and the wind whipped through, chilling Emma despite her hardy equipment, a layer of winter underwear, and the second pair of wool socks tucked inside her hiking boots.

Three of Eleanor's contemporaries spoke. They all testified to her vitality, her commitment, her bravery. Then Leslie lifted the urn. "Bye, Mom," she said, offering a cryptic smile. Then she unscrewed the cap. As Leslie lifted the box and tipped it out, the wind turned treacherous, shifting direction. It slapped the grit that had been Eleanor back into their faces.

Wouldn't you know it, Emma thought, as her eyes teared.

The elderly woman, standing beside her, seemed to

agree. "Always have to have the last word, don't you, Ellie?" she said, in a voice that was loud enough to be overheard. And then there was knowing, affectionate laughter.

Wednesday of that same week, Gina Collins cut a deal with the federal authorities. Emma found herself only partially gratified by having been proved right. Yes, Gina had been the girl who carried the bomb into Eleanor's clinic, then hightailed it out the bathroom window. In exchange for her testimony, the feds dropped the murder charge against her. She pleaded guilty to conspiracy and got a minimal sentence. In three years, she would be free to raise her baby.

Gina swore that the bombing was Diehl's idea, but Emma didn't buy that. She had her own personal experience as a marker. Emma knew about teenagers and their sudden bursts of anger. She understood what a force for mayhem Gina could have been, on her own. But she had no way of proving this. And besides, Emma had her own issues to deal with.

The first session with the family therapist, Lea Wolf, was scheduled in rolling time slots. Liam went first. Emma waited her turn, pretending to read through the magazines, a curious mix of parenting tomes and *National Geographics*. Forty minutes later, the door opened. As Liam stepped out, she saw something odd on his face, a look of relief. Emma thought she was imagining it until he declared, "Don't worry, Mom. She's cool."

As she stood, collecting her purse and her thoughts, he added, "You'll see." Then sat down, popping on his headphones.

* * *

As for Leroy Burnham? He went West like so many enterprising young men. Leroy booked a room at the MGM Grand in Vegas, had a nice meal at the Coyote Café, then spent the rest of the evening losing his money. Cash poor, he ended up on old Route 66.

"I'm guessing he was going to visit your friend Josh," Laurence said. My friend, Emma wondered, but didn't bother arguing. It seemed a trifling detail when you took the entire story into account.

Leroy decided to stop for gas at a Mobil station and help himself to a little extra from the till. The owner's son had other ideas. He emerged from the back where he'd been taking a catnap and shot Leroy once, in the gut with a double-barreled shotgun. "You know how it is out there," Laurence said. "Everyone's a cowboy." In this case, it was a Navajo Indian doing the honors. But Leroy's luck had run out completely. He died right there, on the gas station floor.

So January 2, Emma Price found herself standing in the waiting area at the international arrivals terminal. Scanning the crowd, she finally saw a familiar face.

"Dawn," Emma called. As Emma came close, Dawn unbuttoned her wool coat to reveal a sleeping baby, tucked into a Snugli. Emma could make out a black thatch of hair, and pouting red lips.

"Emma, meet Millicent, Millie, this is Emma."

"Millicent?"

"Millicent Randolph Prescott. A sop to my parents," Dawn told her. Emma reached over, grabbing her suitcase, then taking the diaper bag off Dawn's shoulder.

"You're my savior," Dawn said.

"Are you kidding? I wouldn't have missed this. I'm parked in the short-term parking. We can walk. Or I can pull around."

Dawn shook her head. "Don't ask me to make a decision. I'm too tired."

"I'll pick you up, then," Emma said. "You just have to keep an eye out. I'll take your suitcase."

Dawn nodded, clearly relieved.

"She's beautiful," Emma said.

"Isn't she just."

Emma nodded. "Did she sleep on the plane?"

"Oh no. Not Millie." Dawn laughed. "She was up the entire time. Screeching. Giggling. Wailing at the end. I thought the other passengers were going to riot and kill us. She passed out about five minutes ago, in customs." Dawn's hand was stroking the sleeping cheek. "She's perfect," Dawn added. "Just perfect."

"She is," Emma said warmly. Then she hugged Dawn, who usually shied away from physical contact. Dawn, amazingly, submitted.

"Thank you," Dawn said. "Thanks for being here, Em."

Emma knew she meant it in every sense. "You don't have to say another word," Emma told her, grabbing what she could.

Outside, snow was falling. As Emma reached her car, she hesitated, then tapped the air with her tongue. A delicious nothing, cold, wet, gone. Emma felt elated as she admired the white flakes drifting down. "Okay," she said aloud. There were plenty of ghosts to talk to after all; her parents, her sister, Eleanor.

Then she got in, stuck the key in the ignition. The car coughed, then came to life. And Emma pulled out, following the badly marked exit signs to the toll booth, and then on, to freedom.

SPELLBINDING SUSPENSE FROM

NAOMI RAND

The Emma Price Mysteries

STEALING FOR A LIVING
0-06-103121-6/$6.99 US/$9.99 Can

Having to raise a toddler and a troubled teen by herself
has hit Emma Price like a sledgehammer—a double
whammy to go along with the considerable pressures of
her job as an investigator in the Capital Defenders
Office. Add to that a pressing need to solve the slaying
of an old friend—a controversial political activist—and
Emma's already full plate is seriously overflowing.

THE ONE THAT GOT AWAY
0-06-103124-0/$6.99 US/$9.99 Can

After a dozen years, Emma Price's husband is bailing on
their marriage. To complicate matters, she's pregnant
again. Then her longtime babysitter drowns, a mystery that
inexorably draws the former legal investigator into a hunt
that will take her deep into the crevices of her own life.

Look for more Emma Price mysteries coming soon . . .